# ON THE GRIND

Center Point
Large Print

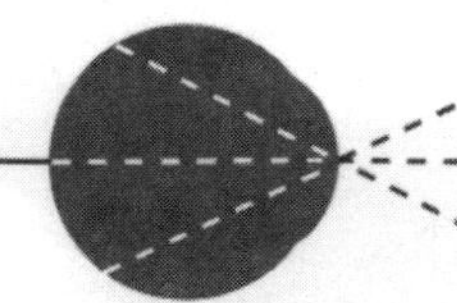

**This Large Print Book carries the Seal of Approval of N.A.V.H.**

A Shane Scully Novel

# ON THE GRIND



STEPHEN J. CANNELL

CENTER POINT PUBLISHING
THORNDIKE, MAINE

This Center Point Large Print edition
is published in the year 2009 by arrangement with
St. Martin's Press.



The text of this Large Print edition is unabridged.
In other aspects, this book may vary
from the original edition.
Printed in the United States of America.
Set in 16-point Times New Roman type.

ISBN: 978-1-60285-385-0

Library of Congress Cataloging-in-Publication Data

Cannell, Stephen J.
On the grind / Stephen J. Cannell.
p. cm.
ISBN 978-1-60285-385-0 (library binding : alk. paper)
1. Scully, Shane (Fictitious character)--Fiction. 2. Police--California--Fiction.
3. Police corruption--Fiction. 4. Murder--Investigation--Fiction. 5. Large type books.
I. Title.

PS3553.A4995O56 2009b
813'.54--dc22

2008045699

*This book is dedicated to Reuben Cannon,*
*my old friend and brother from another mother.*
*He makes me laugh, insists I pray before meals,*
*and always makes me look to my better self.*

*Love you, Reub.*

# CHAPTER 1

Just an hour before my whole life turned upside down, I was making love to my wife, Alexa, in our little house on the Grand Canal in Venice, California. It was the first week of May and a spring storm was washing across the L.A. Basin, filling gutters and runoffs with dirty brown water, pushing a slanting rain against our bedroom window, blurring the view. I knew the police department was about to charge me with a criminal felony, I just didn't know exactly when. I had chosen to make love to my wife partially to ease a sense of impending doom, and partially because I knew it was going to be our last chance.

The Tiffany Roberts mess was already in full bloom, leaking toxic rumors about me through the great blue pipeline down at Parker Center, turning my life and entire twenty-year police career radioactive. Why do I seem to keep volunteering for these things?

So doom and dread hovered as knowledge of what lay ahead turned our lovemaking bittersweet, changing the tone like a low chord that announces the arrival of a villain. We were lying in an uncomfortable embrace, listening to the rain on the windows, when the doorbell sounded.

"That's probably it," I said.

"Guess so," Alexa replied, her voice as dead as mine.

I got up, found my waiting clothes folded neatly over the bedroom chaise. I skinned into a pair of faded jeans and a USC Trojans sweatshirt that I'd grabbed from my son Chooch's room, then padded barefoot to the front hall and unlatched the lock without bothering to look through the peep-hole. I already knew who was going to be there.

The door opened into a whipping rain. Standing on my front steps were three uniformed police officers in transparent slickers.

"I'm Lieutenant Clive Matthews, Professional Services Bureau," the cop in the center said. I'd seen him before, mostly in restaurants around Parker Center. He was an IAD deputy commander. A big guy with a drinker's complexion. He was supposed to be in AA, but the exploded capillaries on his ruddy face were a death clock that told me the cure hadn't taken.

"What's up, Loo?" I said, my voice flat.

"Charge sheet." He thrust three typed yellow forms at me.

A PSB charge sheet lists the crimes being filed against you by Internal Affairs. It's basically an accusation of misconduct which starts a lengthy disciplinary process that usually ends at a career-threatening Board of Rights Trial, which is in effect a police administrative hearing. The fact that a deputy commander in uniform was personally delivering the goods was representative of the gravity of my predicament.

Matthews handed me a sealed envelope. "Your letter of transmittal." The document confirmed the delivery of the charge sheet and started the clock on an array of procedural administrative events.

"You have to sign the top copy for me. Keep the other," he instructed.

"You guys couldn't wait until tomorrow?" I looked past him at the two stone-faced IOs standing a foot back, one on each side of the lieutenant. Water droplets had gathered on the plastic shoulders of their see-through raincoats.

"Nope," the lieutenant replied. "Chief Filosiani and the city attorney request your presence in his office at Parker Center immediately."

"I get to contact my Police Officers Association steward before answering these charges at a Skelly hearing," I said. "That right is guaranteed me under rule six of the city charter. The chief knows that, so what's with this midnight meeting?"

"It's not a command performance. The chief is extending you a courtesy. Your POA steward has been notified. If it was up to me, I'd just body-slam you like the piece of shit you are." He said it without raising his voice or putting any inflection on it. "You might want to get your shoes and jacket. It's pretty wet out here. You can ride with us."

"What is it, Shane?" Alexa was coming out of the bedroom, walking down the hall.

I turned to look at her. Breathtakingly beautiful. Black hair framing a fashion model's cheekbones. Incredible blue eyes that were locked on me. She was belting her robe, her black hair tousled with the memory of sex. I knew these might be the last friendly words we would speak.

"IA. They have a charge sheet. They want me to come with them."

"It's almost midnight," she said, standing behind me. "Can't it wait until morning?" She should have demanded the circumstances. It was a mistake; but then, I knew she was as upset about all this as I was.

"You might also want to come with us, Lieutenant Scully," Matthews said, glancing at Alexa. "The chief is waiting in his office with several people. I think you both need to hear what he has to say."

So that's what we did. Alexa got dressed. I was in the bedroom with her for a minute to get my nylon windbreaker out of the closet. I looked over and saw that she was putting on her sixth-floor attire—dark pantsuit, blouse, gun and badge.

"So it begins," she said, her voice lifeless.

"Yep."

I went into the bathroom to run a razor over my chin. A consideration to this late-night meeting with the chief. For a minute I saw my reflection in the mirror staring back. A familiar stranger with battered eyebrows scarred in countless forgotten brawls. The face of an unruly combatant. My brown eyes looked back at me startled by the sudden confusion I felt.

Five minutes later I was in Lieutenant Matthews's car with the two IOs. One was named Stan. I didn't catch the other guy's name. Not much talk as we headed to Parker Center, with Alexa following us in her silver BMW a few car lengths behind. I had fallen from respected member of society and guardian of the public trust to detestable scum in the eyes of the three men riding in that maroon Crown Vic with me. In their eyes, I was a turncoat. A cop gone bad.

I thought I knew what to expect, but the truth was I had little idea of what lay before me, little understanding of the mess I had so willingly stepped into.

But that's life. I guess if you could see all the dead ends and blind turns, it wouldn't be as interesting. At least that's what I kept telling myself.

The windshield wipers on the detective plainwrap slapped at the rain as we rushed along the 10 Freeway in the dead of night, the tires singing in the rain cuts. No red light, no siren. Just a maroon Ford with four stone-faced cops. All of us in the diamond lane, heading toward the end of my career at breakneck speed.

# CHAPTER 2

Tony Filosiani's office was crowded with pissed-off people. Pissed about being dragged to the chief's office at twenty past midnight, pissed about the reason they were forced to be there. The LAPD sure didn't need another high-profile scandal right now, and that fact was etched on everyone's faces.

I immediately recognized all of the people standing there. The chief of police was dominating the large space. Usually a happy, pixiesque, round-faced presence, tonight Tony Filosiani scowled like a Chinese wood carving, his bald head shining in the bright overhead lights. Next to the COP was an assistant city attorney named Cole Nichols. The ACA didn't want to be there either, but he was filling in for City Attorney Chase Beal, who was up north on some kind of rubber-chicken junket. Everybody knew Chase was planning on making a run for governor and was always out at fundraisers working on his war chest. Next to Nichols was my Peace Officers Union rep, Bob Utley. He was the only one to hesitantly engage my eyes. Bob was a big heavy guy with a Santa-friendly face who had twice successfully defended me against bogus charges at Internal Affairs. Next to Utley was the LAO, or head LAPD legal affairs officer, a tall black captain named Linc Something. Next to him was yours truly in my borrowed Trojans sweatshirt and rain-soaked windbreaker. Behind me stood Lieutenant Matthews, the deputy commander of PSB. But by far the most bitter flavor in this alphabet soup was the chief of detectives. The COD was my own wife, Alexa. She stepped across the threshold seconds later and frowned.

Lieutenant Matthews closed the large double doors to the chief's office, signaling the start of the meeting.

"Detective Scully, I'm not sure you know FBI Agent Ophelia Love," Chief Filosiani said without a trace of the cordiality that usually marked his demeanor. He indicated a tall, lanky blonde in her mid-thirties whom I'd missed during my first quick scan of the room because she was seated against the far wall near a mahogany console.

Agent Love immediately stood at the mention of her name. She wore a cheap off-the-rack tan pantsuit and had a careless beauty that was partially disguised by rawboned farm-girl features, the most startling of which were piercing ice-blue eyes.

"Bob, what's going on?" I asked my union rep. I already knew the answer, but it's always better to play dumb at these things and let the other guy go first.

"Regarding the Venture investigation, you've

been charged with felony case-tampering and blackmail," the chief said, cutting in and answering my question.

"I don't know what you're talking about." My heart rate was inadvertently beginning to rise. *We're into it now,* I thought.

"You can deny it, Detective, but your own partner was the one who brought this to our attention. And her concerns have been independently corroborated by Agent Love and the FBI."

"Detective Quinn turned me in?"

Sally Quinn was my partner at Homicide Special. We had only been working together for about a year. She'd been out of rotation on maternity leave for the last six months and had just returned to duty.

"I only had time to glance at the charge sheet in the car. It says I intentionally lost evidence. I told Captain Calloway how those tapes went missing."

"Unbeknownst to us, the FBI has been running their own surveillance on Harry Venture for half a year and they've got you and his wife on tape," Chief Filosiani said.

What he was referring to was a Homicide Special case, which I had been working for two weeks. Harry Venture's birth name was Aviv Zahavi, but he'd legally changed it when he came to America and went into the film business ten years ago, forming Venture Studios. Harry was a fifty-year-old Israeli national who had made his initial fortune as a black market arms dealer in the Middle East. With the hundreds of millions he'd made in the gun trade, he moved to L.A. and went into the movie business, becoming one of Hollywood's most successful action movie mini-moguls.

Money being the powerful aphrodisiac that it is, Harry soon seduced a budding young actress half his age named Tiffany Roberts, who was starring in low-budget genre movies when he met her. She was beautiful and had a Playmate's body and, as the showbiz saying goes, was willing to do "nude" if it was shot "tastefully." The gossip on the street was that Tiffany instantly saw what Harry could offer and became Mrs. Venture. Big-budget movies and mega-stardom followed. But after she'd done "tasteful" nude scenes with some of Hollywood's hottest leading men, Harry's bedroom seemed to have lost some of its appeal and Tiffany had been quietly hunting around for a hit man to take her pudgy, foreign-born husband off the count. Word of this was quickly leaked to us by a street informant.

Since a murder solicitation by an A-list Hollywood star was an extremely sensitive situation, the squeal ended up going to Homicide Special, which is the elite LAPD homicide squad that typically handles high-profile, media-sensitive investigations.

I'd been working out of that rotation for almost three years and was assigned the Tiffany Roberts case. I was supposed to have been setting Tiffany up, posing as a hit man and wearing a wire when meeting with her behind various discount stores, to work out the terms of the assassination of her husband Harry. I was supposed to get her solicitation on tape, but told my captain that I had carelessly left the tapes in my car one night while I went into a Ruth's Chris to get something to eat. My car was broken into and my briefcase stolen. My boss, Captain Calloway, instructed me to reboot the deal and get her to repeat the offer of murder, but Tiffany became suspicious and broke it off. The case is currently in limbo. Now, apparently, the way they were reading it was that I had deliberately lost the tapes in return for some kind of blackmail payoff.

Of course, I'd seen all this coming. As soon as I'd reported the missing briefcase, the shit had started to ooze downhill just as I knew it would. It had ended up as felony case-tampering.

"Why is the FBI involved with this?" I asked, turning to face Case Agent Love.

She glanced at the ACA, Cole Nichols, who nodded his okay, so she started to tell me. She had a low, husky alto voice that didn't sound like it belonged inside her. The accent was from the South somewhere—the Carolinas or Tennessee, maybe. She was a no-nonsense fed whose demeanor told me she held me in a good deal of professional disdain.

"I'm here because after five years of working Harry Venture for gun smuggling, we finally convinced him to cooperate," she began. "He still has financial dealings with some of his old arms-dealing buddies from the Middle East. New Russian-made Kalashnikov 100 series submachine guns and PP-90 M-1s with nine-millimeter breaches suitable for NATO rounds are currently flowing into L.A. The AK-100-series ordnance is on Homeland Security's watch list and we've pinned this smuggle to the Hispanic Eighteenth Street gangs in downtown L.A. They've established a new pipeline bringing this stuff into the country. They're smuggling it up from the Baja Desert in Mexico. Naturally, we didn't want Harry's wife to murder him in the middle of a federal op where he just became a cooperative witness. For two weeks we've been taping you taping her. Let's say your conduct was less than professional."

I glanced at Alexa, who was standing by the door, her face a frozen mask.

"We can play our surveillance videos for you, but unless you insist, out of deference to your wife I think it's better to say you're in the bag and let it go at that." Agent Love hesitated before continuing. "We accessed your bank statements and discovered you have a recent ten-thousand-dollar deposit, which none of your pay stubs or personal finances support. Unless you can tell us exactly where that ten thousand came from, then we're going to assume that you got it from Ms. Roberts in return for booting your undercover sting against her."

"Don't you have to prove that before just accusing me?" I challenged.

"We think we can," Chief Filosiani said. "Right now Harry Venture is going through his wife's bank withdrawals. If he finds one that was issued on or about the end of last month in the amount of ten thousand dollars, then that fact will be established and added to your charge sheet."

"This is all pretty damn circumstantial," I said. But I knew it wasn't. They would find that withdrawal slip. I was going down for this.

Cole Nichols, the ACA, said, "I'll take that kind of circumstantial case any day. I can also get the FBI video and, along with the fact that you reported your UC tapes stolen, it will make a very compelling picture for a jury."

"Then why am I here?"

"The city attorney and the feds both want to prosecute you, but I convinced the mayor and the federal attorney that this department doesn't need any more bad press or police department scandal," Chief Filosiani said. "I'm willing to offer you a take-it-or-leave-it deal. You have to decide right now, tonight. It's off the table after this meeting."

"A deal?" I looked at Bob Utley, who gave me a hand gesture indicating I should shut up and let them finish. I ignored it.

"I don't want to cop to this flimsy bullshit."

"Your IA file is thick enough to choke a goat," Lieutenant Matthews chimed in from behind me. "Nobody is going to believe anything you say. If I was you, I'd listen to the chief."

"So what are you offering?"

"Resign," the chief said. "Make a statement for the file indicating guilt so we don't have to worry about facing a lawsuit over it later. You'll cop to a lesser charge and then we'll dismiss you for cause and seal the case for the benefit of the LAPD. What really happened in this room tonight, the real reason for your dismissal, will remain a closely guarded secret."

"What about my pension?"

"You lose it. You confess to the lesser charge, waive your pension and quit," ACA Nichols said. "This is a great fucking deal, Detective. You don't deserve it. If the department wasn't still in PR trouble from the Rampart scandal, O.J. and the immigration rights melee, they wouldn't be cutting you this much slack. If I try this case, I promise a conviction. You'll do three to five, easy. Even if the sentence is halved for good behavior, that still puts you in the dog pile at state prison for at least two years. I'll make sure there's no special housing unit for you. A cop in gen pop is a prime target for yard aggression. That five-year stretch will turn into a death sentence."

I looked at Bob Utley. He was supposed to jump up and object, but he said nothing. Every time I glanced at Alexa, her face was cold with fury.

"Could I have a minute with my client?" Utley finally said.

We were shown into a little six-chaired conference room that adjoined the chief's office. Bob shut the door. When he turned, his eyes weren't Santa-friendly anymore. He was staring daggers. Like all honest cops, he hated police corruption. He knew I was dirty, and it pissed him off.

"They can't—" I started.

"Take it," he interrupted.

"Admit I was on the take? That I took money to boot the case?"

"You tanked a solicitation-of-murder investigation and got into a sexual relationship with that movie star. I know it, and they all know it. Take the deal. It's a lifesaver."

"And sign away a twenty-year pension?"

"If you're convicted, you'll lose your pension anyway. If you fight this, you'll go down, Shane. They've got a very tight case backed by videotape of you and Tiffany Roberts swapping spit all over town."

"But—"

"Take the fucking deal! You're damn lucky the department doesn't want to eat any more bad press." His voice was rising in anger. We'd been friends for years, but I could tell he had nothing but contempt for me now.

"What's the lesser charge they're gonna accuse me of?"

"Obstruction of justice. It's a misdemeanor requiring no time served but results in your immediate resignation without benefits."

"Can't I at least have a day to think about it?"

"No. The chief said the offer comes off the table the moment this meeting is over. After tonight, you'll face the full IA charge sheet."

"How come I get the feeling you're on their side?"

"Shane, take the deal." Frustration with me was packed into every word.

"Okay, okay," I said. "Calm down."

"Okay, what?"

"I'll do it. I'll sign the damn confession."

# CHAPTER 3

But that wasn't even the worst of it. The worst part happened outside the chief's office just after the meeting broke up. Alexa and I were caught waiting for the elevator with the others. The rage on her face told me she was about to let me have it right there in the sixth-floor hallway despite the audience of concerned onlookers standing behind us.

"You're moving out of the house tonight, you son of a bitch."

I'd been expecting this, but her voice was so low and filled with hate, it sent a chill down my spine.

"Before tonight, nobody ever said anything about you having an affair. Of course, with that in the picture this all makes much more sense."

"Let's not go into it here, Alexa," I said softly.

"Go home. Pack up your things and get out. I'll spend tonight in a hotel. I don't want to see you when I get home tomorrow."

"Alexa, please, let's talk about this."

"Talk about what? Throwing your honor and integrity away for a few dollars and a cheap piece of bleached-blond ass?"

"That's not—"

"Shut up, Shane. Be out of the house by morning. I'm hiring a divorce attorney."

Then she stepped into the elevator and punched the button. None of the witnesses to this disaster moved to get in there with her. In the face of such rage, they let her ride down alone.

After she was gone, Lieutenant Matthews turned to me. "You still have your gun and badge," he said. It was a statement, not a question.

"Yes."

"Your commander is down on five. He came in specially at the chief's request to accept your resignation and equipment. We can take the stairs."

So I left them all standing there. The rawboned,

ash-blond fed, the city attorney, the Legal Affairs guy and my worthless POA—the whole seemingly ungrateful mess. I followed Lieutenant Matthews down one flight of stairs to Homicide Special.

As I entered the squad I saw the old mismatched cubicles, borrowed from other departments, the bric-a-brac of felony fliers and fugitive want notices pinned on the cork walls. The metal desks and clashing styles of cribbed office furniture. It had once seemed comfortable and familiar. Now it felt as cold as a doctor's examination table. There were only one or two cops working late, because at midnight this place wasn't like other squad rooms. One of the nice perks about Homicide Special was, except for the long hours we spent when a new case was breaking, the unit operated mostly on a day-shift mentality.

The lights were on in Jeb Calloway's office and I could see him through the glass—a five-foot eight-inch muscle freak with a black shaved bullet head. He was originally from Port-au-Prince and, because he was a popular CO with a ripped muscular body, we called him the Haitian Sensation. He'd been my boss for two years and he'd always given me a fair shake. But not tonight. I wasn't counting on anything tonight.

Lieutenant Matthews and I entered Jeb's office and he immediately got to his feet and handed me a sheet of paper.

"That's a Surrender of Property receipt for all your city-issued equipment. I already got your two-way radios and homicide books out of your desk. I'll need you to have a meeting with Sally Quinn at nine tomorrow to pass over any outstanding case information she doesn't have." He was all business. No *Sorry about this,* no *What the hell happened, Shane?* Just, *Here's the property sheet. Get the hell out of here.*

I read the one-sheet. "Some of this stuff is at my house or in my car at home," I told him.

"You can sign it tonight and bring it all in and leave it with Sally tomorrow. I'll be at the chief's weekly meeting."

"Okay."

"I'll take your gun and badge now," he said.

I pulled them off my belt and laid them on his table. Almost twenty years on the job and in a second it all ended with that simple statement. We performed the receipt-of-badge signing ceremony.

"Anything else?" I asked. And then came the one comment that told me he cared.

"You fucked up big, Shane. I can't believe you could be so stupid."

"Right." I turned and left.

Lieutenant Matthews didn't stick around to drive me home. He had a detonator on his liver that needed a barstool. One of the IOs drove me, the one whose name I couldn't remember. I sat beside him in the same maroon Crown Vic. We rode in silence until just before we hit the freeway, when he glanced over and saw I hadn't clicked up. He gave me a piece of advice that would define my life for the foreseeable future.

"Better fasten your seatbelt for the ride," he told me.

# CHAPTER 4

The heavy rain had let up by the time I got home, lessening to a gentle ocean mist.

I sat on the back porch with Franco, our adopted marmalade cat, on my lap. Franco was a midnight prowler and could definitely pick up a victim's vibe. He sat there feeling mine, keeping me company even though the gentle mist was beginning to soak us both.

I knew the best way to deal with my loneliness and sense of loss was to keep moving forward, not to look back or self-examine. I had to stay on this treacherous path I had for some reason chosen. Nonetheless, missing Alexa and not being able to confide in my son, Chooch, was unbearable. He was away at college on a football ride. I knew it was best to just walk the walk. Tomorrow I would begin my job search. I would start the hopeless task of applying to other incorporated cities around L.A., looking for work as a police officer, which was the only job I enjoyed or understood how to do.

I'd known this was all coming, so I'd already looked on the Internet and had found a few departments in the area that were currently hiring—places like Pasadena, Long Beach and Santa Monica. But I knew that the real reason for my dismissal would be immediately posted on a secure Internet site called POLITE, which is an acronym that stands for Police Officers Legal Incident Termination Evaluation. When accessed with a password, POLITE would notify sister departments of the circumstances surrounding any police officer's firing. The official word was I'd been fired for misdemeanor obstructing justice, but I knew the felony case tampering charge and affair with the Hollywood actress I was supposed to be investigating would be on that Web site in all its prurient glory, blocking any further legitimate police employment. I had to try nonetheless. I needed to go through the steps.

When all else failed, my last stop would be the City of Haven Park because everybody in law enforcement knew that the Haven Park PD would hire anybody.

I carried Franco into the house and dried him off with a bathroom towel. He looked up at me with concern in his savvy yellow eyes. They say cats have no expression, but Franco could definitely communicate. We both knew I was in deep shit.

I finally flopped down on the bed and Franco

stuck close, lying in the hollow beside me. I'd found him starving in Carol White's apartment after she'd been murdered and had rescued him. Now it seemed, instead of going out and prowling for lady cats, he had my back, or at least my side. Then he nuzzled me and licked my hand. Cat affection. You know you're down to last straws when your only emotional support comes from a cat.

The next morning, I dressed in a suit, then collected my city-issued gear, took my uniforms out of the closet, folded them and stuffed everything into a bag with my Maglite, cuffs, reg book, and shoulder rovers.

I packed a second personal bag with my shaving gear and a few clothes, grabbed some job-hunting duds, a blazer and a pair of slacks, and put them in the trunk of my car. Then I took one last walk around the canal house. I'd bought this place before I ever met Alexa, but now had to find a lonely hotel someplace.

Just as I was about to leave, I heard the front door open. I went into the entry and found Chooch standing there with his backpack over his shoulder. He seemed shocked to see me.

"You . . . whatta you . . . I came to pick up some laundry Mom did for me."

"Son, I need to talk to you."

"Leave me alone," he said and pushed past me.

He headed toward his room, which was a space

we'd remodeled for him, turning our two-car garage into a third bedroom after his girlfriend Delfina's family died and she'd moved in with us. Now Del was living in a freshman dorm at USC and Chooch was in his second year there. He was currently playing third-string quarterback for the Trojans, but was moving up the depth chart. Needless to say, he was a big guy. Six-four and a half, two thirty. But more than being big physically, he was big emotionally. He and Alexa were the reason I'd survived my dark, dangerous period. I had invested a lot of myself in Chooch, but more than that, he had invested in me. Now I could tell that, because of what had just happened, and because of what Alexa had obviously told him, everything had changed.

"Chooch, I need to talk to you about this," I persisted.

"I talked to Mom. I know what happened," he said. He was pulling folded laundry out of a basket, shoving it angrily into a canvas bag.

"You don't know my side of it," I said. Of course, when you got right down to it, I really didn't have a side.

"Okay." He turned to face me. "Is it wrong what they're saying? Did you take money and have . . . and do things with . . ." He stopped, his face contorted in pain.

"Son, there's more to it. You'll understand it all one day."

"Just tell me you didn't do any of that," he challenged.

"I can't, Son. I wish I could, but I can't."

"Then get out of here, Dad. Leave me alone. Everything you ever told me, all that advice on how to live my life and be a man, was bullshit. It was all a lie. I don't ever want to see you again." He slammed the bedroom door in my face.

I stood there for several moments, unsure what to do. I wanted to go in and tell him he was wrong, but I couldn't. There was nothing I could say. Finally, I just walked out and got into my Acura MDX. I took a long moment to collect my thoughts. Then I heaved a deep sigh to try to settle myself down. I put the car in gear and pulled out. I was so upset I could barely breathe as I drove on still-damp streets under a cloudless blue sky heading back downtown toward Parker Center.

The meeting in the chief's office and the deal I'd made was supposed to be a closely guarded secret. The idea was that my resignation over a misdemeanor was a situation that wouldn't provide any recriminations or public scandal. But I wasn't three steps out of my car in the Glass House garage before an old friend of mine from Robbery-Homicide walked past me without even saying hello. His vibe was toxic. He knew.

More of the same followed as I entered the elevator and took the short ride up to five. Eyes were averted. My hellos went unanswered. This is not the way you treat a colleague who made a mistake and lost some evidence.

The secret we had all sworn to in the chief's office was out. Everybody in the building knew I'd been accused of sleeping with Tiffany Roberts and had taken money to boot her solicitation-of-murder case. The entire ugly mess had leaked in less than ten hours. Who was it that said if three people are trying to keep a secret, two of them had better be dead?

When I walked through Homicide Special I was greeted by an awkward silence. Even people on phone calls hung up and looked angrily over at me. I found my way to the cubicle that Sally and I shared. She was sitting there looking like my crime had somehow also been hers. Eyes down, humiliated, frosted reddish blond hair catching and reflecting the fluorescent overhead lights. When she turned her freckled face up to me, her normally sunny expression was gone. She looked different. Hard to explain. Her demeanor was so altered I was seeing her as a different person.

"Hi," I said.

"Right," she responded. "I've been through your murder books Cal left for me. I think I got most everything I need."

I put the bag full of my city police possessions on my chair. "You want to go over any of the cold cases?" I asked.

"Not this morning. If I need anything, I've got your cell number."

"Listen, Sally—"

"Don't, Shane, okay? I don't want to hear it." She was talking loudly enough that Jim Diamond and Don Stonehouse in the next cubicle were able to hear it all. She was talking loud on purpose. She needed everybody to know she wasn't part of my corruption. She had her own career to worry about.

"See ya," she said. "You can leave your stuff there. I'll give it to the captain. He's at the chief's weekly COMSTAT meeting."

"Right."

I got up and walked out of the cubicle.

I wanted to keep moving forward, wanted to get my job apps started, so I left Parker Center and took the 110 Freeway to the Pasadena Police Department, which was twenty minutes east from the interchange downtown and was located behind a beautiful domed turn-of-the-century city hall.

The PD administration building was in an old-style structure with magnificent two-story glassed-in stone arches. I found the personnel office and sat across from a uniformed sergeant. When I told her I was recently off the LAPD for personal reasons and was looking for a job in Pasadena, she quickly entered a secure password, logged in to POLITE and found me on the site.

I don't know exactly what was written there, but

her face hardened. Suddenly we were just going through the motions—fill this out, sign that. I left twenty minutes later with no hope of ever being employed there.

Long Beach was the same deal. So was Santa Monica. Except in that quaint beach city the personnel officer was an old sergeant with six three-year stripes on his uniform sleeve. We were about the same vintage and I saw a flash of sympathy pass through his gray eyes. He told me Santa Monica PD wasn't looking for anybody with my qualifications right now, which of course was B.S. But then he took an ounce of pity on me.

"Why don't you try Haven Park?" he suggested. "They'll hire guys with bad POLITE write-ups."

"I was thinking about that," I answered. "But isn't their starting scale like really low? Less than fifty-five thousand a year?"

"You want to stay in law enforcement, that's your best bet." Then he leaned forward. "Listen, Scully, you got some serious shit on you." He pointed at the computer screen in front of him. "You're wasting your time here or on any other legitimate department. Haven Park's your only shot."

I thanked him and left.

No luck in the Valley or at the sheriff's department, but I put in my application everywhere just the same. I had twenty years of service on the LAPD and two Medal of Valor citations, but because of what was posted on POLITE, nobody was going to give me a second look. Regardless, I had to apply everywhere else first. Had to go through the steps.

Tomorrow, I would go to what had been called by the press "the most corrupt police department in California."

Tomorrow, I'd give the dreaded Haven Park PD a try.

# CHAPTER 5

I spent the night at a downtown hotel. The Biltmore on Grand. I can't even remember what the room looked like, I was that upset.

The next morning, I dressed in my charcoal-gray suit, a fresh shirt and tie. I got my Acura out of the parking garage beneath the hotel and loaded all my stuff from home in the trunk and began the short four-mile trip into downtown L.A. where the tiny, one-square-mile, incorporated city of Haven Park was located.

I took the freeway past the City of Commerce with its rail yards and warehouses. On the other side of the freeway were the small, incorporated cities of Maywood and Cudahy. I left them behind, finally getting off on Ortho Street. How fitting, I thought, to be traveling into a criminal cesspool on a street named after a fertilizer. I turned left and, after driving about a mile, took another left on Lincoln Avenue and I was in Haven Park. Only it looked more like a small town in Mexico, or at the very least, a Texas border town. I'd read somewhere that the population of Haven Park was largely made up of illegal aliens. Thirty thousand Hispanics living in a one-square-mile stucco town.

As I drove down the main drag, I saw nothing but urban sprawl, most of it run-down businesses that had been painted in bright south-of-the-border colors—yellows, greens and oranges. Most of the building signs were in Spanish. I passed the Mendoza Clínica Del Dentista, a yellow one-story building with heavily barred windows. Most people run from a dentist's office, but Dr. Mendoza was worried about people trying to break into his. A huge King Taco on one corner advertised TENEMOS TACOS DE POLLO, and under that was a sign for Mexican ribs.

I passed a string of run-down strip malls and then saw the alabaster-white, wood-sided city hall building coming up on my right. It dominated most of a city block. It had a wooden cupola on each corner and a big weather vane on the roof making it look like a Mafia wedding cake. The city hall and the Haven Park PD shared opposite ends of the large structure.

There was a small glass door right in the center that did not appear to be the main entrance for either the city hall or the police station. There was an open meter right in front, so I parked, got out, fed the slot a quarter, and walked down to the police station. Then I took a short detour around the Haven Park PD side of the building past the fenced and landscaped parking lot. I looked in at the police vehicles parked behind the chain link. It was better rolling stock than we had on the LAPD. There were two or three new Ford Crown Victoria squad cars that were not currently out on patrol. Two new SWAT vans, as well as some EMT trucks, black-and-white station wagons and surveillance vans were parked in random slots. A large black-and-white Vogue motor home that appeared to be a tricked-out mobile command center with two satellite dishes on the roof loomed above the rest. All of it looked less than a year old.

I headed back to the police department's front door, which had HAVEN PARK P.D. stenciled in gold letters above the city seal. Under that it said RICHARD ROSS—CHIEF OF POLICE.

I knew all about Ricky Ross. In fact, I had a tortured history with him that went back ten years to my patrol days on the LAPD when I had partnered with Ross for six months while working in Van Nuys. I was the one who'd gotten him thrown off the LAPD. Back then I was just a few months sober, but Rick Ross was still the chief engineer on the Red-Nose Express. He liked to get liquored up, and on his way home in plainclothes would sometimes pull his sidearm and wave it at people who cut him off on the freeway. This practice earned him the nickname "Freeway" Ricky Ross.

One night, when I was catching a ride with him, I actually witnessed this behavior and, in an over-the-top moment, saw him accidentally discharge his weapon, barely missing a banker from West Covina. I'd immediately turned Ricky in to Internal Affairs and testified against him at his Board of Rights hearing. He'd claimed he was just removing his backup gun from his covert carry holster and it had accidentally discharged. He caught a huge break and went on suspension for six months, but that only made him worse.

He was drunk all the time after that. His wife finally divorced him. He lost his house and a month later he'd lost his LAPD badge for good. Rick Ross blamed me for all of it. It would seem that this man could be a tough mountain for me to climb if I wanted a job in Haven Park. But I had a way around him.

As I pushed open the door to the police headquarters, I ran smack into a big police sergeant in uniform, another cop that I'd known back on the job in L.A. He was a large, muscle-bound guy with a steroid abuser's body named Alonzo Bell. Alonzo was half white, half some other, dark race that he would never exactly identify—Arab or Persian, maybe even Hispanic. Bell is an Anglo name, so he'd probably changed or shortened it, or the complexion came from his mother's side.

Alonzo had been thrown off the LAPD years ago for losing it in an I-room and almost beating to death a gangbanger who'd shot and wounded his partner. The partner survived, but Alonzo's L.A. police career didn't. I remembered him as a giant attitude problem you didn't want to mess with.

"Do I know you?" he asked, seeming to remember me, hard eyes giving me the once-over.

"Shane Scully. How you been, Al?"

"Shane fucking Scully," he said, a smile widening his flat brown features. "Whatta you doing here, dude?"

"Looking for work."

He grinned. "What happened to bring you this far down? You bang the captain's wife?"

"Lost some evidence. Little misdemeanor. But I was running out of road in L.A. anyway. It was better if I just moved on."

His dark features arranged into a frown and then he glanced at the name engraved in gold on the door. I guess he knew about my history with Ricky Ross. But then anyone who was on the LAPD when Ricky got the boot knew the story. After the IA hearing Ross went nuts, and confronted me in the Parker Center garage, where he threatened my life in front of about ten guys. What went on between us until he finally got fired had been pretty ugly.

"You know Rick Ross is the acting chief down here," Alonzo warned.

"Yeah, I heard. It's even on this door." I tapped the gold letters and grinned.

"He's an asshole," Alonzo said matter-of-factly. "The old chief, Charlie Le Grande, was okay. He just wanted to keep the shit on the sidewalk and off his shoes. But the feds busted him for having criminal ties to Eighteenth Street gang members. He's under indictment. Mayor Bratano appointed Ricky Ross to be our acting chief. Ross was on patrol two weeks ago, next thing you know he's chief. Nobody saw it coming. He's a hemorrhoid with ears."

"Look, Alonzo, I'm kinda down to last chances, and I really want to stay in police work. I didn't know about Ross being acting chief, but this is kind of my last shot. I hear there's ways things can happen down here. Can you help me?"

Alonzo surveyed me carefully for a long moment. "Yeah, maybe," he finally said.

"How do I do it?"

"Go ahead and fill out the paperwork. I'll help you get to the front of the line. C'mon." He walked back inside the building and I followed him.

The interior of the department wasn't art deco. The funky architectural swirls stopped at the front door. Inside it was pure cop shop—pictures of the command structure, a bulletproof glass divider separating the public areas from the police cubicles in back. Alonzo buzzed us through using a plastic key card and we walked down a scuffed, painted hallway.

"We've currently got forty-one active duty patrol cops on the job down here, plus command staff—a few captains and lieutenants," he told me as we walked. "But despite your history with Rick Ross, the timing's great because we're adding people right now, trying to get our numbers up. Reason for the expansion is we just got the contract to police our neighbor city of Fleetwood."

I'd read about the new Haven Park–Fleetwood contract in the *Blue Line*, the LAPD magazine.

Both cities shared the same population base of illegal immigrants and were roughly the same one square mile in size. Although Fleetwood didn't adjoin Haven Park, it was just one city over, separated by the equally tiny township of Vista, which was policed by the Los Angeles Sheriffs Department. Fleetwood had also been using the county sheriff's as its police force, paying them under contract until about two months ago, when suddenly Enzo Diaz, Fleetwood's Hispanic mayor, asked Cecil Bratano, the Hispanic mayor of Haven Park, if Haven Park's police department would take over the policing duties in Fleetwood.

For reasons of corruption and common profit, Cecil Bratano agreed. The county sheriff's contract was immediately canceled and Haven Park entered into a municipal alliance presided over by both mayors and policed by the Haven Park PD.

Hence Haven Park PD's sudden need for more officers.

Alonzo Bell stopped in front of a door marked PERSONNEL RESOURCES.

"The girl in there is Mita Morales—Aztec blood, kinda fat. But she can screw you up and lose your file if she doesn't like you. She likes me, so I'll sprinkle some fuck dust on this deal, and she'll be your buddy."

"Listen, Alonzo, I guess I should tell you I've got a pretty bad write-up on POLITE."

"Don't worry about POLITE. If we dinged guys off this force because of that bullshit, there wouldn't be one cop riding in a Plain Jane down here, including our esteemed acting chief. Just fill out the forms and meet me at Club A Fuego at seven tonight."

"A Fuego?"

"Yeah, it's a hangout. Big barn-sized bar full of off-duty cops, politicians, drug dealers—everybody goes there. It's where the real business in Haven Park and Fleetwood gets done. There're some people you need to meet. If we get them on your side, it won't matter what Freeway Ricky Ross says. You'll be set."

"Just like that?"

"It's very different down here. Welcome to Haven Park." Then he pushed open the door and introduced me to a stone-faced woman with Aztec features named Mita.

# CHAPTER 6

Mita never smiled, never changed her expression as she asked questions about my background and typed the answers on a tattered, throwback IBM Selectric. She filled out the top of the first form, then rolled the paper down and typed some more information on the bottom of the sheet. She never turned on the computer that sat on her desk; never typed in the secret password for POLITE; never read about my career-ending felony case-tampering charge.

"Fill the rest of that out and sign it," was all she said and scowled at me as if I were week-old bird plop cooking on the hood of her car. I went to the table across the room to do the work, but as I looked back, I caught her sneaking a peek at my ass. Gotcha, Mita.

After filling out the report and smiling at Mita's Aztec stone-face, I left.

Next, I drove around Haven Park looking for a suitable place to stay. I still needed employment before I could look for an apartment or motel room to lease in the area. Unfortunately, the hotels that I passed looked pretty Third World. I picked one called the Haven Park Inn, which was a cut above the rest. If things worked out down here, I'd give it a try.

I continued to drive around the one-square-mile

city. It was blocks and blocks of the same thing. Very little money had been wasted on landscaping. The business streets like Lincoln and Pacific were wall-to-wall one-story markets, stores or auto body shops, all pretty low-end. The residential neighborhoods were mostly bungalow-type houses with Spanish arches and barred windows, painted in traditional Mexican hues, bright, but also strangely depressing.

I passed Club A Fuego. It was only eleven o'clock in the morning and there were very few cars in the parking lot. The nightclub was located on Willow Street and as Alonzo had told me, it was huge, a gymnasium-sized red barn. In Spanish *a fuego* means "on fire," but it can also mean "cool."

The parking lot could easily hold two hundred cars. There was a porte cochere that shaded the entry. I saw a Haven Park police car parked under the overhang in the shade. A uniformed police officer was leaning against the front fender of his unit smoking a big black cigar. He didn't even look at me as I sharked through the parking lot and out the side entrance.

I think in all the years I've been a cop I've never before seen an American police officer in uniform leaning against the fender of his patrol car smoking a big cigar. It was like a bad Mexican movie down here.

I left A Fuego in my rearview mirror and headed

through Vista. I passed the ritzy Bicycle Club Casino that sat on the lip of the freeway. A very impressive structure with a neon sign that advertised POKER & PAI GOW. Then I drove around Fleetwood.

After about two hours, I had a pretty good idea of the layout of both towns. There was very little to distinguish them from one another. The Los Angeles River ran through the east end of Fleetwood and then through Haven Park. The river was a sludge-filled mess that afforded little esthetic relief from the relentless feel of poverty.

Once, as I was passing back into Haven Park, I thought I caught sight of a tan Chevy four-door sedan tailing me. It looked like some kind of cop plain-wrap with blackwalls. I slowed down, trying to see inside, but it immediately turned off.

One other thing caught my eye as I cruised. The Hispanic gang that was operating down here was a branch of the large and powerful 18th Street gang. The clique in Haven Park called itself the 18th Street Locos. They had spray-painted almost every available wall or overpass with 18-L. Agent Love had said that the 18th Street gang were the new gun and drug players in L.A., moving their product into our city from criminal warehouse towns they'd constructed south of the border. The flow of new Russian machine guns had been so relentless it had finally captured the interest of Homeland Security.

The Locos were a powerful inner-city gang, so I wasn't surprised to see their graffiti. But there was some other tag art that did surprise me. Intermixed with all the 18-L's were several freshly painted SSCC graffiti tags. I knew that stood for the South Side Compton Crips. Compton was a few miles south. It struck me as strange and faintly ominous that black gangsters from Compton had started tagging walls in a predominantly Hispanic territory like Haven Park.

*What's going on with that?* I wondered.

# CHAPTER 7

Club A Fuego was already jumping when I arrived at a little past seven o'clock that evening. I pulled into its huge, half-full parking facility. Out of some sense of caution, I decided not to park in the underlit lot where my car might be tampered with and instead pulled out and parked under a streetlamp by the curb. Then I went inside.

The interior of the club was a big open three-story space, one end of which was occupied by a large dance floor. The other side was the bar area, where most of the crowd had gathered. There was mariachi music blasting over the sound system. It was cranked up way too loud, emitting earsplitting Tijuana Brass. The music managed to cut through the din of the hundred or more people, mostly men, some who were shouting conversations at each other to be heard. A threadbare carpet that had withstood years of careless bar service gave the building a musty smell. Even with the hundred-plus people at the east end of the room, the place still looked almost empty. It was that big. Mexican waitresses in red vests circulated with trays. A few people had sought some privacy from the relentless music and were sitting at the tables around the basketball-court-sized dance floor, nursing drinks and conversing earnestly.

I made my way to the far end and passed into the bar. I could smell fried Mexican food that was being served along with beer and mixed drinks. I found a place at the stick and ordered a Heineken, then looked around at the loud, milling crowd.

A few guys I'd known on the LAPD were scattered around, most in plain clothes. Some were engaged in shouted conversation over the blaring music, others were playing pool on well-worn tables. Spanish was the primary language being spoken by the largely Hispanic patronage. Gangster types in street vines with gang tats talked with older-looking, slightly overdressed *jefes* in expensive silk suits and mixed with a smattering of off-duty cops in polo shirts and windbreakers. Strange crowd.

I didn't see Alonzo Bell, so I took my beer and began a slow tour of the lounge. At one end of the bar a Mexican soccer match was playing on the digital flat-screen TV. Upholstered booths lined one entire side of the room. I felt a hand grab my arm.

"There you are. I been looking for you, dude." I turned and looked into the big, flat, brown, frying-pan-shaped face of Alonzo Bell. He was in street clothes and his massive weight-lifter's arms bulged the sleeves of his short-sleeve shirt. "I got a table back here, follow me," he shouted into my ear.

He moved us through the room, stopping a few times to introduce me to people I'd never seen before and probably wouldn't remember later. Some were Anglo, some Mexican.

"Meet Shane Scully," he would say. "He's gonna try and catch a ride with us. Shane just came off the big blue zoo downtown."

We finally made it to his table and he slid in. I took the seat opposite him.

"My spot," he shouted. "Nobody takes it when I'm here."

"Interesting place." I raised my voice over the din and motioned to the room. "How many of these guys are cops?"

"The whole day watch and most of the swing shift will be here eventually," he called back. "This is where the real business gets done. That guy over there"—he pointed at a small Mexican man with sharp features—"he's the mayor's assistant. Carlos Reál. We call him Real Deal Reál. Carlos will sell you anything from a gun permit to a stolen baby. He's always on the grind, that guy. We all are." *On the grind* was street slang for working your hustle.

It went on like that, Alonzo pointing out cops, politicians and 18th Street Locos.

"The Locos run everything down here," he told me. "The main *veterano* in the Haven Park clique is that guy over there. His name is Ovieto Ortiz."

He pointed out a man in his late thirties who was just moving up to talk with the mayor's assistant. Ovieto Ortiz was a wiry, dangerous-looking man with a big black 18 tattooed on the side of his neck.

"His street name is 007 'cause of his double-O initials and 'cause he's got a license to kill. Ovieto is a big piece of the way business gets done down here, so the cops tolerate him. You spell tolerate with a dollar sign in front of it."

"I saw some South Side Crip graffiti here and in Fleetwood," I shouted across the table at him. "If Eighteenth Street Locos run this town, why are Crips tagging walls?"

"The blacks used to run this place till all the illegal aliens moved in and pushed 'em out. Now they're trying to reclaim their old corners. It could get ugly. We have our orders straight from Mayor Bratano's office to shut these blacks down. We hook 'em and book 'em, the city court cooks 'em. The idea is to keep Haven Park and Fleetwood safe for Eighteenth Street business."

"You kidding me? You're running this street gang's interference?"

"We got our own culture down here. It's called cafeteria policing. Everything is laid out on a big buffet table, cops get to pass by and just fill their trays. You probably heard that the starting pay scale is low," he yelled, smiling as he said it.

"Yeah. Fifty-five grand."

"Don't let it bother you, dude," Alonzo said with a laugh. "If you're in the cafeteria line, you can make more money than a crooked banker. We got millions of scams. Last month, one of our damn patrol officers who was just a fucking two-striper, took home twenty-five hundred in kickbacks in two weeks. Get in the cafeteria line, brother. Fill your tray. You won't be sorry."

"You're shitting me."

"It's like Mexico. Haven Park's a Third World city with a whore's mentality. Everything that gets paid flows upstream. Everybody gets a taste as it goes by. Crooks kick up to cops, everybody kicks up to city hall and the mayor. Protection, bribery, tow tickets, the works. The two brothers who own A Fuego are Manny and Hector Avila. They also own Blue Light Towing, which has the exclusive tow truck contract for Haven Park and Fleetwood. That contract is worth a fortune."

"What is?" I shouted back. "Towing cars?"

"The cops boot a car, it's a two-hundred-dollar impound. The Avilas give a third of that to the mayor and kick back ten percent to the cop who writes the ticket. If a blue writes ten towing tickets a day, you can get an envelope from the Avilas with two hundred bucks in it at the end of your shift. If you stay on it, at the end of a five-day week it's an extra grand. After a year, you got fifty G's. This shit can add up, and that's just the tow truck stuff. There's lots of other ways to make up for the low starting pay."

The mariachi CD ended and for a moment A Fuego quieted down and people stopped shouting at each other. It occurred to me that all the noise would make it impossible to record a conversation in here.

In that momentary lull of the music I asked, "You can get ten cars towed in a day?" It surprised me because it seemed like a lot.

"Depends on how committed you are. Some guys can do it. The dumb *bolupos* who live down here are mostly undocumented. Haven Park and Fleetwood are full of fruit pickers, scared of their shadows. They pay the two hundred to get their car back or we auction their rust buckets off and get our cut out of the sale. Gardeners and maintenance guys are the best targets 'cause they need their trucks to work. Show me a fucking Chevy pickup with a leaf blower and I'll own the fucker. I towed this one asshole six times in two months. He finally moved. Hated to see that brown boy go." Alonzo took a gulp of his beer and smiled sadly.

Then a new tape started and we were back to screaming at each other. It went on like that. He detailed the scams, explaining the ways a cop could make extra money in Haven Park. He told me about health code and fire department tickets on Mexican restaurants or any other food business. They would threaten to close kitchens or shops unless they got paid cash. There was a protection scam being run in Fleetwood. Gang money came in envelopes distributed by the watch commanders—weekly payoffs for letting 18th Street Locos have their run of both towns.

"But if you put something on your tray you gotta remember to only take half and kick the rest up to the guy above you. A piece of everything else has to end up in Mayor Cecil Bratano's pocket. And you gotta get in with the Avilas," Alonzo told me. "If they want you on the PD, you're on."

"No matter what Ricky Ross says?"

"Ricky's just a lushed-up paper-pusher who Mayor Bratano picked because he can't find his ass with either hand. The real power on the job are Hector and Manny Avila. They kick back big to the mayor. That's why they got the exclusive towing contract. They run the political machine and most of the graft in both cities."

"I'm surprised you can get away with all this," I said. "Especially after all the bad publicity Maywood and Cudahy got in the newspapers for police and government corruption."

"What was going on in Maywood and Cudahy was small-time B.S. compared to this."

He grinned as he looked up and spotted somebody. "Hector and Manny just got here. Lemme bring these guys over. Say the right shit and before you know it, you're gonna be riding in a new Plain Jane, policing the great cities of Haven Park and Fleetwood."

# CHAPTER 8

Alonzo got up from the table and greeted a middle-aged dark wiry guy with a Brillo Pad mustache who, after leaning in and listening for a minute, turned and waved an arm at another guy with the same wire-brush hair. There was a strong family resemblance, but the second man was older and heavier. His hair and mustache were steel gray. After a moment, Alonzo led them both over and made room for them on his side of the upholstered booth. The Avilas sat down and studied me carefully across the wooden table.

"Hector and Manny Avila, meet an old friend just off the LAPD, Shane Scully," Alonzo said, his voice rising above the escalating mariachi music.

*"Como se?"* Manny said.

*"A viente,"* I replied.

He smiled. *"Habla español."*

*"Sí, poquito. Es necesario para la policía en Los Angeles."*

*"Buena,"* Manny said. Then he turned and smiled at his stone-faced older brother.

"Shane had some problems on the LAPD. He got caught fixing a case, taking money, screwing the suspect, *la bonita, chica de cinema*." Alonzo Bell grinned.

It was pretty obvious somebody in Haven Park had gone ahead and accessed my POLITE file. Except down here my bad deeds served as a recommendation, because Manny smiled and said, "This is not such a big problem."

"We checked around," Alonzo continued. "Shane has already tried a bunch of other police agencies, but with that felony case-tampering beef, nobody will put him on. He really wants to stay in law enforcement. He gets the picture. He knows how to sing from the hymnal."

"You have Alonzo swearing for you. You have a very good *compadre*," Manny Avila said. Hector still hadn't said anything. He just studied me aggressively.

"I've got some problems with Rick Ross," I said. "He probably isn't going to want me on the force."

Manny made a dismissive gesture with his hand as if that was of no concern. *"Ross es abadesa,"* he said. "A worthless pimp. You need not worry about the feelings of such a man."

"That's good to know," I said.

"If you have our friend Alonzo speaking for

you, there is little more to say," Manny yelled over the music. Then he grinned at Alonzo and put a familiar hand on his shoulder, a gesture of friendship. "If Alonzo is telling us that you are a good man, then consider it done."

"That's what I'm saying." Alonzo smiled.

Suddenly Hector, the older, more serious brother, spoke for the first time. "You must know that from this point on, things will be expected of you. There are rules, things that must happen. Alonzo can explain, but you must realize these rules cannot be broken. *Comprende?*"

"I understand."

"Money will have to change hands," Hector said. "When you do well, then others must also do well."

"Fair enough," I said.

"Okay. Then tomorrow you will go and see Captain Talbot Jones. He will accept your application." They both shook my hand.

"Welcome to the Haven Park PD," Manny Avila said, and just like that I'd made the worst police department in America.

I drank beer with Alonzo and met half a dozen guys on the force, including Talbot Jones. He was a huge, glowering presence. A black cop who Alonzo told me later had been thrown off L.A. Vice for excessive violence. Talbot Jones was a patrol captain and Haven Park's acting deputy chief.

I ended up drinking a few too many Heinekens by the end of the evening. Alonzo and I left A Fuego at a little past midnight. When I went to the curb outside where I'd left my Acura, it was gone.

"I left it right here," I said. "What happened to my ride?"

"Got towed. Sorry about that." Alonzo grinned.

"I was parked legally. This street isn't posted. What's the deal?"

"Welcome to Haven Park," he said, still smiling.

It was the third time today somebody had told me that.

# CHAPTER 9

Alonzo dropped me at the Haven Park Inn and instructed me to show up around nine A.M. at the station, where Talbot Jones would take care of me. "By then, the Avilas will have the whole deal rigged," Alonzo said before driving off.

After he left, I went to my room and fell onto the bed with my clothes on, looking at the cracked brown ceiling. I could smell grease in the upholstery and curtains. Somebody had been cooking tacos over a hibachi in here. It had been a long but eventful day. I didn't know what lay ahead, but I was definitely in the cafeteria line.

I slept fitfully. I heard gunshots and sirens once about two A.M. and woke up, not sure exactly where they were coming from. It sounded like a good-sized police response not too far away. I stayed awake until five, and then slipped into a restless sleep.

In my dream I was at the L.A. Police Academy in Elysian Park, holding my recruit gear in a small canvas bag, dressed in jeans and an LAPD sweatshirt. I was very excited because I had just been accepted on the department and, with my arrival at the academy, had finally found an identity I could believe in.

"This is going to be bitchin'," I said to the guy standing next to me. I could hardly wait to get started.

When I woke up at seven I could barely face the grim prospect of starting work on the Haven Park PD.

I arrived at city hall after a short walk of two and a half blocks down Pacific Avenue. I felt dirty even though I had taken a shower. The heavy glass door with the police department seal and Ricky Ross's name in gold letters greeted me. I pushed it open and entered. I stated why I was there and was led by a civilian employee down a long corridor decorated with old black-and-white photos of Haven Park arrests dating back to the forties.

She showed me into Talbot Jones's office. He was in a captain's uniform this morning, seated behind a large mahogany desk. The office was typical of a deputy chief. Plaques everywhere, pictures of the captain shaking hands with politicians and business leaders. I saw one photo of Jones with Ricky Ross, who was a skinny, dweeby-looking guy with thin sandy blond hair styled in a comb-over. He looked innocent enough, but you couldn't fool me. I'd seen violence flare behind those hazel eyes.

There was also the mandatory Haven Park Little League photo. This particular team was sponsored by Big Kiss Bail Bonds. Two coaches were holding up a KISS JAIL GOODBYE sign behind a bunch of grinning ten-year-olds. I wondered how many of these players would grow up to one day need the services of their Little League sponsor.

There were several pictures of a short but compactly built Hispanic man who seemed to favor white Panama hats. I knew from pictures I'd seen of him in the L.A. paper that this was Haven Park's mayor, His Honor Cecil Bratano.

"Scully, huh?" Talbot said in a deep baritone after I reintroduced myself. He seemed to have forgotten we'd met each other at A Fuego the previous night. He glanced down at a computer printout on his desk. "Says here you got jammed up in L.A."

"Misunderstanding," I said.

"Let's not sling a lot of bullshit at each other, okay? I've got your IA package right here in front of me. You left a long slimy trail on the sidewalk over there."

"If you say so, Captain." I was not sure how to play the guy. I needed this job. He was a big, imposing, six-foot four-inch, muscle-bound ass-kicker. One of those black guys who can project simmering anger without saying a word. Since he'd been thrown off the L.A. cops for beating up street people while on the Vice squad, I really didn't think my IA record should scare him off. He flipped through my application. "You know the score down here?" he said, not even looking up.

"Alonzo Bell told me a lot of it last night. I'm not a troublemaker, Captain. I know how to go along to get along."

He grunted, said nothing, as he continued to peruse my application for a long minute more.

"Your app says you were a marksman on the LAPD gun range and were current on all of your field expediency ratings before you resigned. That right?"

"Yeah, I was in good standing until I had my little problem."

"Uh-huh," he said, still glaring down at the pages. "I understand you talked to the Avilas last night. They give you the story from their end?"

"Yes, sir. I got a pretty good idea how it all works."

He finally looked up at me. "Okay, Scully. Then here's the riff from my end. This ain't police work like you're used to in L.A. We got our own way of doing the job down here. Most of the residents in Haven Park and Fleetwood are undocumented. But that doesn't mean we're the fucking immigration police. We're not busting these people for being here without papers. The reason they live in Haven Park in the first place is because this is a sanctuary city. We straight on that?"

"I understand."

"This department is vertically integrated with city hall. Know what that means?"

"Everything flows up through one chain of command, right to the mayor's office."

"Exactly. You step out of that chain, you create any kind of backwater or eddy of discontent, you're gone. We don't need Wyatt Earp down here. We also don't need William Kunstler. All you gotta do is play by the rules that the city council puts forth and it all glides and slides."

"Are those rules written down somewhere so I can see them?" I asked.

"You bet." He pushed a small booklet over at me. "You a smart guy, Scully?"

"I try to be."

"Stay in line and don't change the way things are done in my city. It says in that booklet that you will adhere to our police guidelines and deal with street crises according to the mandates set down in writing there. You don't freelance, you don't go into business for yourself. Except for towing kickbacks, when something is put on your tray, the prescribed amount, which is half, gets passed up to the guy above you."

"Cafeteria policing."

He didn't say anything, just sat there staring at me. Finally, he cleared his throat. "You know where the Haven Park Elementary School is?"

"No, sir, but I'll find it."

"Two blocks over on Pine Street. It's an old decommissioned school that our department's using as a training and locker facility. Report to Arnold Bale, he's our equipment manager. He'll give you a gun and uniform and get you set up. Since you're LAPD-trained and field-savvy, I'm going to waive our Haven Park Police Academy program for the time being and just put you right on the street. We're a little short-handed with this new Fleetwood contract and can use the man-power. There might be some tests and stuff you'll have to take later."

"I appreciate that."

"Your training and probation officer is Sergeant Alonzo Bell. He swore for you, so he can train you."

"That suits me fine, sir."

"A few other things. One: We're not here to protect and serve like in L.A. This is an ash can. You try to protect and serve the lettuce-pickers who live in this toilet, you're gonna get played. Don't make friends with any of them. They're assholes. Two: This department is not an equal opportunity employer. We got no Dickless Tracys on the job down here. You want to work with a woman, go somewhere else. We got very few Hispanics, one or two. Mostly we're made up of black and white officers, and a few Asians. I understand you speak some Spanish, which will come in very handy. We are not looking for any civil libertarians. We don't want or need a fucking police union. We're happy with things the way they're currently run. If any of that doesn't sit well with you, there's the door." He pointed behind me.

"All sounds good to me, Captain," I said.

"Raise your right hand."

I did.

"Using the power vested in me for and by the City of Haven Park, California, I do solemnly swear that I, Shane Scully, will abide by all the terms, covenants and conditions set forth in the policing guide and will faithfully fulfill the duties of a Haven Park peace officer to the best of my abilities, so help me God."

I started to repeat that long, confusing oath, but Captain Jones stopped me.

"Don't say it back. This isn't the fucking Boy Scouts. Just say I do."

"I do."

"Welcome to the Haven Park PD. Get out of here and go check in with Arnie Bale at the school."

I left Talbot Jones's office. I was tired of

walking and wanted to get my Acura back. I tried to do this by borrowing a phone at the front desk to call Blue Light Towing. I got a recording saying that they were closed for the holiday.

"What holiday is today?" I asked, frowning at the civil employee on the other side of the desk.

"Cinco de Mayo," she said, acting as if I'd just asked when Christmas was.

I walked out of city hall a newly minted member of the Haven Park Police Department. I was back on the job. I'd been vouched for by crooks and sworn in by a scoundrel.

# CHAPTER 10

Haven Park Elementary was a long-abandoned sprawl of one-story stucco buildings badly in need of paint and repair. The exterior walls of the fifties-style structure served as canvas for endless amounts of gang graffiti. The rest of the property, including a half-sized athletic field with a baseball diamond and an old-style bow-truss gymnasium, was enclosed by a rusting chain-link fence.

I walked up to an ancient civil service employee who was sitting by the gated entrance to the school reading a Mexican comic book. "I'm a new police officer. Looking for Arnie Bale," I told him.

"Got some ID?" he asked.

I showed him my driver's license. He wrote my name on a sheet.

"To the right, up the stairs. The equipment building is that one over there that says 'Fuck the Police' on it."

"Interesting sentiment."

"Taggers. We clean it off. They spray it back on. Entertainment for everybody. Arnie should be inside."

Arnie Bale, when I found him, reminded me of my first junior high school baseball coach. A stringy brown-skinned guy who was all cords and muscles. He had an Adam's apple the size of a prune. I couldn't take my eyes off the damn thing when he talked. Up and down, up and down—like a ball on a rubber band.

"You look like about a size forty regular," he said, giving me the once-over.

"Close enough."

"Here's the equipment list." He shoved a printed sheet of blue paper into my hand and said, "We got most of it. Some is out of stock, so check what I can't supply, and I'll reorder. Follow me."

He led me down a narrow hallway, opening one cupboard after another. He gave me a dark blue Haven Park patrol officer's uniform with the Haven Park Police Department seal emblazoned in white and gold on the right shoulder and a half moon patch that said FOREVER VIGILANT on the other. I received a gunbelt, a steel-blue Smith & Wesson .38 with a four-inch barrel and two speed loaders, along with a Maglite, baton and shoulder radio rover. All standard issue. Then Arnie reached into a box and handed me a three-inch-long leather object with a wrist strap.

"What's this?" I asked, looking at the thing, which weighed about two pounds.

"Sap," Arnie said.

"You mean like to hit guys over the head with?"

"Yep."

"I don't think I've seen or heard about a police officer using a sap since the NAACP and the ACLU were formed."

"Yeah, well . . . I won't tell 'em if you won't."

"I really get to use this?"

"Part of our standard equipment package. Swing it in good health," he joked.

By the time I got to the end of the corridor, I was loaded up with gear. Arnie took me into the old elementary school locker room outfitted with benches that ran in front of rows of battered gray metal lockers. He showed me to an empty one and handed me a combination padlock.

"Set your own combination number. Our roll calls are in the gym. Then we walk the two blocks over to city hall to get our black-and-whites out of the police lot there."

"Okay."

"Put on your uniform. We don't supply shoes, but those you got on look fine. Meet me in my office when you're in harness."

He left me in the locker room. I dressed quickly.

It felt a little funny because I hadn't been in street blue, except for police funerals, since I last rode Patrol in L.A. over ten years ago. It felt strange to be harnessing up for a street tour, as if my life hadn't progressed much since those early days on the LAPD. Arnie had a good eye for sizes and everything fit pretty well.

When I finished dressing I found him in an old coach's office located inside a wire cage. He was seated behind a scarred metal desk, and looked up at me as I entered.

"Shit fits you good," he said, proud of his guesses. Then he pulled out a black box from his desk drawer, opened it and handed me two gold metal uniform ornaments.

"Badge and hat piece," he said. "We're outta hats right now 'cause of the Fleetwood expansion. I got more lids coming in. You about a seven and six-eighths?"

"You're pretty good, Arnie."

"Yeah, I rock. Pin that on your shirt. Put the hat piece in your pocket till the new brims come in and get your ass outta here. Your training officer is gonna swing by in twenty minutes to pick you up. You can wait for him by the handball courts out front. Have a good one."

I threaded the badge through the metal eyelets on my uniform shirt and clipped it closed. Number 689. Pinned, tinned and ready to sap Mexicans.

When I went into the Los Angeles Police

Academy in Elysian Park, it had taken me eight grueling months to earn my uniform and badge. This was a joke.

I exited the gymnasium and found the handball courts. There was an old wooden bench under a leafless elm, so I sat in the meager shade from the dying tree and waited. I wasn't sure exactly what to expect, so I decided to follow the advice on my left shoulder and be forever vigilant.

# CHAPTER 11

"I gotta straighten a guy out in Fleetwood, so let's run over there and I'll show you around," Alonzo Bell said as I got into the passenger side of his black-and-white. He pulled out of the elementary school and continued. "Our shop is Car Nine. In Haven Park we use a regular ten-code like LAPD. I've got us out of service, ten-seven, for the beginning of the tour so I can show you the turf."

"Good deal."

We drove down a commercial street called District, then skirted the edges of Haven Park, went through the neighboring city of Vista and entered Fleetwood.

"I heard shots and some sirens last night," I said as we rode past the mostly residential blocks of single-story, brightly painted stucco houses with dead lawns.

"We had a little street-cleaning action. I didn't hear about it till this morning. The night watch caught some South Side Crips doing corners over on Lincoln Boulevard. It got frisky." *Doing corners* was street slang for drug dealing.

Bell smiled. "We don't want those guys over here. Two C-homies got splashed, two got hooked and booked. Lotta red sauce got spilled. Big night."

"But you leave the Eighteenth Street Locos alone."

"Eighteenth Streeters are kicking back to us, so they get the hospitality mat. I thought I ran this all down for you at A Fuego," he said, frowning.

I nodded and looked at the passing houses. More dead grass, rusting Chevys. Urban blight.

We drove through Fleetwood to the city administration complex, which was located next to a rundown industrial complex.

Alonzo nosed our unit into a slot. We got out and I followed him inside the two-story city hall building. He approached a pretty, dark-eyed girl with shiny jet-black hair, who was wearing a tight sweater that showed off her jutting breasts.

"Mariana Concheta Brown," he announced. *"Maravilloso Mamacita."*

"Hey, Al. Where you been? How come none of you hot Haven Park guys come calling anymore?" She smiled at him and he winked at me. Obviously she was more than a friend.

"Meet my new partner, fresh from L.A. Shane Scully, this is Mariana Brown. Her husband's in Iraq."

He winked again, all of this, I guess, to tell me he was laying this war bride.

"Nice to meet you," I said.

"Mariana runs the sorry sack of incompetent dogs who work here. Armando around?" he asked.

Mariana picked up a phone and buzzed. "Sergeant Bell to see you, sir."

A few seconds later, a fat brown middle-aged toad of a guy exited the door behind Mariana. His greasy black hair was slicked back and he had one of those deeply pockmarked complexions that looked like he'd had trouble learning to eat with a fork as a kid.

"It didn't come," Armando said without preamble, growling the words at Alonzo.

"You need to talk to Cal or Gordon 'cause they were bringing it."

"Don't hide behind those *mallates*. You know how this shit's supposed to work. It's your responsibility to make sure my end gets to me."

"Say hi to Shane," Alonzo said. "He's my new partner." Trying to use me to avoid the short ugly man's anger.

Armando glanced at me, then addressed Alonzo again. "This shit's gotta stop."

"I'll check with those guys, see what happened."

Armando turned to face me. "You'll do good

down here if you don't forget how things work. Alonzo here, sometimes he's got a bad memory." Then he slapped Bell hard on the shoulder. It wasn't a very friendly gesture. "I want that package before I go home. Make it happen."

Then, without saying goodbye, he turned and went through the door behind Mariana, who was studiously at work not looking at Alonzo, pretending not to have heard the humiliating slapdown.

We walked outside and got back into our shop. "That guy's on the Fleetwood City Council, but he needs to chill. He's getting way too full of himself," Bell growled, working off some anger. "Put us ten-eight."

I picked up the mike. "This is Car Nine. We're ten-eight and clear to take calls at El Norte Park in Fleetwood."

The RTO came back. "Roger, Nine, we show you ten-eight and clear in Fleetwood."

I clicked the mike off and looked over at Alonzo. Whatever had transpired at city hall was still chewing on him and he glowered darkly as he drove. We headed back into Haven Park. On the way, we passed a large political billboard with a picture of a Mexican middleweight boxer named Rocky Chacon. He was in a classic fighter's stance with his feet squared, his red gloves up, facing the camera. Under the picture, written in both Spanish and English, it said:

VOTE FOR A CHAMPION
ROCKY CHACON FOR HAVEN PARK
MAYOR

"What's with that?" I asked Alonzo, jerking my thumb at the sign as we rolled past.

Bell glanced at the billboard and said, "That's a big problem. That's something all of us better do something about, quick."

He drove in silence for a minute. "You heard about him, right? When he was still fighting? Juan 'Rocky' Chacon—'El Alboratador.' "

"*Alborotador* means brawler, right?" Alonzo nodded, so I went on. "Yeah, I remember him. The middleweight champ for about six seconds. He was from some little dirt-street town in Baja."

"He lives here now. Became a U.S. citizen. Runs a little grease-pit taco joint with his mother called Mama's Casita. He's some kind of hero to these beaners 'cause they thought he had big *ganas* in the ring. Now this guy is running for mayor on a reform ticket, and according to the last poll in the *Haven Park Courier*, he actually has a decent shot at winning."

"I thought Cecil Bratano had it all locked up down here."

"He did, but the thing you gotta realize is most of the shit-sticks in this city are illegals, which means they can't vote. Only a couple a thousand registered voters in all of Haven Park. Doesn't take much to swing an election. Nobody counted on this Rocky Chacon character. He's a reformer pledging to stop all the ticket towing and corruption. All of a sudden he's leading in the polls. One of our jobs is to convince Rocky to either drop out or move out. But he's a gutsy little bastard, and so far he's been hanging tough."

Alonzo put on his blinker and slowed as we turned onto Lincoln Boulevard. Then he took a right onto a side street called Flower Avenue and pulled up across from a small but freshly painted Mexican restaurant. Mama's Casita. There was a lot of city roadwork going on in front of the place. A backhoe had torn up the asphalt and was roaring back and forth, throwing up a cloud of dust while blocking the little parking lot beside the restaurant.

"All that roadwork is us," Alonzo said, smiling. "Mayor Bratano authorized it. Gonna tear out the sidewalk and more of the street next week. This asshole and his mama are gonna be serving their tacos in a big dusty hole. Gonna go broke if he doesn't get the message."

"You think a little dust and noise is gonna run him off?" I asked skeptically.

"Probably not, but we don't stop with that. There's more. Rocky is my little project." He grinned. "Come on, I'll show ya."

He put the car in gear and pulled out. A few blocks away on 58th Street was a strip mall. There was a storefront in the center with a campaign poster of Rocky in the window. The same stripped-to-the-waist, fight-night pose. CHACON FOR MAYOR OF HAVEN PARK was painted on the window. Bell grabbed the mike off the hook and said, “This is Car Nine at the mall. Fifty-eighth and Flower. Send me two tow trucks, more if you can spare. We got a bunch a illegally maintained vehicles. We’re code six at the location.”

“Roger. Car Nine is code six and requesting tow trucks at the Flower Avenue Mall,” the RTO said.

He hung up. “Follow me. I’ll show you how this works.”

We got out of the car and walked into the parking lot. Alonzo immediately started writing a towing ticket for every car that had a CHACON FOR MAYOR bumper sticker on it.

“You just write ’em?” I said. “Don’t have to be illegally parked or anything?”

“This one has a broken taillight,” Bell replied, and shattered the light with his baton. “Against the law to drive an illegally maintained vehicle. Gotta tow it.”

“Blue Light Towing is closed for Cinco de Mayo.”

“Impound lot only. The garage never shuts down. Those greedy *culos* even work Easter Sunday.”

Just then Chacon came running out of his campaign headquarters. He was only about five feet seven inches tall and 160 pounds. He was around forty years old, and had a ruggedly handsome face dominated by a broken nose. He still looked to be in very good shape.

"What are you doing? I just saw you break that," he shouted at Alonzo. "You been doing this for over a week now."

"You better calm down, sir," Bell said with exaggerated politeness. "Go back inside. This doesn't concern you."

Several campaign workers came out behind Rocky, but they just stood there saying nothing while Alonzo brazenly broke taillights and side mirrors off their cars, then wrote tickets. Rocky Chacon had machismo and wasn't used to taking abuse from another man.

"You are police. You can't do this. It's against the law," he said, rage shaking his voice.

"We *are* the law." Bell grinned and broke another taillight. Then he wrote another ticket. "It's illegal to drive a vehicle with broken mirrors or brake lights," he said. "These cars cannot be driven, so they're all gonna be impounded. The owners can retrieve them at Blue Light Towing tomorrow. Bring cash."

Chacon started to move toward us with an intense, dangerous look in his black eyes. It looked like he was seconds from going physical. Just then a gray-haired, heavyset woman rushed out of the campaign headquarters and grabbed Rocky's arm.

"No. No, Juanito. This is exactly what they want. No."

"But Mama, they break the law. This is the policeman I told you about. He comes here every day. They can't do this."

"Come inside!" she ordered him. "Leave them! Come! You must do this! Juanito, do as I say!"

She pulled him again. He was clearly torn by the moment, but then reluctantly acquiesced. However, he was full of murderous rage as he walked inside, leaving Alonzo Bell and me to finish writing up the cars. We got seven done before the first tow truck arrived.

"You see how close to the edge he is? He almost lost it and came after us," Alonzo said as he wrote a last ticket, then closed his metal book.

I saw Rocky Chacon looking out the window, talking loudly to his mother and to several people whose cars were about to be towed.

"That guy is a day or two away from assaulting a police officer. Once I get his skinny ass into an I-room I'll give him a bare knuckle lesson in city politics he won't ever forget."

Minutes later, two more Blue Light tow trucks pulled into the lot and all three started hooking up the offending vehicles.

"And that is how it's done in Haven Park," Alonzo said proudly.

As we crossed the street to our patrol car I noticed the same tan Chevy with blackwalls parked half a block away, watching us. I turned to walk in that direction and confront whoever was inside, but before I could get there the tan car quickly sped off.

# CHAPTER 12

At the end of our straight eight we both changed into street clothes in the locker room. Alonzo suggested we complete our first day over a few beers at A Fuego. We headed out to the parking lot and he drove me to the club in his brand-new white Cadillac Escalade. I estimated the fancy SUV must have cost him upward of ninety thousand dollars with its state-of-the-art sound system, deluxe interior and chrome spinners. It was a lot of car for a sergeant making sixty or sixty-five thousand base pay. There was little doubt that the Haven Park cafeteria line had paid for his ride. He drove half a mile and turned into the parking lot at A Fuego.

"So after your first tour, whatta you think?" Alonzo said, looking over and grinning as he parked the car in a red no-parking zone up near the front entrance.

"It's a good way to go. Pretty hard to go wrong if you can change the rules to fit the crime," I said, smiling back.

"Got that right," he said.

We walked to the front door and entered. The same relentless, deafening mariachi music rocketed out of half a dozen speakers, bouncing off the walls and against my chest.

"I'd really like to get my car back," I shouted in his ear to be heard over the music. "Blue Light is closed till tomorrow."

"Nothing is closed when you know the right people," he said. "If you want, I can boot that up for you right now, no sweat."

I nodded, so he held up his hand for me to wait right where I was and headed across the nightclub, where he found Manny Avila in a booth by the kitchen. He shouted something into his ear and pointed at me. Manny smiled in my direction and waved. They exchanged a few more words, then both got up from the table and walked into the club's office through a door behind the bar.

Five minutes later Alonzo returned and handed me an envelope. "All set up. He's calling a guy right now to open the impound lot."

"What's this?" I asked, holding up the envelope.

"Your half of the eight tows we wrote today. Eighty bucks. Keep this up and in six months you'll be driving your own new Escalade."

I grinned and put the cash into my pocket without opening the envelope.

"We can go get your car back right now. Come on, I'll drive you over there. It's only a few blocks."

We headed out of the club and got back into Alonzo's SUV. He pulled out onto the street, and as he made the turn I again saw the tan Chevy following us.

"See that Chevy with the blackwalls?" I said.

"Yep."

"Third time I've spotted that thing. I know this is a small town, but it ain't quite that small."

"Let's see what they want. Better unstrap," Bell said. He pulled out his off-duty backup piece and wedged it under his thigh. I did the same. Then he floored the Escalade and swung a right, squealing rubber as he skidded into a side street. I turned in the seat and saw the tan Chevy fly past. Alonzo spun a smoking gunrunner's one-eighty and roared out again. We were now right behind the car, which was accelerating, trying to get away from us up the street.

"Oh, no, you don't. You're mine now," Alonzo said as he reached under the dash and hit a toggle switch. Red and blue police lights mounted in his grille flashed on the trunk of the Chevy. After half a block of chasing the car, Alonzo leaned on the horn, blasting it relentlessly until the Chevy finally pulled over.

Alonzo and I clutched our backup pieces and jumped out. As soon as our feet hit the pavement, a man and a woman were coming out of the Chevy, and both had guns in their hands.

"Police!" Alonzo shouted.

"FBI," Ophelia Love shouted back, holding up her FBI badge. "Holster those weapons!"

"I know this bitch," I said. "Federal heat."

"Yeah. Cunt is always up in our business down here."

There was no way any of us were about to initiate an interagency shoot-out, so we all put our guns away. An awkward moment followed. Then Alonzo pasted a big, insincere grin on his face.

The fed with Agent Love had a crew cut and an unsettled expression on his face. He looked implausibly young, just out of Quantico. Agent Love turned and glared at me.

"Is this dickhead on the job down here already?" She sounded amazed. Her voice was full of contempt and she never took those ice-blue eyes off me.

"You're talking about one of Haven Park's finest," Alonzo said. "And I should caution you against calling my probationer a dickhead, because it pisses me off."

"Didn't take him long, did it? But then, you flush a toilet anywhere in L.A. and the shit always comes out here in Haven Park."

"Why are you still following me around?" I growled. "My case in L.A. is closed. No charges filed. This constitutes harassment."

"I work down here," she shot back. "This is my beat. I'm on the federal gun squad, remember? All the illegal firearms in So Cal are coming into L.A.

through this town. I'm here to shut that down."

"You need to go get straightened out with Mayor Bratano on that," Alonzo said. "We got a big jurisdictional overlap here. Our department is all over the Eighteenth Street gun-smuggling problem. We don't want federal help."

"You aren't doing anything, except cashing envelopes full of payoff money."

"You got some evidence to go with that, or are you just showing off for your crew cut over there?"

Love's lanky build was tense. She stood with her feet spread defiantly, facing us down under dull streetlamps.

"I'm now a duly sworn member of the Haven Park Police Department," I said hotly. "If I see you behind me again, I'm going to take appropriate action."

"Do whatever pleases you," she snapped back.

"Ophelia, let's go," her young partner said, shifting his weight uneasily.

She took her time as she turned and they both got back in the Chevy and pulled out.

"Little history between you two?" Alonzo asked.

"That bitch is the reason I got thrown out of L.A."

Alonzo Bell dropped me in front of the impound yard and waited as I got my car. There was a Hispanic man waiting just behind the fence. He opened the gate, handed me the key to the MDX and watched as I started it. I noticed one or two of the cars we'd towed this afternoon sitting under the halogen lights in the lot, all of them sporting CHACON FOR MAYOR stickers.

As I pulled out, Alonzo stepped over and leaned into my passenger window. "Coming back to A Fuego?"

"Think I'm gonna look for a new hotel and hit the sack," I replied. "See you in the morning."

"Good first day, partner," Alonzo said, holding up his envelope.

"Good first day," I agreed, holding up mine. Then I put the MDX in gear and pulled out, leaving him standing there.

# CHAPTER 13

It took me all of five minutes to get out of Haven Park. My head throbbed and my shoulders were tight with tension. I drove toward downtown L.A. and finally pulled into a garage on Sixth Street that housed a high-tech custom car stereo shop.

I'd called ahead and a guy I'd known since I busted him for illegal wiretaps ten years ago was waiting for me. He'd done six months in county, but he was an electronics genius, so after he got out I helped him get a job here. His name was Calvin Epps, but everybody called him Harpo because, except for his ebony skin color, he was a dead ringer for the late Harpo Marx. He was still the best wiretap guy I knew.

"How you been, Shane?" Harpo said as I pulled in and shut off my headlights.

"Okay, I guess."

"I heard what happened at Parker Center," he said. "Couple a blues walking a beat down here told me about it. You'll make it, man. Same as me. Everything looks better after some time passes."

"Thanks, Harpo." I'd already told him what I needed on the phone. "You straight on all this?" I asked, as I got out of the MDX.

He nodded. "Leave your car here. I'll loan you my extra van. I'll be done by eight tomorrow morning just like you wanted."

We swapped keys and after saying goodnight I got into his old, primer-painted '86 Chevy van and drove out.

It took me almost thirty minutes with the Dodgers baseball traffic to get on the 110 Freeway. I kept a wary eye on my rearview mirror to make sure I wasn't followed as I finally transitioned to the 105 and settled in for the long drive past LAX before exiting onto Sepulveda.

I drove past the endless stretches of oil fields, where huge pumps seesawed up and down like giant metal insects drinking from an underground pond. Then I turned west toward the little city of Manhattan Beach. I finally found Ocean Way and looked for an address I'd already memorized. It was halfway down the Strand. I turned into the driveway of an expensive new three-story complex with a Century 21 real estate sign announcing new beachfront condos for sale and pulled up to the security gate. Then I punched in the access code I'd been given. The garage door opened and I drove Harpo's rusting, primered van down into the sterile, freshly painted parking structure, where I left it and took the elevator up to Penthouse 2.

The Otis box was mirrored and carpeted and, like everything else in this overpriced mecca, smelled brand new. The doors opened onto an attractive foyer. There were two penthouse condos on this floor that, from what I knew about Manhattan Beach real estate, I estimated had to be worth at least three million dollars apiece. I'd been told the key for number 2 would be hidden inside a carved figurine opposite the mirrored wall. I felt inside the figure's open back until I found it, then unlatched the mahogany-paneled front door.

Inside, the lights had been dimmed and there was a fire burning in the fireplace. A Sheryl Crow love song was coming through the elaborate stereo system. The condo was beautiful. Rich upholstered furniture sat on the white plush pile carpet. Fine art hung on padded silk walls.

I saw her sitting on a porch chaise, her back to me, looking out at the ocean. She must have sensed my presence, or maybe she even saw my shadow move.

A woman so breathtaking, men might easily agree to kill for her. Movie-star gorgeous—that beautiful. She stood and turned toward me, looking through the sliding glass doors into the living room.

Then she ran into the condo, struggling for a moment with the doors before she raced toward me, flinging herself into my arms.

"Oh, Shane . . . my God, I've missed you so," she whispered.

I hugged her tight, feeling her warmth. I could barely speak, couldn't wait to make love to her.

"This was the hardest thing I've ever tried to do," she whispered in my ear as we stood there clinging to one another.

Then she kissed me, and with that kiss my tension evaporated. As if a cool dressing had been laid on an open wound, I was instantly better.

"I love you so much," I told her.

"I love you, too," Alexa said.

# CHAPTER 14

After we finally separated, Alexa said, "She's down on the beach patio. We shouldn't keep her waiting."

I got three Beck's beers from the fridge and we headed down to the sand where Ophelia Love was waiting. I handed her a beer and we clicked bottles.

"That was intense," she said, smiling.

"Sorry about the guns. Alonzo's idea."

"Not the first time I've looked Mr. Smith in the eye." The sentence was etched with her Carolina twang.

We arranged the patio chairs together in a circle so we could all look at each other. Then I filled Alexa and Ophelia in on what had happened since I went undercover. I finished by saying, "It's much worse even than Rick Ross told us. It's crooked as a Bayou card game down there."

Alexa leaned forward, her shining black hair falling in luscious sheaths at the sides of her face.

"I'm a little worried for this guy who's running for mayor, Rocky Chacon," I said. "Alonzo and the rest of thc Haven Park department aren't about to let him win."

"Now that you're on the inside, you can't do anything that might blow your cover," Ophelia cautioned. "We're already doing what we can to protect him."

After we finished our beers, Agent Love stood to go. "I'm gonna keep hassling you and pulling you over, Shane. It's the only way I can stay close enough to give you any cover." She smiled wanly. "See if you can keep that walking woodpile you're partnered with from blowing my head off."

I handed Ophelia the envelope containing the

eighty dollars in towing kickbacks. "I didn't open it. Before you book it into evidence, get the bills dusted. You might get some latent prints."

She nodded and handed me a business card. "Here's my cell number. Memorize it and throw the card away. In a crunch, you can call or text me, but if you use that number I'd suggest that you ditch your cell afterwards. The Haven Park cops can easily track the SIM card."

I knew she was right. It would be dangerous walking around with a phone message to her that could be recovered from the cell's memory.

After Ophelia left, Alexa put her head on my shoulder and we sat on the beach chairs, holding hands and listening to the pounding surf.

It didn't take long before we moved our escalating foreplay upstairs to the penthouse bedroom. The condo complex we were in was less than a month old and was about half sold. P-2 belonged to Assistant Chief Malon Arnett, who ran the Administrative Affairs Division. The A-chief came from a wealthy family and had invested his inheritance wisely. Arnett had agreed to loan his place to us for secret meetings.

We didn't even bother to strip the comforter off. We just fell on the quilted spread and grabbed for each other. Our lovemaking lasted for almost half an hour and afterward we lay naked on top of the king-sized bed, both propped up on an elbow facing each other, smiling.

"It's good to have you back," Alexa said, "even if it is just for one night."

Then I took her through my blowup with Chooch and finished by saying, "He said he never wanted to see me again."

"I've been talking to him, trying to spin it up so he won't be quite so angry," Alexa said. "But he thinks you cheated on me and it's ripping him up inside."

It was hard to believe that all of this had started just fifteen days ago when Ricky Ross had popped up and asked for a secret meeting with Chief Filosiani. He had just received his up-from-the-ranks promotion to chief of the Haven Park PD, and told Tony that two months before that he had finally taken the cure. Once he'd sobered up, he knew he had to do something about the massive corruption in Haven Park. Mayor Bratano had only appointed him interim chief because he thought Ross was still such a drunk he wouldn't make any trouble. The mayor didn't like strong people around him.

Once Ross got sober he said he knew he had to step up and try to change what was going on in Haven Park and Fleetwood. However, as acting chief he was rarely told about what was happening on the street-policing level. After the indictment of ex-chief Le Grande, the mayor preferred to keep his new chief in the dark. Rick said he got his envelope of cash every week, but that he couldn't prove where the money came from.

Ross thought he was being set up by Bratano to take a fall if the feds ever put their gunrunning narcotics case together. Alexa and I discussed it and we thought that was the real reason he'd come to Tony Filosiani and the LAPD for help. Ross also agreed that something bad was about to happen to Rocky Chacon. That his life might be in real danger.

He told Tony that he wanted me to go undercover because I had been the one to flag him for discharging his firearm on the freeway when nobody else in our patrol division had been willing to step forward. I found that explanation very hard to believe.

During the week that followed, Tony, Alexa and I had several intense meetings with Ross. After listening to it all, I still wasn't sure of his motives and didn't trust him at all. But the evidence of massive corruption in Haven Park and Fleetwood was overwhelming. After two days of indecision, I had finally accepted the assignment.

Tony recruited Agent Love from the FBI to be my backup because she was already working the gun beat in Haven Park and her presence down there wouldn't alert anyone. Nobody else knew that my dismissal from the LAPD had been staged.

Ophelia's roommate in college had been Tiffany

Roberts. She had gone on to become a famous movie star. Ophelia had asked if she could use Tiffany's name and the story about her wanting Harry dead to dress up the sting. We agreed to try and keep the whole story out of the press. But if it did leak, the LAPD Public Affairs Office had a lot of preprepared denials ready. We didn't think, with those department denials, any news organization would risk a defamation-of-character lawsuit. In less than two weeks her true role in all of this would be revealed. I had never met Tiffany in the parking lots of any big-box stores, nor was there ever any FBI surveillance tape. The plan all along was for me to confess at the chief's midnight meeting, making the need to display the video evidence unnecessary.

The only other sticking point had been Chooch. The chief had refused to cut me loose to work the undercover assignment if Chooch knew the truth.

Tony had reasoned that Chooch would not be able to resist telling his friends that what they were hearing about his father being fired was B.S. "He'll swear them to silence and then let the secret out," Tony had said, adding, "Any leak can get you killed." Alexa and I had finally and reluctantly agreed to keep our son in the dark.

Alexa had moved some of my clothes over from the house in Venice. We dressed in sweats and went out on the upstairs balcony to sit under the stars.

"You said your car got impounded by Blue Light Towing. You know they probably hung a bug on it," Alexa said.

"I left it with Harpo. He's sweeping it now. But he's not going to take anything out if he finds one. It would tip them off."

Of course, the other huge risk in all this was Freeway Ricky Ross himself. He'd threatened my life in the Parker Center garage ten years ago. He'd lost his career, his wife, everything he owned. I'd been the witness who had taken him down. What better way to get back at me than to lure me into a Serpico-like situation, then find a way to let Alonzo or Talbot Jones know that I was an LAPD spy? I'd be shot in the field. Fragged in some staged gunfight.

I spent the rest of the night with Alexa in Deputy Chief Arnett's king-sized bed. We made love again, held each other, and then fell into a restless sleep.

# CHAPTER 15

I arrived back at the stereo shop on Sixth Street at a little past seven A.M. Harpo was in his office, hunched over a Mexican breakfast of refried beans and rice.

"Want some of this?" he asked, pushing the plate across his desk and offering me a plastic fork out of a box. "This guy Gonzales, on the corner, is a genius with a frying pan."

I grabbed one of the forks and took a bite. Amazing.

"Find anything?" I asked.

"Your Acura has better recording capabilities than the big room over at Capitol Records. Whoever installed that shit knew what they were doing." He led me over to my car, still carrying the plate of beans, then leaned in and pointed at two carefully concealed microphones. One was in the rearview mirror light sensor, the other was tucked up under the dash on the passenger side out of sight.

"It's all voice-activated. I erased the recording back to the spot just before you pulled in here, then turned it all off." He closed the car door and we stepped back. "All of the units are high-frequency radio bugs. They have receivers in the trunk, stuck to the inside of your spare tire. I left it all right where it is just like you wanted. For the fun of it, I installed a separate voice-activated radio unit of our own. It's buried up in the passenger side of the front seat piggybacking off their mikes."

"Thanks, Harpo. You're the best."

"Then how come I got busted?" He grinned.

I took a few more bites of the refried beans while he reactivated the digital recorders, then paid him in cash.

I pulled out of the Sixth Street garage and tuned the radio to an angry rap station, then set the volume at the threshold of pain just to piss off the dirtbag who eventually had to listen to all this.

My guess is they would go into my trunk and switch out the recorder late at night while I was sleeping, or when I was out on patrol with Alonzo and the MDX was unguarded in the police parking lot at the elementary school.

The big disadvantage of hanging a wire on someone is, if the bug ever gets discovered, it's very easy to get fooled by your own trickery. I started thinking of ways to get something on that recorder that would help my cause.

After pondering my top five options, I finally decided to give Sammy from Miami a call. Sammy Ochoa was a forty-year-old Cuban street character whose grind was every low-end street hustle ever worked on the ice-cream eaters from Minnesota who wandered the tarnished streets of Hollywood searching for scraps of movie glamour. He would sell these marks everything from a counterfeit Best Picture Oscar to fake Britney Spears memorabilia. He ran his business out of a gay movie theater he owned on Melrose Boulevard. I'd first busted Sammy when I was still in patrol, right after he got here from Miami Beach. Something about his flat-footed, take-no-prisoners larceny was comically appealing to me and we'd entered into an uneasy friendship where mutual benefit and cash were the glue. He slipped me street intel, which I paid for out of my snitch fund. I also kept Hollywood Vice off his back, claiming him as a street informant.

As I drove back to Haven Park, I decided to put on a little theater production, with Sammy from Miami as my featured guest star.

I got back to the Haven Park Elementary School before eight and parked in the police parking lot that adjoined the school. After I locked the Acura I hurried up the sidewalk.

I had to show my driver's license to the old guy at the gate, who didn't seem to remember me from yesterday.

The locker room was in turmoil like all police shifts getting ready for a tour—guys dressing in patrol uniforms, talking too loud, horsing around, slamming lockers.

Once I was down to my shorts and T-shirt, Alonzo Bell, already in harness, ambled over. Without warning he threw a beefy arm around my shoulders, then turned me roughly and presented me to the room of about ten other patrol officers. "Meet my new boot, Hardwood Scully," he announced. "He fucks movie stars."

The cops in the room hooted. "He's a beaut, Al!" one said. "Tiffany Roberts was fucking that?" Another laughed.

Alonzo suddenly slipped me into a headlock. Before I knew it, he was wrestling me playfully around the locker room, giving me a painful head noogie.

“This is the guy.” He joked as he threw me roughly against a locker, pushing his huge right palm into the middle of my chest, pinning me there. “Let’s check out the merchandise here.” Then he ran his hand quickly across my chest.

The cops in the room hooted with laughter. One shouted, “Leave him be, Al. He’s got an ass like a forty-dollar cow!”

I was grinning, pretending I was having fun while at the same time trying to keep from punching Bell’s lights out. But I knew exactly what he was doing. He was checking me for a wire.

“You about through?” I asked, forcing a smile.

He grinned and turned me loose as the rest of the room laughed. “For now. Let’s get you in harness. We got some important shit to attend to. You and me are working fire and health this morning.”

I went to my locker feeling the eyes of the squad on me as I put on the rest of my uniform. Sergeant Bell was a strong flavor. The other cops took their lead from him.

“Where’s your hat?” Alonzo asked, coming back from the men’s room just as I closed my locker and slipped on my combination padlock.

“Arnie Bale is ordering one. Didn’t have my size.”

“Let’s go, then,” he said. “Roll call.”

I carried my equipment duffel, known in police circles as a war bag, and followed the stragglers into the gymnasium, where I sat beside Alonzo on the bleachers with other members of the day watch. I'd been told that in Haven Park, like in most departments, the patrol force was divided into three shifts. The day watch went from eight A.M. to four P.M. Mid-watch, from four to midnight. The graveyard was from midnight to eight. The shifts rotated every month. Haven Park now had forty-two patrol officers plus command staff.

In Haven Park, cops rode in single-man cars, what we'd call an L-unit in L.A. This facilitated business in the cafeteria line because with just one cop in a car there was never a corroborating witness. Since I was a probationer being trained by a sergeant, Alonzo and I were the only X-unit, or two-man car, on the day watch.

Our watch commander was a skinny bald guy with narrow shoulders and a little bit of a potbelly who was standing swaybacked on the shiny varnished-wood basketball floor before us, wearing lieutenant's bars on his blue collar and holding a clipboard. His name was Harry Eastwood. Without even asking, I knew his handle had to be Dirty Harry.

"Okay, shut the fuck up," he started by saying. "We expect to get some blowback from that Crip shooting two nights ago, so look for Crip mother ships cruising in your areas." The room quieted down. "Bust any black guy in a Chrysler four-door wearing a red head-wrap. Pull 'em all in and we'll sort the fashion victims from the assholes later."

He looked down at his clipboard. "We've got some homeless guy lighting cooking fires on the L.A. River bank," he went on. "Keep an eye out for this dink. Whoever he is, we need to get that to stop. We're in high fire season and don't want some brain-dead shopping cart driver burning down our cafeteria." Cops were taking notes.

"The midweek update on the hot car sheet is posted on the bulletin board. Write down the tag numbers for all those G-rides. The night shift reports there's a white Corolla that just started holding up liquor stores over in Fleetwood—couple a border brothers in stocking masks. You know that's gotta be tweakers, 'cause only meth addicts would use a getaway car with a fucking leaf-blower for an engine." Scattered laughter from the cops gathered on the bleachers.

"I'm hearing from Blue Light we're still not up to quotas on our tow tickets. Let's get with the program, guys. I'm looking for every one of you to write at least three, maybe four boot jobs a day. Keep the flow going here."

Then he stopped and looked at us. "Anybody have anything?"

"Me and Scully are gonna be working fire and health codes this morning, so somebody needs to cover Sector Four till around ten o'clock," Alonzo said.

"I got it," a guy with red hair and a rosy complexion said. I thought I recognized him from L.A. or maybe from a joint op I did once in Santa Monica. Something Larson—a drinker.

"Okay, that's it," the WC said. "Get out there and try and make Haven Park the safest place on earth for assholes to multiply." He turned and walked back to his office.

We left the elementary school gym. I stood in the hallway with the other patrol officers and copied car tags off the hot sheet posted up on the cork bulletin board. Then everyone moved as a group through the front doors onto Pine Street, heading to city hall to collect our patrol cars.

We walked single file, right through two residential blocks, carrying gear, flashlights, and duffels. I couldn't help but think, if you wanted to eliminate the Haven Park day shift, one quick drive-by with a street ventilator on full-auto would pretty much do it.

When we got to the parking lot Alonzo led me to Car Nine and opened our patrol unit. The midnight-to-eight guys who had been using it were just walking away.

"Those fuckers on graveyard always leave this shop looking like a dirty ashtray. Look at this shit," Alonzo growled angrily as he pulled out the floor mat and shook sunflower seeds, gravel, and gum wrappers off the plastic onto the asphalt. Then he brushed off the seats. We stashed our stuff in the trunk while all around us black-and-whites were driving into the lot. Graveyard shift cars were one by one being turned over to day watch officers. Finally, Bell slid behind the wheel and I got in the passenger side.

"I decommissioned the air bags in this shop so we won't eat a ton of plastic if we ram anyone who tries to take off."

"Sounds good."

Then he smiled at me. "Ready to help change the political landscape in Haven Park?"

"That's why I signed on."

"Good, 'cause this morning Rocky Chacon makes a mistake he can't walk away from."

# CHAPTER 16

"This is Car Nine. We're ten-ten in the four hundred block of Flower Avenue," I said, and hung up the mike as we pulled to the curb across the street from Mama's Casita.

"Car Nine is out of service subject to a call on Flower Avenue," the RTO came back.

While I was doing this, Alonzo Bell was busy shuffling through his briefcase. Finally, he pulled out a manila envelope and opened it.

"What's that?" I asked.

"Expired fire extinguisher tags. Mama doesn't work the breakfast shift, so if we're lucky it'll just be El Alboratador himself. The way this is gonna work is I'll keep Rocky busy while you swap the current fire extinguisher tags with these expired ones. It's okay if the kitchen wetbacks see you do it. We aren't looking for style points. Their word isn't worth shit in court anyway. What we're gonna do is pull out all the extinguishers and see what transpires."

"Close them down for being outside of fire regs," I said.

"You got it. And Scully, I don't need a referee. I want this guy to knuckle up and come after me. I'm looking to hang an assault-on-a-police-officer beef on that little beaner. I got him by a hundred pounds or more, so he shouldn't be too hard to control. But you never know. I saw him fight once and he's got very quick hands, so stay ready."

"Got it."

"The extinguishers are located in the kitchen and by the exits. Last I checked there should be six or eight of 'em."

We got out of our shop and headed across the street to Mama's Casita. The backhoe was still roaring back and forth, not digging up anything this morning, just pushing dirt around, making a racket and throwing a lot of dust up into the air. Alonzo smiled at the mostly Mexican city workers as he passed.

*"Buenos días, caballeros,"* he said, tipping his hat with exaggerated politeness. Then he turned to me. "You know you got it made when you got

this bunch a tea bags doin' your dirty work for ya."

We went inside the restaurant. Mama's Casita was done in a south-of-the-border theme, using the primary colors of the Mexican flag. Fresh green tablecloths, red curtains, white walls and napkins. There were booths around two sides of the room, wooden tables and chairs in the center. Blackboard menus were hanging behind a soda-fountain-like counter with the specials written in yellow chalk.

Business was being clobbered by the city work going on out front. This was a popular spot and it should have been full. It wasn't even nine A.M., and there were absolutely no customers inside.

"Where's Mama?" Alonzo said to the lone Hispanic waitress.

"Che no come mornings. Maybe noon," the girl said.

"Rocky around?"

She nodded and went to find him. After a minute, Rocky came out of the back.

"When you gonna let us up?" he said as he approached. "That backhoe is killing us, man." He was full of seething anger. "You got to get that out of here. Nobody's coming in. Look at this place. All this confusion and noise, people don't want to eat in a damn construction zone."

"It's a problem, I can see that, sir, but you're talking to the wrong city employee," Alonzo said patiently. "You need to speak with Street

Maintenance. On the other hand, I'm always willing to listen. Why don't we get a cup of coffee? Maybe I can find a way to help."

"I don't want to pay you money to stop something that should have never started to begin with," Rocky said hotly. "There was nothing wrong with that street. Those crews out there aren't even doing anything. Just driving back and forth, moving dirt, making noise. You think I don't know what's going on? This is complete bullshit."

I was worried for him because, like Alonzo, I didn't think he was very far from losing it. This police harassment had been going on for weeks and he'd pretty much had it.

"I know who you are," he continued. "I already filed a complaint against you. You're the same cop who keeps towing my campaign workers' cars. What's your problem, man?"

"I deeply resent the suggestion that I might be harassing you on purpose or be willing to take a bribe to get needed city roadwork to stop." Alonzo winked at me and gave me a nod, telling me to get started. "Why don't we sit and you can tell me how I can help?" Alonzo said disingenuously.

As they sat at a table, I went off in search of the fire extinguishers. I went through a kitchen door into the pantry area. Three Mexicans swung wary eyes at me as I entered. *"Donde esta los extintores?"* I asked.

A fry cook pointed toward a wall in the back, where I saw a big red $CO_2$ bottle hanging in a bracket near the refrigerator. I walked over and checked the tag. The extinguisher was only a month old. I pulled the current date certification tag off the bottle and replaced it with one of the expired ones Alonzo had just given me. The counterman saw what I was doing.

"You just changed that," he said in perfect English.

I ignored him and moved on. Then I did the same thing to another $CO_2$ canister. I hated this, but if I backed off now or tried to alter Alonzo's plan, then I was instantly through down here. I had to go along and hope I would soon have enough to put an end to the criminal corruption in Haven Park while at the same time keeping Rocky Chacon alive.

I found four more extinguishers and retagged all of them. Then I grabbed all six units by the handles and lugged them out to the front of the restaurant. When I got there I saw from Rocky's body language that he was close to snapping, gesturing wildly as he talked.

"Now you say you also gonna close the street all the way to Forty-eighth? How do people even get to my business at all, then?" he shouted.

"It's certainly going to be a problem," Alonzo said. "However, you have my word that we will get all that roadwork done as quickly as possible."

A slight smile tugged at the corner of his ruler-straight mouth. This was the kind of stuff Alonzo lived for.

"And how long will that be?" Rocky snapped. "A fucking year?"

"I'm only a police officer. You need to call the Street Maintenance Department, and you better watch your tone, Mr. Chacon. I don't appreciate being cursed at."

"And I don't appreciate being lied to!"

I set the extinguishers on the table next to them.

"We got a problem with those?" Alonzo asked, looking over at the six delinquent extinguishers and frowning theatrically.

"Yep. All these maintenance tags are out of date," I said.

"Boy oh boy, that's a tough one, Mr. Chacon. Probably gonna have to close you down. If you have a grease fire with no extinguishers, people could die in this firetrap."

"These are all brand new," Rocky shouted, and with that he reared up, standing in anger. Alonzo immediately stood with him.

"You're just trying to close us down. You're a fucking liar!" Rocky shouted.

"I'm gonna call that verbal assault," Alonzo said. "Now sit down before I arrest you." Rocky didn't move.

I could see a flash of unreasoning anger in

Alonzo's eyes. He hated guys who didn't do exactly what he said, when he said it.

Then my partner did a totally inappropriate thing. He threw a hard right across the table at the little Mexican fighter, hitting him high on the forehead, snapping his head back. Rocky sat back down hard, but the little middleweight was tough and could definitely take a punch. He didn't stay seated long. He scrambled back up and in a flash was out of the booth.

Alonzo pulled his nightstick from his belt ring as he came lumbering out after Rocky, a murderous look in his pinched eyes. My partner was about to give Rocky a police-baton beat-down, which consisted of a combination of swift strikes known as three from the ring.

I had to move fast. I grabbed Rocky from behind and lifted him off the ground, then threw him to the floor. Since he was down, that should have ended it, but Alonzo was immediately straddling him, roaring in rage and swinging the baton at Rocky's kidneys. I knew the body shots could rupture his spleen.

I grabbed the sap from my back pocket and swung, aiming to clip Alonzo behind his left ear. I tagged him perfectly, but Sergeant Bell had a thick skull and he shook off the shot, rolled slightly to the side, stunned for a moment, then glowered up at me.

"The fuck you doing, asshole?"

"Sorry. Missed. Trying to hit him."

While this had been happening, the counterman and two fry cooks had charged into the restaurant from the kitchen. Both were wielding dangerous-looking boning knives. We were on the verge of a full-scale race riot.

"Alonzo!" I warned, pointing at the kitchen posse. He stood, yanked his gun out and aimed it at the fry cooks and counterman, who all came skidding to a halt. While that was happening I quickly cuffed Rocky and yanked him to his feet. He was groaning in pain, but still conscious.

Even though Alonzo had the three restaurant employees at gunpoint and under control, he still wanted to finish what he'd started. With a gun in one hand and the street baton in the other, he turned back toward the handcuffed fighter. I got ready. I couldn't let him attack a restrained, unarmed man. But before I had to intervene, Alonzo hesitated. Some survival instinct, born from years of committing felonies in uniform, told him not to do it. Especially in front of three independent employees who could testify. Illegal or not, Alonzo knew they could cause trouble if they passed a polygraph. He had fucked this up by losing his temper. His sour expression of resignation signaled it was over. I knew he was probably going to find a way to make this my fault.

I led our handcuffed prisoner out to the car and

put him in the backseat. Then I dropped the six confiscated fire extinguishers into the trunk.

"I'm gonna post this fucking grease pit," Alonzo snarled at me as he came out and opened his brief-case. He took out a big red sticker. Then he walked inside the restaurant and ordered the employees to shut down the kitchen. They turned off the lights and locked the front door. The last thing Alonzo did was post a huge red fire sticker across the door that said:

CLOSED BY ORDER OF THE HAVEN PARK FIRE DEPARTMENT

While all this was going on, I stayed with Rocky, who was seated in the backseat of the cruiser, handcuffed but smoking mad.

"You okay?" I asked him, concerned about the half a dozen kidney shots he'd already taken.

"Fuck you, *chamorro*," he growled.

"Listen, Rocky. You're in a lot of trouble here. Do yourself a favor. Calm down and do what you're told."

He sat there, staring straight ahead. He didn't answer, contempt for us fueling the already deadly mixture of rage and injustice burning inside him.

# CHAPTER 17

"We don't have shit. Just a lousy misdemeanor verbal assault. I needed felony battery," Alonzo growled at me. "We also got three kitchen slaves saying Rocky didn't do nothin'. You were supposed to keep the wetbacks out of there."

We were in the small jail facility on the second floor of the Haven Park PD. Rocky was in the larger of our two interrogation rooms with a video surveillance camera running. On the TV screen I could see the ex-middleweight sitting in the I-room looking at his shoes. His left hand was chained to a ring in the wall.

"We need to get him on a Class A felony," Alonzo continued. "So you're gonna get a chance to fix your fuckup and do that."

"Calm down. Let's not make this worse than it is," I said.

"Shut up," he snapped. "Here's what you're gonna do. You walk in there, unhook him, then insult his manhood. Beaners can't deal with that. Call him a *maricón.* Stay away from the table mike and keep your voice down. We don't want the surveillance video to show we provoked him. I know this asshole. He'll throw down. After he's attacked you and we got our felony, I'll be in there and put a big hurt on him."

"It's a bad idea, Al."

"Hey, I'm not coming to you for fucking approval. I'm telling you the way you're gonna do it. This guy is gonna eat a Class A felony and go away for five years. He sure ain't gonna be the mayor of Haven Park from a cellblock in Soledad."

For a minute, I didn't answer. I just stood there trying to come up with a valid reason for not going through with this.

"You gonna become a problem here? I thought you wanted to make it on this department. I'm the guy who has to sign you off probation!"

"Jeez, man. Calm down."

"Get in there and do it." He pulled out his sap and held it up, showing it to me. "You take one punch for the camera and I'll close his show."

It was an impossible situation. I had no choice but to go ahead, because if it wasn't me, I knew Alonzo would just get somebody else to do it. At least if I was in the I-room I might be able to stop him from killing the guy.

"Okay," I said, reluctantly.

Alonzo opened the I-room door. Rocky looked up at me with a malevolent stare as I stepped inside, leaving the door unlatched behind me. Then I reached over and quickly uncuffed him. That got his attention.

"Stay where you are," I said. Alonzo was outside watching this on the monitor. I had to find a way to make it look right, but still keep my partner from killing Rocky with that damn sap.

"I thought I told you to hold it together. What's wrong with you? You stupid or something?" I kept my voice low so it wouldn't record on the surveillance tape.

"Do not talk to me this way," Rocky said.

"Why not, *joto*?" I whispered. "You gonna do something about it? You're nothing but a *jugador a los bandos. El maricón.*"

Chacon exploded up out of the chair and started swinging. I ducked his first shot but caught the second one square in the teeth. It was a clean right, efficiently delivered, and it snapped my head back. Then two or three more combination punches hit me. The guy was lightning-fast. I was trying to cover up, but he was scoring at will. I was getting creamed.

*Where the hell is Alonzo?* I thought as more blows rained off my shoulders and elbows. He was supposed to be in here after the first punch.

Just then Rocky caught me on the side of the head with a great left hook, which stunned me. I pawed back at him with a weak right cross that did nothing. Rocky circled right and peppered me with three quick jabs, splitting my lip and bloodying my nose.

*"Quien es el joto ahora, flaquito!"* Rocky shouted as he circled left, bouncing jabs off my forehead, then delivering a devastating uppercut.

I was getting cut to pieces, so in order to minimize the damage I rushed him and slammed him against the wall, trying to pin his hands to his sides.

At last the door opened and Alonzo came in swinging the sap. He bounced two pounds of leather-wrapped lead off Rocky's head. In an instant the smaller man was down on his knees. Then, before I could intervene, Alonzo kicked him in the stomach and sapped him again. Murder flashed in my huge partner's eyes. He was winding up for a last mighty kill shot when I threw myself at him and knocked him off balance. He swung anyway. The sap whistled through the air but missed both Rocky and me.

"Knock if off! We're code four!" I yelled.

Alonzo finally stopped and looked down at the little Mexican fighter, who was unconscious and prone on the concrete floor.

"That's how we do it Haven Park–style," Alonzo growled.

"We need to get some EMTs in here," I said, spitting out droplets of my own blood as I talked.

Ten minutes later Chacon had been revived by paramedics and was sitting up on a bunk in one of the holding cells. He refused to talk, refused to look at us. He had sustained a concussion, but his eyes were pinpoints of hatred.

"Where the hell were you, Al?" I said as the EMTs iced my split lip and put cotton sticks up my bloody nose.

"I thought you needed a little object lesson in

how to take an order. When I say to do something, you need to do what I tell you instead of giving me a bunch a guff. You're lucky I didn't pay you back for the sapping you gave me at the restaurant."

Alonzo held up the videotape of our I-room brawl. "After we file the assault charges I'm gonna leak this to the *Courier* and some local TV stations. Let them see what a violent, unstable prick their mayoral candidate is."

"I'm not sure showing a tape of Rocky taking on two cops twice his size is going to screw him up with his constituents."

"Yeah? Well, that's why you're stuck down in this shit hole, being retrained by me."

While I wrote up the assault report, Alonzo sat at the desk next to mine and dialed somebody at the *Haven Park Courier*. After explaining the situation, he added, "He's under arrest right now. This guy committed felonious assaults on two police officers. Yeah, yeah." He paused and listened a moment before saying, "You bet. I think I can steal a copy of the tape for you guys. But I'm looking for a nice clean piece. You gotta stop with all this Rocky Chacon, man-of-the-people propaganda and print what really happened."

# CHAPTER 18

Rocky contacted a beautiful, raven-haired lawyer named Carmen Ramirez. His *abogada* was only about twenty-eight but full of Latina pride. At one point I heard her tell Alonzo that even if Haven Park's city attorney filed these assault charges, it wouldn't prevent Rocky from running for mayor. "In America," she explained hotly, "you are still presumed innocent until *proven* guilty, and a presumed innocent man is not prohibited from running for public office."

She promised Alonzo she would delay the trial for at least two years and finished by telling my increasingly glum partner that once Rocky was mayor, the whole crooked police department would be out of a job. None of this information did anything to improve Alonzo's demeanor.

Later, I noticed Rocky and his firebrand attorney talking in his cell. Years of police work have made me a pretty good student of body language. When she was alone with him she adopted a more open posture and as they talked, their nonverbal communicators conveyed intimacy. At one point, she leaned forward and touched his arm. It seemed Rocky had something going with his beautiful lawyer.

Carmen Ramirez quickly arranged bail, which for a felony assault in Haven Park was preset at one hundred thousand dollars. Because there was no loss of life involved, a court hearing was not required.

Rocky called Big Kiss, wrote a check for ten percent of the bond and kissed our jail goodbye. He was out of the police building one full hour ahead of Alonzo and me.

We finally finished our paperwork at two and when we walked outside into the afternoon sun, ten or fifteen picketers were already out front holding signs that said POLICE PERSECUTION and FREE ROCKY CHACON.

"Told ya," I said to Alonzo, who was glaring at the picketers.

He didn't answer, but motioned to our black-and-white. We got in, cleared the station and pretty much blew off the rest of the day watch going code seven at one of the few Anglo-run restaurants in town, called the Coffee Barn. Alonzo said very little to me as we ate and sipped coffee from chipped mugs.

He had not considered the fact that until Rocky was convicted of the felony he could still legally run for mayor. The protestors outside the jail further underlined the fact that Rocky's I-room brawl wasn't going to disqualify him as much as endorse him. It gave Alonzo a lot to think about.

In the stifling silence of this meal, I realized I'd lost a lot of ground with him. It's never a good idea to sap your training officer, even if you're trying to keep him from killing an innocent civilian. As he poked at his greasy hamburger in silence I knew I'd have to find a way to make up the points I'd just lost and I had to come up with a way to do it fast.

At end-of-watch I loitered in front of my locker waiting for Alonzo. I figured I might buy him a few drinks at A Fuego and try to smooth all of this over, but I didn't see him. Somebody on the day watch finally told me Sergeant Bell had left Haven Park to see some people up in L.A.

I grabbed my jacket and walked to my car in the parking area next to the school. I got in and pulled out, heading to the Haven Park Inn, where I was still registered.

I was tired and angry as I climbed the stairs to the second level. My lip was killing me and my nose was swelling. I knew I'd probably wake up tomorrow with two giant shiners. I unlocked the door and entered.

The lights were off, but as I dropped my jacket on a chair, I knew instantly someone was inside the room. I spun and snatched my backup Smith & Wesson .38 out of the clamshell holster at the small of my back, extending the titanium AirLight in the direction my senses told me the danger was. I almost fired. But at the last instant some instinct stopped me. As my eyes adjusted to the dark, I saw a man in silhouette sitting calmly across the room from me.

"Don't shoot," he said lazily. "I give."

It was Rick Ross. He was wearing a blue windbreaker, tennis shoes and khakis from the Gap. A Dodgers ball cap was pulled down over thinning blond hair.

"You just break in here?" I said, taking a deep breath to calm my nerves. "What the hell's wrong with you?"

"We need to talk."

I was still trying to get my heart rate to slow. I didn't like Ross. I certainly didn't trust him. I hated that he thought he could just break into my room uninvited.

"I don't want you in here without asking me first."

"It's such a palace," he quipped, looking around. "I can certainly understand why you'd feel that way."

"Don't do it again. I was less than a second away from shooting you."

He stood and moved up to where I was standing. "You forget I rode with you for six months in the Valley. You aren't a shoot-first guy."

"What do you want?" I asked, still surging with wasted adrenaline.

"Brief me," he said, treating it as an order. "Let's go. I want to hear what you got. I don't have much time."

"You might want to slow your roll, Rick. I don't work for you. I'm here to help you if I can, but don't get the dimensions of this arrangement stacked up wrong."

"You're riding with Alonzo Bell," he pushed. "Start with that. Bell's a violent officer."

"I knew him from the job in L.A. Ran into him when I first got here. Since he's our day watch sergeant it actually worked out pretty well. Bell was a good shortcut."

"I hear you're on the pad with the Avilas."

"If you know all this, why did you break in here?"

We stood in silence looking across two feet of mud-brown carpet. I didn't want to tell Rick Ross anything.

"The jail sergeant called me this afternoon," Ross said. "He told me you and Bell shut down Mama's Casita on fire regs, busted Rocky Chacon for verbal assault and then got him for battery in an I-room."

"Pretty much what happened."

"Whose brain-dead idea was that?"

"Alonzo's," I said angrily. "He didn't exactly think it through."

Rick Ross hadn't changed much physically and maybe that's why I felt he hadn't changed emotionally. He was still a very twitchy guy who sent a strange vibe. "Alonzo's already leaked the I-room tape to the press," I added.

"What the fuck for?" Ross snapped. "That isn't gonna help put Chacon out of business. It's just gonna make him stronger, more of a hero down here."

All my warning buzzers were going off. If Rick Ross was on the level with me and was really trying to clean up Haven Park, then he should want Rocky to win the election.

"What do you want from me?" I said. "I can't control Alonzo. He's not real bright."

"You got anything else?"

"What's with this gang problem you've got? How come the South Side Crips are moving back in?"

"I'll deal with the Compton Crips," he said. "You're here to put the hat on Mayor Bratano and these crooked cops."

I stood there trying to sort out my mixed feelings. Finally, I said, "Is there anybody on the job down here I can look to for help or is the whole damn department in the cafeteria line?"

"There's one Hispanic officer, Oscar Juarez. He's a clean-cut kid. Most of the cops I've got are rejects from other departments who can't get employment elsewhere. Juarez started out here because he was born here. He seems to be heading in the other direction. He's applying to departments all over Southern California. So him, maybe. One other thing. His second cousin is Anita Juarez."

"Who's that?"

"She's a reporter on the *Courier* and Rocky

Chacon's current girlfriend." That helped to explain the great press he was getting from that paper, not that he needed much help.

"What about his lawyer, Carmen Ramirez? It looked to me at the jail like that was more than just professional."

"If Rocky has a personal shortcoming, it's women," Ross said. "He goes through a lot of them. He's left a trail of broken hearts. Anita is his current squeeze and her second cousin is Oscar Juarez. It might mean something. I don't know."

We stood in awkward silence, still studying each other. Then he asked, "You got anything concrete to give me? Something that could actually serve as evidence?"

I knew it was foolish to hold back on him, especially since he was the one who had arranged to put me undercover in the first place, but some part of me, some cop instinct, told me he might have an ulterior motive. If he wasn't just trying to carry out his original threat from ten years ago, maybe he needed me to cover his ass in case the FBI ever came against him, as they had with his predecessor, Charles Le Grande.

I decided not to tell him about the envelope with eighty bucks in towing kickbacks that I'd turned over to Agent Love for fingerprinting, or about Alonzo's scam of switching out the tags on the $CO_2$ bottles at Mama's, or that the assault on Rocky in our I-room was really an attempted murder, which I couldn't prove anyway because it would come down to Alonzo's word against mine.

Instead I said, "I'm just working into it with Sergeant Bell."

"I'll check in with you later."

"Don't do it this way next time. Get a message to me. Set up a meet somewhere, outside where I can see it coming."

He nodded and walked to the door, but he stopped again before opening it. "I guess all this attitude is about what I yelled at you in the Parker Center garage all those years ago. You probably still think I've got it in for you."

"You said you were gonna see me dead, no matter how long it took. Hard to forget stuff like that."

"I was drunk. I was losing it. That's not me anymore. This isn't gonna work unless you start trusting me, Shane."

"Hey, Rick, you think I'd be down here at all if I didn't trust you?"

"I got eyes, man. You think I'm dirty. It's all over your face. But I've changed."

"The *new* Ricky Ross."

"Maybe that's *your* character flaw," he said, smiling slightly. "You lack the ability to forgive."

"Look around you, Rick. Lack of forgiveness is a big Haven Park problem. I'm just trying to stay alive in this fucked-up place."

“Good luck with that,” he said, then turned and left.

Ten minutes later, I’d loaded everything in my bag and was checking out. I needed to find a better place to live.

I also needed to set up my meeting with Sammy from Miami. I was running out of time and my nerves were rattling like dice in a tin cup.

# CHAPTER 19

I ended up at the Bicycle Club Casino Hotel in Vista. The hotel favored southwestern colors and somebody had decorated my room in a weird mixture of tan and orange-peach colors. But the space was clean and the room service fast. I also liked the fact that there were a lot of hotel cops as well as closed-circuit video in the casino and hotel corridors.

Of course, I knew that for the right price anyone could be bought off, including the plastic badges who worked hotel security, but it’s the little lies we tell ourselves that help to get us through. Whatever the reason, I felt safer here, and it was a big trade-up physically from the Haven Park Inn.

I called Sammy Ochoa from a pay phone in the casino and while I explained what I wanted, and we argued over price, I watched tables full of stone-faced men playing blackjack, wearing ball caps and sunglasses, who reminded me of the walking dead in a George Romero movie. After some haggling, Sammy and I agreed on a price and arranged to meet an hour from now on Melrose.

I left the casino and drove across town in the MDX playing my rap station loud. I spotted Sam standing on the West Hollywood street corner we'd agreed upon, just half a block down from his porno movie theater, which was currently running a gay-biker double bill: *Hot Chaps* and *Chrome Chain Cowboys*. Probably gonna miss those two.

Sammy from Miami was a short, wiry Cuban with skin the color of a Starbucks latte. His teeth were yellow from years of smoking Cuban cigars. Tonight he was dressed in leather pants and a vest, looking like a South American gaucho. I thought Sammy would be good for what I needed because he also had a long yellow sheet. If somebody in Haven Park checked him out, he'd come back dirty as a public toilet.

I pulled up and let him into the car, then drove down the street with the rap music pounding.

"Jesus, Scully. What's with this music?" he said, reaching out and turning off the radio.

I pointed out the two hidden microphones as I drove. One under the glove compartment, one in the rearview mirror. He nodded. I'd warned him on the phone that the car was bugged and he understood we were only putting on a show.

"So, is it done?" he said, getting right to the heart of it.

"Yeah, wait a minute. I wanta find a place to park so we can talk."

I turned onto La Brea and drove until I found a strip mall on the corner of Santa Monica Boulevard. I pulled in and turned off the engine.

"Okay, Sam, yeah, it's done. The guest of honor's in harp class. Coroner booked the stiff in at two A.M. last night."

"I need proof of death," he said. "I ain't payin' till I know that scumbag is really breathin' dirt."

"I got pictures just like last time," I said. "Plus, I can give you the coroner's tag number. After I pulled his drapes, I took his wallet. He's a Cuban illegal, and you were right, his prints aren't in the system yet. He's booked as Juan Doe Seventeen and is in the freezer at Mission Road. Just go in and tell them your cousin is missing or something. Describe this guy and they'll show you the stiff."

"I'll send a guy down. After we see him on a tray, I'll pay for the hit."

"Since I got thrown off the LAPD I got no cash. My wife is divorcing me and her attorney is locking everything up. I'm working down in Haven Park now, but the pay sucks and I haven't even got my first check yet."

"None of this is my problem."

"We've done business before. You know I guarantee results."

"Show me the shots."

I loudly unzipped a bag I'd brought with me and Sammy did some good acting, laughing slightly as he pretended to look at digital photos on my non-existent camera.

"Jesus. What did you hit him with? Back of his head is gone."

"Two hollow points behind the ear. That's what ten grand buys you. I want my money."

He waited a beat and then said, "Okay, tell you what. I'll give you half now and half when I have proof of death. That's the best I can do."

I sighed loudly. "Gimme it."

I had five hundred in fresh currency ready and counted the bills, snapping them loudly for the benefit of the mikes. I slipped the cash silently over to him—payment in full for a great performance.

"You can just let me out here," Sammy said as he opened the door. "I got some jokers working up on Sunset selling Madonna's underwear to tourists. Got her name embroidered on it and everything. Interested? Actual Madonna thongs, crotchless panties and tit-hole bras. I swear it's her gear."

"I look terrible in crotchless panties."

"Suit yourself. But this shit will kill on eBay." He closed the door. "Talk to you in a day or so." Then he walked away.

I stopped at an all-night drugstore and bought a

cheap pre-paid cell phone. When I got back to my room in the hotel, it was around ten o'clock.

I called the Haven Park PD and gave them the new cell number, then got something to eat in the casino restaurant. I looked around at the zombies gambling away their futures in a joint that clearly favored the house. As I watched the rows of dead-end players, it suddenly hit me that their odds were a whole lot better than mine.

# CHAPTER 20

The next day I didn't see Alonzo Bell. I reported to roll call and harnessed up, but was told that my training officer had taken a sick day for personal business. I was still a probationer and Harry Eastwood didn't want me out in the field, so I was sent over to the Haven Park police building, for an eight-hour shift answering phones and filing paper.

I spent a frustrating day riding a desk wondering what Alonzo was doing. The longer I sat there, the more I wondered if my performance at Mama's Casita and in the jail had forced some kind of dangerous reevaluation.

The mayoral election was in eight days and there was a front-page story in this morning's *Courier* written by Anita Juarez, detailing Rocky's arrest and calling for new leadership in Haven Park. The editorial page had a slew of angry letters protesting his treatment at the hands of the Haven Park PD. I knew the Avilas and Cecil Bratano weren't about to sit back and watch this election go sour. Rocky Chacon had a much better chance of winding up in Haven Park's morgue than its city hall.

At the end of the day shift I walked back to the elementary school, changed in the locker room, clocked out and drove back to the Bicycle Club. Even though it was only five o'clock, the parking lot was already full of cars belonging to dedicated gamblers. I went up to my sand- and peach-orange-colored room, kicked off my shoes, flopped down on the bed and spent half an hour trying to think what my next move should be.

One of the biggest problems working undercover was managing stress. Most uniforms, if they want to, get a chance at working a stint in Vice while still in the Patrol Division. Since Vice is a plainclothes gig, it's thought to be a good stepping-stone to the Detective Bureau.

When patrol cops got this opportunity they were generally excited about it. But it quickly became obvious that some of them didn't have the temperament. It was emotionally devastating to be sitting across from a dangerous drug dealer in a dark shooting gallery full of murderous characters, wearing a wire, knowing that at any moment you could be discovered and killed.

A lot of officers who had been eagerly looking forward to UC assignments ended up asking the watch commander to let them work support instead. Living a lie under the constant threat of exposure and death could become unbearable. It's why most law enforcement agencies limit UC work to only a few weeks.

For the past several days I'd been feeling the pressure. Not sure who was watching me, not able to trust anyone, including the guy who'd asked me to take the assignment in the first place. I missed my wife and had temporarily lost the respect of my son. Why the hell was I doing this?

At a little past seven I was so fatigued that I fell asleep sprawled across my peach-orange bed-spread.

Suddenly I was jangled out of a troubled dream by my new cell phone. I sat up and looked at my watch: 7:40 P.M. I'd only been out for half an hour. I stumbled over and fumbled the cell open.

"Yeah?" I mumbled.

"Scully?" a voice I vaguely recognized asked.

"Yes."

"Lieutenant Eastwood. You've got a call-up."

"What's up, Loo?" My nerves instantly on edge.

"You'll be briefed when you get here. We've got an 'all hands' situation. Get to the training facility on Pine Street and get in harness. Roll call is in the gym in twenty minutes."

"On my way, sir."

I hung up and wondered, was this finally it? Had I just been called in to be kidnapped, killed, then dumped in the L.A. River?

# CHAPTER 21

Most of the Haven Park police force was already crowded into the elementary school locker room when I got there. Judging by the tight expressions, something major was going down. As I stripped off my street clothes, I heard two guys at the next locker discussing an upcoming gang fight at Haven Park High tonight—a perfect setting for me to take an accidental bullet in the back.

I needed to give Agent Love a quick heads-up, so I grabbed my brand-new cell, stuffed it into my Jockey shorts and hurried into the bathroom. I found a vacant stall, locked the door, sat on the toilet and sent her a text message using the number I'd memorized at the Manhattan Beach condo. I typed out:

911-SSCC-18L-MWHS-415-M

A 415-M was LAPD code for a major disturbance. Just as I hit send I heard Alonzo Bell enter the bathroom.

"Scully, where the fuck are you?"

"In here," I yelled through the stall door.

"Get your ass out here. Roll call's in five minutes."

"Coming."

I couldn't walk out carrying my damn cell with a 911 message to the FBI in its memory chip, so I looked for a place to ditch it. The high school was a fifties building and the toilets in the locker room had old-style surge tanks. I lifted the lid and dropped my new cell into the water, replacing the porcelain top. When I came out of the stall, Bell was standing there, frowning impatiently. "Let's go," he said. "Move your bowels on your own time."

I dressed quickly and followed my partner into the gymnasium. As soon as we got inside, Alonzo moved up to the podium and stood with the other shift sergeants and our command staff officers.

Dirty Harry Eastwood was strapped up in black Second Chance riot gear. Despite the Kevlar, I had a feeling if any trouble went down, he'd stay safely inside his tricked-out mobile command center. Standing next to him was Deputy Chief Talbot Jones.

I spotted Hector and Manny Avila in expensive sport coats to one side of the podium, looking worried. I had no idea what they were doing at our roll call.

The entire Haven Park patrol force assembled expectantly in the bleachers and the room quieted immediately as Harry Eastwood stepped to the podium.

"Deputy Chief Jones is going to take the first part of this briefing. Tal?" The lieutenant moved aside to allow Talbot Jones to come forward.

"Okay. You guys all know this has been coming for a while," Jones began in his rich baritone. "According to sources the Avilas have on the street, this rumble is going down tonight." He paused and looked at Bell. "Al, pull that blackboard out here."

Alonzo went to the big double doors of the gymnasium and rolled in a large blackboard, placing it in the center of the basketball court. Taped to one side of the board were blown-up mug shots of eight Hispanic males in their twenties, all with names and numbers printed underneath. On the other side of the board were ten same-sized mugs of African-American Crip G-sters.

"Okay. For the past few weeks Manny and Hector Avila have been working under contract with the city of Haven Park as gang violence consultants," Jones said, explaining their presence at our briefing. "As most of you know, they have very good Eighteenth Street connections. A few hours ago, they picked up a rumor that a rumble is planned during halftime at tonight's home football game between Haven Park and South Compton High. Ten or twelve armed Crips are heading our way right now. These shots on the left side of the board have been identified as the probable Crip shooters by our Inner-City Gang Intelligence Division."

He tapped the blackboard with his knuckle. "The shot-caller is this guy." He pointed to a picture of a scowling black banger in his late twenties with close-cut hair. "His name is Harris Karris, street handle K-Knife. The guy is bad news, with a long list of agg assaults and unfiled murder allegations, so if you see him, cut this asshole no slack."

Ballpoints clicked as cops wrote down Harris Karris's name, street handle and identifying characteristics.

"The Locos know this is going down and have agreed to lay back and work with us." Jones tapped the side of the board with the pictures of eight Locos. "We have a shared objective with these guys, so let's make sure we're focusing on the right people tonight."

I couldn't believe he was telling us to give the Locos a pass and only go after Crip shooters. But it got even worse as the briefing continued.

He motioned to Hector and Manny Avila. "As you know, the Avilas have been very helpful trying to diffuse Eighteenth Street gang violence. Their participation in the youth center has helped to contain what was once a very dangerous citywide problem." He turned toward the Avilas. "I'm going to turn the briefing over to Manny Avila, so he can give you his take."

"Thank you, Captain Jones," Manny said as he stepped behind the podium.

"To begin with, let's get something straight. The Eighteenth Street gang is not a bunch of innocents. I'm not going to stand up here and tell you they're choirboys. But we need to remember they're from our neighborhood. These South Side Compton Crips are outsiders who come into our city and incite violence.

"Tonight can be a defining moment for Haven Park. Of the officers gathered here, my brother Hector and I have been privileged to know and work with most of you."

He pointed to the side of the blackboard that displayed the eight scowling *eses*. "We're making progress with this bunch. *Veterano* shot-callers like Ovieto Ortiz are finally seeing things our way." He tapped 007's picture.

"Using our influence, we're convincing them to forgo violence and walk a new path."

I had seen the LAPD crash reports on 18th Street arrests outside of Haven Park and the gang was growing and becoming more violent, not less. But I kept my mouth shut and my expression blank.

"What happens tonight can begin a new era," Manny said. "One without Crip violence. Eighteenth Street *eses* will be able to stop fighting over territory and focus on living more productive lives. But before that can happen, these *mallates* from Compton need to be taught a lesson."

He looked at Harry Eastwood and said, "The quality of life in Haven Park is in your hands." He turned and stepped away from the podium. Not exactly the Gettysburg Address, but all the cops in the gym were nodding enthusiastically.

"Good stuff," Eastwood said, as he again addressed the room. "We all certainly owe Manny and Hector Avila for everything they've done in gang intervention down here.

"After roll call we're gonna deploy into smaller groups in classrooms for specific shift briefings, then we'll van over to the Haven Park High football field. After the players go onto the field we'll muster in the locker room under the stands and be ready when these South Side Crips show. We have spotters up in the press box and plain-clothes officers in the crowd. Keep your radios on tactical frequency two."

Eastwood turned and motioned to Alonzo, who rolled another blackboard out in front of us. It had a big schematic map of the Haven Park High football field and parking lot. Several photo reconnaissance blowups were also taped there.

"Day watch will be covering the parking lot and the refreshment stands out front," Eastwood continued.

He pointed to several recon pictures of the front of the high school stadium. There were metal bleachers on one side of the field that looked as if they could hold six or seven hundred people.

"Alonzo Bell is in charge of the day shift. Your radio call signs will be Thrasher One through Twelve.

"Mid-watch will cover the football field and bleachers. Sergeant Dobson is in charge. Mid-watch, you're Constrictor One through Twelve. I want the mid-watch guys stationed under the bleachers behind these concrete equipment rooms," he said, indicating the location. "Your job is to protect the people in the stands."

"The graveyard shift is Stone Breaker. Sergeant Lunderman has that group and you'll be held in reserve back at the command post."

I couldn't believe that Eastwood was going to keep the entire graveyard shift at the CP as his personal security.

But then he cleared that up by saying, "Graveyard is going to do the critical response work. I'll spot-deploy that bunch as the situation demands. Okay, let's make this a neat, clean operation. Remember that Haven Park parents and students will be in the stands. I don't want any innocents to get shot.

"Unfortunately, we need to let this situation happen so we can make felony arrests and finally put an end to all this Crip violence on our street corners. Stopping that game in advance and clearing the stands will only alert the Crips and we'll lose a golden opportunity. I think, with this many guys, we can swarm them and get a good, quick result without risking collateral damage.

"Lastly, let me say that these Crips are hardened killers. If any of them go to God tonight, I'm not gonna be writing down badge numbers."

A murmur of approval came from the cops seated around me.

"Let's do it and let's do it right. Meet in your individual groups for briefings with your sergeants and then see the armorer and pick up the new Heckler & Koch MP5 submachine guns and Second Chance Kevlar vests that just came in. We'll reconvene out front in twenty minutes."

I couldn't believe that they weren't going to stop the game and clear the stadium. But as Talbot had told me when I first got here, the Haven Park PD wasn't out there to protect and serve. This was all about our envelopes.

The day shift, most of whom I still barely knew, met with Alonzo in one of the old elementary school classrooms that no longer had any desks or furniture. He had some chalk in his hand and had already drawn our sector of the parking lot onto the blackboard.

"Okay, everybody gets a number," he said. "Belkin, you're Thrasher One; Ashcroft, you're Two; Scully, you're Three . . ." He continued until all of us had a radio designation.

"I've got your call signs written down on a card,

but to tell the truth, I'll never remember them. The call signs are just more of Dirty Harry's movie bullshit. How we're gonna use 'em is to marshal troop strength. Like I'll say, 'One through Three respond to the east side of the parking lot'—that kind of thing. But if you call me, use your fucking name so I'll know who I'm talking to."

He turned to face us. "Okay, we all know what this is about. We're gonna throw down on these Crips and bag this K-Knife character, I got a raise in grade for the guy who dumps him. Is everybody straight on what we're trying to do here?"

"You got it! Done deal!" the officers of the day watch shouted back.

The adrenaline was really pumping in our little classroom.

"Okay, study the parking lot layout on the board and saddle up. Everybody gets totally flacked for this one. These new Second Chance vests will stop armor-piercing rounds, so even though they're bulky, wear them. I don't want to lose a guy to a stray bullet. Roulon Green is gonna be passing out vests and MP5s."

He motioned to a tall black officer who was a Policeman II, standing in the doorway in front of a large rolling cart stacked with H&K shipping crates and boxes of Kevlar vests. There were plenty of extra magazines.

"See you all out front."

Everyone got an MP5, a vest and two spare

mags, then started to disperse. Once they were gone, Alonzo took my submachine gun out of my hand and leaned it against the wall next to me. As I started to shoulder into my vest, he took it as well. "Gimme your cell phone."

"Left it in my hotel room. Why you always on me?"

"Why you always such a hard-on?" he replied.

I shrugged, but didn't answer.

"You're with me tonight," he finally said. "You stay close by. I don't ever want you outta my sight."

Then suddenly, without warning, he ran his big hand over me, under my arms and down my chest, looking for either my cell phone or a wire. This time he made no attempt to disguise the frisk. All cops know that people wearing a wire will often hide the recorder in the crotch because most men have a homophobic dislike of frisking another guy's package. But that wasn't going to stop Alonzo. I grabbed his wrist as he went for my groin.

"When are you gonna give this a rest?"

He smiled and said, "You gotta get with the program, man."

"I'm trying." I grabbed the MP5, my extra mags and Second Chance vest.

Then he said, "I got your back out there tonight."

It was the scariest thing he could have told me.

# CHAPTER 22

Lieutenant Eastwood and the graveyard shift officers were under the bleachers, locked inside the black-and-white bus that served as his sixty-foot mobile command center. The rest of the Haven Park police force gathered with Deputy Chief Jones in the Haven Park football team's locker room under the stands where pictures of the ten Crip shooters were taped up on the coach's chalkboard. We had nothing to do but study their scowling faces and wait.

I thought it strange that our chief, Ricky Ross, had not even made an appearance. Not at the elementary school briefing, not here. Did he even know this was happening?

We could hear the five hundred or so people in the stands above us cheering as the ball was kicked off and the game began. The department spotters high up in the bleachers were keeping us apprised of outside activity.

"Still all clear out here," someone said over the radio. I didn't have a clue who the spotters were.

"We got a good complement of Locos roaming the stands. They're mostly in their regular black gang coats with blue neck scarves, so watch out for them," the spotter said.

The tension inside the locker room was growing. It was hard to sit in twenty pounds of

Kevlar and wait to go into action. I tried to stay calm, but was overdosing on a mixture of stomach bile, anxiety and adrenaline. Even though I was flacked, I knew that if I was a target, my own teammates could cancel my pension with one head shot.

As I looked at the tense faces around me, I wondered which, if any, of the cops gathered with me had my kill number. I wondered which one was Officer Oscar Juarez.

"We got bogeys entering the parking lot," a spotter said ten minutes later. "Three black Lincoln Town Cars. Mother ships. Four guys to a car."

"Roger that," Talbot Jones said, then turned to face us. "Okay, Alonzo, you and your bunch are up. Remember, let this get started. Make sure these Crips get some chrome out before you go into action. We need felonies to get clean DOAs here. Once it gets going, lead enemas all around. Move out."

We left the locker room and ran beneath the stadium seats toward the parking lot. Our operation plan had been discussed beforehand and the deadly mission was reflected on our drawn, expressionless faces. Our boots were setting up a rumble, echoing underneath the bleachers as we ran.

Alonzo was in the lead. I was second, with the rest of the day watch strung out behind me. As we sprinted away from the football field toward the parking lot, Alonzo directed our squad with arm gestures. Some flanked right, some left, peeling off in both directions.

We had been told to deploy into the lot, and set up a pincer movement. Then the center column, made up of myself and three other guys, led by Alonzo, would make a frontal assault and initiate a firefight away from the stands. The pincer groups would close in after the shooting started and surround the Crips, catching them in a crossfire. Once we had them contained, the swing shift would leave their position where they were protecting the stadium and bleachers and offer tactical support. Graveyard would cover critical response and swarm a position if any of us got pinned down.

I was hanging with Alonzo, running right behind him, and soon only four of us were left in the center column, still heading straight toward where the twelve Crip shooters were supposed to be waiting in their smoked-windowed Lincolns. We were all clutching new MP5 burners in death grips as we ran. Equipment rattled, adrenaline surged.

The lot was badly underlit and it was hard to see. When we reached the center of the parking area, we finally saw the Lincolns. We moved up fast to clear all three Town Cars. They were already empty. The four of us began scanning the area. If the Crip shooters were here, they were crouching low out of sight. Since we had split into smaller groups it was impossible to tell where the rest of the squad was. I felt exposed and vulnerable.

When we finally got to the far end of the parking area, we still had seen no Crip G-sters. Alonzo radioed the two flanking groups and soon all of us were standing in a huddle next to a chain-link fence.

Alonzo triggered his mike. "This is Thrasher One. We're ten-ninety-seven. Nobody in sight in the parking lot."

"Stand by, Thrasher One," the spotter came back.

Then we heard a long static burst of gunfire coming from the direction of the stands as somebody over there dumped at least fifty rounds. It was followed by the short, tight, burping sound of an automatic weapon on a four-shot burst.

"They musta got around us," one of the cops said.

"We're hearing gunfire," Alonzo announced into his shoulder mike. "Give us a location."

"We're ten-ninety-nine under the bleachers," Talbot Jones said, using our ten-code for an emergency. "Redeploy! We've got men down!" Jones screamed.

Alonzo spun and all of us ran as a group back toward the bleachers. I knew from my Marine Corps training this was a tactical blunder. We were clumped together and out in the open, all of our operation plans forgotten as we ran headlong to help fallen officers.

Just then, a machine gun on full auto opened up. Bullets sparked, pinging off parked cars all around us. We were under direct fire. Two of our guys went down.

I kept running and shouted into my shoulder rover, "This is Thrasher Three, we have men down!"

I had to decide if I was going to follow Alonzo on this suicide charge or take my own evasive action. More guns opened up and that sealed my decision. I veered off, sprinting between cars looking for muzzle flashes.

I saw one. The gun was firing from behind the refreshment stand to my right. I headed in that direction, running low between rows of parked vehicles. I wasn't sure what I was supposed to do. I was pretty much just trying to stay alive.

# CHAPTER 23

Suddenly I was hit from behind.

A round caught my Kevlar vest high in the shoulder and knocked me flat. The MP5 flew from my hands, landing somewhere out of sight under a tricked-out low rider. I couldn't tell where the gunfire was coming from. Bullets were flying everywhere. My Kevlar vest had saved me.

With my MP5 lying out of sight in the dark and my shoulder aching from the impact of the bullet hit, I pulled my police-issue Smith & Wesson .38 and crouched low, regained my footing, then slowly rose up to look over the hood of the car. Police in riot gear were swarming all over the place. A machine gun cut loose across from the refreshment stand, firing in long bursts. It sounded like an AK-47, which puts out six hundred rounds per minute at twenty-three hundred feet per second. Nothing sounds quite like it. I heard Lieutenant Eastwood screaming instructions over the police rover on my shoulder.

I started moving again, slower this time, checking my back and protecting my sight lines. I finally reached the refreshment stand where I had seen the initial machine gun muzzle flash. There were three Crip gangbangers hunkered down behind the stand. One of them looked like Harris Karris. Their eyes were wide with fright as they looked for a way out of this. None of them had been expecting to run into heavily armed cops.

I started moving up slowly, trying to get the drop on these guys. Suddenly Alonzo Bell appeared on the far right, sneaking up behind the Crip G-sters. As I watched, he knelt down and got ready to unzip all three. It was happening so fast that I didn't see how I could stop it.

Just as I was about to call out a warning, four

SWAT vans roared into the parking lot and screeched to a halt close to where I was standing. The Crips hit the deck just a split second ahead of Alonzo's gunfire. The bullets from his MP5 barely missed K-Knife and the others. The van doors burst open and four seven-man FBI SWAT teams poured out, deploying quickly.

Ophelia Love had finally arrived with backup. The Crip shooters threw down their weapons and thrust their hands in the air. The parking lot was quickly secured.

Alonzo Bell was caught short. It had happened so fast, he had been unable to get off his kill shots. FBI agents swarmed the scene.

"We're code four," somebody yelled, and all over the parking lot FBI SWAT officers in flak gear started to hook up Crip shooters. All ten were quickly cuffed and arrested. Two had been injured.

I grabbed a spare Maglite and ran back to where I had dropped my MP5. I didn't want to try and explain that loss to my new department bosses. I shone the beam around under some cars until I saw it, then rolled under a low rider to retrieve the gun. When I came out, Alonzo Bell was standing right in front of me.

"Where the hell did those feds come from?" An angry vein was pulsing on his forehead.

"How the hell do I know?"

"Somebody tipped 'em."

Just then Ophelia Love, looking pissed off and tough in black Kevlar, strode angrily over to where we stood. She was holding a Glock nine in one rawboned fist, a field rover in the other.

"Scully. I should've known you'd be in this," she growled. Then she wheeled on Alonzo. "Are you just bagging Crip shooters or are you gonna bust some of these *esse*s as well? I want every gang-affiliated Eighteenth Street Loco out in this parking lot in cuffs and I want it right now," she ordered.

"Those guys had nothing to do with this," Alonzo defended. "They're just here watching their high school football game."

"If any one of those dirtbags has a student body card, I'll eat it. Now get 'em out here," she shouted. "I'm not fucking around. Do your job or I'll have my guys do it for you."

When he didn't move, she gave the order to her own SWAT team. They all surged toward the stadium and twenty minutes later the feds had a dozen angry 18th Street Locos in custody and had herded them to the FBI SWAT vans. Most were carrying the new Russian-made AK-100 series machine guns hanging from cords tied around their shoulders, protected from view by their duster-length gang coats. The new Russian ordnance was going to put them in serious trouble with Homeland Security.

The Crip arrestees were being transported to the

Haven Park PD for booking as the feds started processing the 18th Street L's.

An announcement was being broadcast over the loudspeakers saying the game was canceled and instructing all spectators to vacate the area immediately.

Frightened parents and students began filtering through FBI checkpoints and moving quickly into the parking lot to retrieve their cars and get out of there.

When I reached our mobile command center under the stands, I found Talbot Jones and Ophelia Love in the middle of a fierce argument.

"We had this under control. We were deployed," Jones responded angrily.

"That's not what it looked like to me," she fired back. "It looked more like an ambush."

She glared at me. "Get outta my way, Scully." Then pushed past me and walked to her SWAT vans.

The entire mess ended up back at the Haven Park PD. Talbot Jones decided to book the Crips and the Locos at our mobile CP in the police department's main parking lot. There wasn't enough room in the Haven Park jail to hold all of the arrestees, so Ophelia Love made arrangements to have the overflow prisoners transported to the L.A. County Sheriff's facility in Vista.

As the mop-up continued, I couldn't believe how lucky we had been. The Second Chance Kevlar had saved all our guys. No spectators had been injured despite an incredible amount of careless gunplay. Two Crips had been shot and were transported to County USC by the EMTs. Both appeared to be in stable condition and looked like they would survive.

The 18th Street Locos had one fatality; a nineteen-year-old named Carlos Rosario was dead where he landed and left the football game in the coroner's van.

As we were finishing with the booking, Alonzo approached me. "We need to talk," he said.

"Okay."

"Meet me over in the elementary school parking lot in twenty minutes." Then he turned and walked away.

I desperately needed backup for that meeting, but couldn't talk to Agent Love about it. We were locked into our roles as sworn enemies.

Ten minutes later Ophelia drove off in one of the FBI SWAT vans, leaving me to deal with Alonzo alone.

It was after midnight when I walked over to the elementary school and changed from my uniform into my street clothes. I needed to recover my cell phone because, waterlogged as it undoubtedly was, the chip might still contain my text message. I waited until that bathroom stall was empty, then went in and locked the door.

When I opened the surge tank and looked inside, my cell phone was gone.

# CHAPTER 24

"What were you doing in Manhattan Beach two nights ago?" Bell demanded. We were standing in the deserted parking lot of the elementary school next to my car.

I started groping for an appropriate response.

"You left here at end-of-watch, then went downtown, switched cars and went to Manhattan Beach. You spent the night in a condo on Ocean Way."

"Are you having me followed, Alonzo?"

My heart was racing. I'd left the bugged MDX with Harpo, made sure I wasn't followed on the freeway when I drove his van. So how the hell could they know about my trip to Deputy Chief Arnett's condo in Manhattan Beach? Yet somehow they'd managed to tail me there. Either that or they'd planted a tracking device on *me*. I knew from police ops I'd done recently that the new GPS trackers had been reduced to the size of small collar buttons. Was I wearing one of those in the sole of a shoe or something?

"I'm waiting for an answer," Bell growled.

"I don't have to tell you what I do off duty," I stalled, still trying to assess the jeopardy.

If they knew I'd gone to that condo in Manhattan Beach, then they also knew I'd been meeting with Alexa. My whole story about

Tiffany Roberts was going to start looking like a lie. What about Ophelia Love? Did he know she'd been there? I could see Alonzo's off-duty piece clipped in an easy-to-reach place on his belt under his windbreaker. Mine was in my clamshell at the small of my back, just a little tougher to get to.

"I was seeing a woman," I finally said, keeping it vague.

"Not good enough."

I knew I had to tell this ape something and, if he didn't buy it, be ready to deal with some major fallout. However, the more I thought about it, the more I was certain he didn't have a clue what I'd done or I'd already be tits-up under a bridge somewhere. So he didn't know what I'd been doing, only where I'd gone.

"It's none of your business," I said, trying for a better read.

"I did you a solid to get you on this department. If you're a federal plant, then it's my screwup. So it damn sure is my business."

"I was in Manhattan Beach seeing Tiffany Roberts," I said. "She's still hooked to that producer Harry Venture, trying to keep her marriage together for the sake of her career. I met her there."

"You're lying. We ran the real estate taxes to see who owns the units. There's no Tiffany Roberts or Harry Venture on the books for those condos. There is, however, an LAPD assistant chief named

Malon Arnett who owns a penthouse there. Let's talk about him."

"Hey, Sergeant, I just got thrown off the L.A. department. What would I be doing hanging out in an apartment owned by Chief Arnett?"

"Debriefing. Telling him shit about what's going on down here."

"Right." I shook my head in disgust. "Me and the A-Chief from Administrative Affairs. He's a paper pusher. He runs budgets, not undercover ops. What the fuck are you talking about?"

"Then come up with something, because I talked to some people an hour ago who are very upset about this. I want the truth."

"I told you the truth. I was meeting with Tiffany. I don't know shit about A-Chief Arnett having a condo there. The condo we were in was a furnished model in the building. Tiffany has a friend who works at Century 21. We gotta be very careful since this all went down. Her husband knows about us now. She just barely kept him from throwing her out. Her friend unlocked the model so we could use it. Check it out, Al. There're empty units all over that building."

My heart was slamming inside my chest.

"You can bet your ass I'm going to check it out."

We stood for a minute studying each other. Then I said, "Is this meeting over?"

"Yeah, it's over." Bell turned and walked to his Escalade and drove off.

I headed back to the hotel and went straight up to my room. I stripped off all my clothes, took everything out of my dresser and closet and put it all out on the bed along with my briefcase and shoes. Then I started looking for the tracking device.

I found it inside my belt. They had sliced open the leather on a seam, buried the tracker and stitched it back up. As I suspected, the unit was the size of a collar button. I left it in there. It wasn't too hard to realize how they'd done it. They'd broken into my locker while I was out on patrol. The padlock they'd given me obviously could be opened by a second combination.

Now I needed to warn Alexa and have Ophelia set up a new cover story for Tiffany Roberts and me about the condo.

I dressed again and stuffed a change of clothes into a paper bag, then exited the room, leaving the belt containing the tracking device behind.

I went downstairs to the lobby, crossed to the casino and made two calls from a pay phone. One was to Alexa, the other to Ophelia.

Next, I rented a car from Hertz through the hotel concierge, who handed me the keys and informed me it was a blue Mustang, parked in slot 23 at the side of the hotel. I went into a downstairs men's room in the casino and changed into the black T-shirt and Bermuda shorts I had in the paper bag. I rolled my original outfit up inside my windbreaker and jammed it under my arm. I pulled a ball cap low over my eyes and slipped on a pair of dark glasses, transforming myself into another card zombie. Then I slipped out a fire exit and hugged the side of the building, watching my back as I made my way to the rental car slots. I found the Mustang, got in and sat there watching out the rear window to see if I was being followed. My heart hadn't stopped flopping around in my chest since the meeting with Alonzo. Textbook paranoia.

When nobody showed for five minutes, I put the car in gear and got the hell out of there.

# CHAPTER 25

This time I was very careful getting to Santa Monica and employed a freeway anti-tailing technique I'd discovered through hours of trial and error. Simple and impossible to defeat. I drove at over seventy in the fast lane until I finally saw a hole in traffic, then, without signaling, dove suddenly across three lanes and shot down an off ramp onto surface streets. Then I got back on the freeway going in the opposite direction. The idea was, any car attempting to follow would not be able to find a similar hole in traffic and would overshoot the exit. I repeated the maneuver three times.

I'd just rented the Mustang, so I knew both the car and my clothes were clean.

Twenty minutes later I was on the Coast Highway driving through Santa Monica. I turned into the parking lot by the Santa Monica Pier, looking for the LAPD eight-wheel truck that we used for clandestine meetings with undercover operatives. Because Switzerland was neutral territory, we had nicknamed the truck Little Swiss. Some smartass in vehicle maintenance had gone to the Swiss chocolate company for the decals that now decorated both sides of the cargo box.

I quickly spotted the truck looming above the other cars and pulled into an empty spot nearby. As soon as I got out of the Mustang, the back doors of Little Swiss opened and I was let inside. Seated in back were Alexa and Ophelia, two very tense-looking women.

I wanted to hug my wife and kiss her, but I could see from both their faces that they were in battle mode, so I just sat on the wooden bench opposite them. There were three television monitors on the front wall of the interior, which displayed surveillance views of the parking lot, being recorded by three roof cameras.

"Thank God you sent me that 911," Ophelia said without preamble. "Those guys were about to commit a mass execution."

"That's exactly what they were up to," I confirmed.

"This is supposed to be a country of laws," she stated vehemently.

"I'm running out of options," I said to get her off the 'country of laws' party line. "Alonzo Bell is all over me. He suspects I'm a plant. They even put a tracking device in my leather belt. I found it and left it in my room."

"Then we're pulling you out now, Shane," Alexa declared.

"I haven't gotten close to the real corruption yet. I haven't even met Mayor Bratano. If you pull me out now, we'll have accomplished nothing."

We sat silently on the hard wooden benches looking at each other across two feet of open space while the TV screens showed infrared panning shots of the parking lot.

"What about Rocky Chacon?" I asked Ophelia. "The way I see it, they're getting set to take him out."

Alexa said, "Maybe Ophelia can find a way to put more FBI security on him. But if you get involved, they're gonna *know* you're a plant."

Ophelia nodded. "I think Alexa's right. You're probably already compromised. Talbot Jones didn't believe my story about being there because of a street tip. He suspects somebody on the inside of leaking the ambush."

"I need a few more days."

Both women sat trying to decide what to do. I must have been frowning, because Alexa leaned forward.

"What?" she asked.

"Sergeant Bell knows I went to Manhattan Beach. He knows Deputy Chief Arnett has a condo in that building."

"Then you're definitely out of there," Alexa said, rising as if the meeting were over.

"Hold on," I said. "I told him I went to that condo to meet Tiffany—that we were using one of the furnished models. I told him Tiffany has a girlfriend at Century 21 who opened it up for us. He looked like he bought it, but he's going to check it out. We need to put a female FBI agent in at that real estate management company, somebody who can swear she opened the apartment for her movie star friend. If you guys can set that up, then my story will check out and I can give this a little more time." I didn't tell them that I'd lost my cell phone with the text message to Ophelia on it.

"They're bound to suspect you just because you're the new guy," Alexa rightly pointed out. "That's why they put a sattrack on you."

"I have some other action working. I put my street creds on display. I'm hoping to get an offer that will incriminate Mayor Bratano."

"What the hell does that mean?" Alexa said.

I waved this off. "I'm beginning to get a read on these guys. They think they have the game so rigged nobody can get to them. That's why they pulled this bullshit tonight. They think they can't lose. It's making them careless."

"I don't think there's even a furnished model in that condo building," Alexa said.

"So what? Just put up a sign that says there is. I saw the Century 21 vacancy ads when I went there. All Ophelia's phony real estate agent has to do is say she let us use one."

"What happened to your face?" Alexa was staring at my swollen nose and the beginnings of two black shiners, slightly visible in the dim light in the truck.

"Slipped getting out of the shower."

"Shane, damn it!" Alexa was losing patience.

We all sat in silence for a minute.

"What's this work in progress you were talking about?" Ophelia finally asked.

"Can't tell. Sorry. It compromises one of my street contacts."

"That's such bullshit!" Alexa was now flat-out angry.

"Look, I think if this happens, it's gonna go down soon," I told them. "Give me two more days. After that, I'll fold up and get out."

"One day," Alexa said.

"Come on—"

"One," she said, firmly. "I'm not kidding, Shane."

She looked over at Ophelia, who, after a moment, nodded her agreement and said, "Listen, Shane. Put the belt back on. I can use that tracking signal just as well as they can. I'll get the satcom guys at Quantico to dial in the frequency for me."

"What about Rick Ross?" I asked. "You just gonna leave him down there to sweat it out?"

"I'll talk to Tony," Alexa said. "We'll figure something out for him. You've got one day."

# CHAPTER 26

"Leave your car here. We're gonna take a short trip," Alexa said, after Ophelia left. "We've got to go see someone."

"I can't be seen with you."

"Shut up," she said, and kissed me on the mouth. Then she stepped out of the truck and slammed the back door.

I heard her climb into the front seat and a minute later Little Swiss started up and we were rolling. As I sat there, it was very clear to me that I was betting my life on what Agent Love could set up overnight with Century 21. But I needed enough time for my Sammy from Miami ploy to pay off. I doubted if one day was enough. My strategy with Alexa was to take the one day she'd given me, then try to come away with enough good stuff to extend the time frame another one or two days after that.

But Alexa and Ophelia were right. I'd made mistakes in order to save lives. I'd compromised my cover to save Rocky and those twelve Crips. Both women knew I was skidding around on bullshit. My best choice was to stay the course and see where I was when the clock ran out.

We drove for another twenty minutes and then the truck stopped and the engine shut off. Alexa opened the back door and said, "Follow me."

When I climbed out of the truck, I realized immediately we were at the beautiful Malibu Beach Inn, a swank contemporary luxury hotel located on a strip of beach known as "Billionaire's Beach." Because it was situated in an exclusive enclave, the hotel afforded its guests a good deal of privacy.

I followed Alexa to Room 26. She opened the door with a key from her purse and led me inside. The suite was gorgeous and had a private balcony with expansive ocean views.

Then I saw him. Chooch was standing in the room, leaning against the wall, looking very tall, handsome and uncomfortable.

"Tell him," Alexa said.

"The chief—"

"Forget the chief," she interrupted. "This isn't his family that's getting destroyed. It's ours. Tell him."

"Tell me what?" Chooch asked, obviously still in the dark about what was going on, not sure why his mother had asked him to meet us here.

Alexa had realized that it would be stronger coming from me so she hadn't told him any of it yet. But I couldn't speak. I just stood there.

"Your father didn't do any of the things they said he did," she finally blurted. "It was all faked with my approval. He's gone undercover in Haven Park and he's down there risking his life to expose a corrupt police department and city government. I won't take the chance that he could be killed without having the opportunity to set things straight with you in person." She had a very determined look on her face.

"I'll wait in the other room," she said.

I took my son out onto the balcony. The surf was breaking on the cliffside rocks, frothing in the landscape lights from the hotel deck above us. I told Chooch everything that had happened—how we'd set up the sting. I explained that I'd never even met Tiffany Roberts, and why we had been instructed by Chief Filosiani to keep him in the dark.

"I would have never said anything, Dad," Chooch said after I finished. I could tell that our lack of trust in him badly hurt his feelings.

"How could they believe that I'd risk your life over stuff like that?" he said.

"Because they don't know you."

After a while I saw a sad look descend on him. "I'm sorry for what I said, Dad."

He stood up and reached out to me. We hugged each other, locked in a long, silent embrace.

"You know something funny?" I said after we finally parted. "I'd have been very disappointed if you'd acted any other way."

Alexa joined us on the balcony ten minutes later and we talked about everyday, unimportant stuff. What was happening at USC, what courses his girlfriend, Del, was taking. It was great to be able to leave Haven Park behind for a little while. We told each other how happy we were to be a family again.

"You can never tell anyone about this. Not even Del," Alexa cautioned Chooch. "Not until this is all finished and the department releases the truth."

"Do you think there's anything that would make me risk Dad's life? Are you kidding, Mom? I'd die first."

And I knew that's exactly what he would do.

An hour later, when Chooch left, Alexa and I made love. I'd felt so empty these last days, so without hope, that the act of our lovemaking filled me, cleansed me, made me reborn again. Afterward we went out onto the balcony and sat holding hands.

"You remember when we were in Aruba, that other time you were undercover going after bad cops?" Alexa reminded me.

"Sure, I thought I'd lost you."

She was referring to the case we worked several years ago, before we were married. I'd been undercover working the black market peso exchange where Fortune 500 companies were using their products to launder Colombian drug money. To set my cover, I had been asked by six rogue cops running the scam to shoot Alexa as my loyalty test. We had set up an elaborate hit where Alexa was wearing a Kevlar vest. I pulled the trigger, but didn't know that the rogue cops had put armor-piercing bullets in my gun. For two weeks, I thought I'd killed her. It plunged me into a deep depression. But we'd both survived.

"I'm trying to tell myself that this isn't anywhere near as bad as that," she said, smiling at me. "If we could get through that, we can get through anything."

But Alexa hadn't been down in Haven Park. She hadn't seen the way things worked there. Tow tickets, protection rackets, and extortion. Murder was just another dish on the cafeteria line.

As I sat holding her hand, watching the waves explode in foam grenades against the craggy rocks below, I wondered if we would be able to survive again.

# CHAPTER 27

Time was short, so I couldn't spend the night with Alexa no matter how much I wanted to.

I sat in the back of Little Swiss while she drove to the lot by the Santa Monica Pier and parked. She opened the back door and joined me inside. We kissed goodnight and held each other.

"I'm never gonna sign off on something like this again," she told me. "I can't take it."

"It's an interesting thought," I said, "but if it's right, you'll do it again, because it's your job."

It was a little past three A.M. when I got back to the hotel. I went straight to my room, set my alarm for seven A.M. and fell asleep.

My next shift was a complete waste. As soon as I got to the station I found out Alonzo was scheduled to be in court all day testifying. Lieutenant Eastwood set me up for another dull day of shuffling paper.

Over in city hall all anyone talked about was the big SWAT event at Haven Park High and how the feds' Special Tactics team had jumped our play. Most of the uniformed cops I talked to thought we had a rat in the department. Because I was Haven Park's greenest boot, I was getting some serious stink eye.

At end-of-watch I got into the Acura and pulled out of the parking lot. I'd used up most of my twenty-four hours and had accomplished nothing. I was scheduled to check in with Alexa as soon as I was EOW, so I returned to the Bicycle Club and called her from one of the pay phone banks in the casino lobby.

"What happened?" she asked.

"Alonzo was in court. I spent the day filing paper."

While she was mulling that over I asked, "How about one more day?"

I knew from the prolonged silence that followed that something was up.

"Gimme another twenty-four hours," I pressed. "Today was a complete loss."

"They still don't know you have that Mustang, right?"

"I parked a few blocks away. Unless they get into the Hertz computer and start looking at contracts, it should still be clean."

"Get in it and drive north. Take Pacific Boulevard. I'm notifying Agent Love. She'll make a field stop."

"What's up?"

"Homeland took over the case. They got spooked by all the AK-100s that were booked at the high school. You work for them now."

I certainly didn't want my undercover op run by people I didn't know.

"I told Ophelia I want you out of there, but it's a federal case now, so her people have to sign off."

"I'll be careful, honey."

"Shane, I need to be in the loop. You know what information hogs the feds are. You've got to stay in touch with me no matter what."

"I'll call twice a day. I love you."

After we hung up I walked the two blocks from the casino to where I'd left the rental. I got into the Mustang and drove out of Vista on Pacific Boulevard, heading north toward a commercial district filled mostly with warehouses and freight yards.

I'd only driven four blocks when two black Navigators with tinted windows hedged me in at the curb. Four FBI guys in dark clothes swarmed the Mustang. I was pulled out of my vehicle at gunpoint, handcuffed and then pushed into the back of the lead Navigator. As soon as I was inside, it roared away. Seated beside me was Ophelia Love.

"Sorry, but this bust was the best idea I could come up with on short notice."

She reached over and uncuffed me. "Those weapons we took off the Locos last night are new Russian guns. Some of them were minted less than two months ago. My bosses think the Locos are moving this stuff for Russian mobsters who have ties with local Al-Qaeda cells. Homeland wants this pipeline shut down now."

"I need more time."

"Your wife wants you out of here. I told my local supervisor that I agree that you might be compromised. But he still wants us to try for a result. As point agent, it's my call, but everybody is breathing hard."

"Today was a complete waste," I said. "Alonzo was in court."

Ophelia sat for a long moment before she said, "I like your wife. I'd like to do what she wants. Every day you stay under, your jeopardy increases."

"I'm up for it if you are," I told her.

"We need to wrap this up fast. I need you to wear a wire. You have to lure these crooks into conversations. Try to implicate somebody like Talbot Jones or Sergeant Bell. Somebody who, once we bust him, will roll over to save his ass. If you agree to the wire, I'll let you stay for one more twenty-four-hour period. Otherwise I'm pulling you now."

Wearing a wire is an invitation to disaster because there's absolutely no excuse that works if you get busted. For that reason, I shoot my head no.

"Then I'm pulling you."

"You're not gonna pull me. This is a career case for you."

"Then you're done," she said.

"Wear the wire or clear out? That's my choice?"

She nodded, her mouth set in determination.

"Gimme it," I said, holding out my hand.

She opened her purse and pulled out a digital recorder and a mike. It was just a little larger than a Bic lighter.

"You want me to send somebody from Tech Support over to wire you up?" she said.

"No," I said, putting the recorder into my jacket pocket. "The last thing I need is another meeting with the feds. I'll figure it out."

They dropped me at my rental car on Pacific. I got inside and, watching the mirrors for a tail, drove into Vista, parking again on the side street two blocks from the Bicycle Club. Then I hoofed it back to the hotel.

I probably should have called Alexa from the lobby pay phone, but I didn't want another argument and I knew Ophelia would tell her what was happening, so I just went back up to my room and flopped on my bed. I was out in minutes. I slept like a dead man—which was what I almost became.

# CHAPTER 28

When I woke up there were four sets of hands holding me down. I was looking up into Alonzo Bell's brown frying-pan-shaped face.

As soon as I opened my mouth to speak, he shoved a pair of socks between my teeth. I fought, but was rolled over onto my face. Handcuffs were snapped onto my wrists.

Someone pulled a pillowcase over my head and my world went peach-orange. I had recognized two guys in the room from the day watch. One was a mid-watch officer named Gary Singleton, a Pasadena PD reject. Another was a black cop from the day watch, Roulon Green. Over by the door was a huge, overbuilt, linebacker-sized guy I'd seen once or twice during shift changes. I think his name was Horace Velario. I'd heard he was Alonzo's best friend from high school.

Then Bell leaned down and whispered into my

ear. "Here's the drill, *m'ijo*. You walk where we lead you. Trouble buys pain."

I was pushed blindly out of the room, led across the carpeted hall and down some concrete fire stairs. I had no idea where we were or what time it was. Once we were out of the stairwell, our footsteps echoed loudly on hard concrete. I figured from the sound that we were leaving the casino through some kind of basement corridor.

Then I was being pushed up into the backseat of either an SUV or a high van. I was sandwiched in with a man on each side. The engine started and we were in motion. I kept trying to talk through the sock jammed in my mouth, but every time I did, I caught a sharp blow to my rib cage.

"Stay quiet," Alonzo growled.

Maybe an hour later, the car turned off the paved street and we were driving on some kind of a rough dirt surface. My mind was racing, trying to figure this out. Had they found my cell phone in the elementary school bathroom and despite its waterlogged condition managed to retrieve the text message? Had they seen Agent Love's wire recorder that I'd carelessly left on the dresser, or had they missed it in their hurry to get me out of there? I was starting to panic.

The car finally stopped and I was pulled out and forced to walk across uneven ground. I smelled the rich odor of moist soil mixed with the pungent, sweet smell of orange blossoms.

I was pushed to my knees. The pillowcase was suddenly ripped off. My eyes adjusted quickly to the dark. I saw by the faint light of the quarter-moon that we were out in the middle of an orange grove someplace. I was surrounded by the entire Haven Park day watch as well as a few other cops from other shifts. All were dressed in street clothes. The sock was pulled out of my mouth, but my hands remained cuffed.

Alonzo Bell took a position about ten feet away facing me. "We know you're the one who's been ratting us out," he said.

I didn't respond. Same rule. Let the other guy go first. Learn as much as you can before saying anything.

"We know you blew us in to the feds on the Crip ambush," he continued. "We know you met in that deputy chief's condo in Manhattan Beach and were debriefed. We know almost all of it. If you want an easy death, you're gonna tell us everything else."

My mind was racing through this problem, looking for an exit. Had Ophelia Love failed to lay down my condo cover story in time? Had Ricky Ross finally made good on his threat to kill me? Was there anything that would get me out of this?

Whatever I said next, it needed to be convincing. They weren't going to make stupid mistakes.

"You tell me everything," Bell said. "If it matches

exactly what I already know, then you get a nice clean head shot and you're gone. You fuck around with me and I will blow off little pieces of you until you're begging me to finish it."

My only shot was to bluff. "Go fuck yourself," I said angrily.

"Not the response I'm looking for, Scully."

"I'm not your rat. I don't know who's been selling you out, but after you kill me, your problem isn't gonna go away, because you got the wrong guy."

"And that apartment you went to didn't belong to Chief Arnett?"

"I told you. I was with Tiffany Roberts in the furnished model. You can believe me, or you can stick it up your ass. I'm fuckin' done arguing with you about this."

He pointed his gun at me and fired. I think he was just trying to scare me, but the bullet came very close and nicked my left ear. I could feel blood running down the side of my face.

Then he pointed his nine-millimeter at my heart. I could see his trigger finger turn white as he added pressure.

*Here I come, Jesus,* I thought as I knelt in the moist soil. I took my last breath and got ready to die. He pulled the trigger and I watched the hammer fall.

# CHAPTER 29

CLICK.

Nothing happened.

I looked into the muzzle of Alonzo's handgun, right into the black eye.

I could smell the oranges and feel the beat of my heart.

*A misfire?*

Alonzo slowly lowered the gun and just stood there. I didn't know what was happening, didn't know what to expect.

Then a huge smile spread across his round face and he said, "Somebody uncuff him."

Two guys rushed forward, pulled me to my feet and took the handcuffs off, freeing my hands. My knees were shaking. I could barely stand.

"You're no longer on probation," Alonzo announced. "You just became a full-fledged member of the Haven Park PD."

The guys who were standing there all started to applaud.

"You okay?" Alonzo asked, grinning. "A few guys have puked. Larry Miller shit his pants."

I was still trying to absorb it.

"We had to know you were solid," he explained. "Loyalty test. We had to take you right to the edge to be sure." Then he shook his head as he repeated my own words back to me. " 'You can believe me, or you can stick it up your ass.' Beautiful. Best yet."

All the cops gathered around and slapped my back, congratulating me.

Alonzo led me over to his Cadillac Escalade. The private cars of the rest of the day watch were parked in a large dirt clearing. There were no houses or lights visible in any direction. We seemed to be miles from civilization. Somebody opened a Styrofoam chest and started passing out ice-cold Coronas.

Horace Velario, Alonzo's three-hundred-pound best friend from high school, nodded his shaved head and shoved a cold one in my hand. "You could probably use this."

I was staring dumbly at the semicircle of beaming police officers. I was beginning to realize that before you get to ride in the corrupt squad cars of Haven Park, everybody had to go through this same loyalty test.

"The final initiation," Alonzo said. "You're in the posse, man." He opened the door of the Escalade and announced, "Come on, we're going to a party."

I didn't much feel like going to a party. I just wanted to go home, lie down and try to get my nerves to settle. But I did as I was told. The other cops got into their vehicles. I heard doors slamming all around me and then six or eight cars, driving with just their parking lights on, caravaned out of the field and transitioned onto a small paved road, which ran alongside acres of orange groves.

"Where are we?" I asked.

"In the appropriately named city of Orange," Alonzo said with a grin. He got on the freeway and we were soon flying along, heading back toward downtown L.A.

For the first time since waking up I was beginning to accept the fact that I actually had some tomorrows.

"There's a party in Ladera Heights being thrown in your honor," Alonzo said, grinning.

"You guys are pretty careful," I said.

"There's a lot on the table down here, Shane, and nobody wants to see the inside of a prison cell, so you're damn right we're careful."

It was the first time he'd called me Shane.

We drove right past the cities of Haven Park and Fleetwood and were soon on a twisting road, climbing up to the better neighborhoods in the hills of Ladera Heights. The small, single-story houses in the flatland neighborhoods slowly gave way to million-dollar mansions that overlooked the city. Finally, Alonzo pulled up to a huge double gate that was framed by a mosaic Spanish-style arch. I could see maybe twenty cars in a large parking area behind the wrought iron. The rest of the day watch pulled in behind us. Alonzo leaned out of his driver's window and triggered the security speaker.

"Bell," he said. "I got Scully with me." The gates opened and we pulled up the long drive and parked by a beautiful two-story house with lots of Spanish arches and a red tile roof.

"Whose place is this?" I asked, looking off to the right at a crowd of maybe forty men and women, who were drinking and chatting in clusters around the Olympic-sized pool and cabana.

"Cecil Bratano's," Alonzo said proudly. "He throws these bashes maybe twice a month."

As I got out of the Escalade, Talbot Jones came out of the house and approached me.

"Good going, Scully." He was dressed in slacks and a blue blazer. I think it was the first time I ever saw him smile.

I could hear music coming from the pool through gigantic speakers. Frank Sinatra was singing "Leave It All to Me."

# CHAPTER 30

Sinatra sang about it being "a very good year."

Dancers from some strip club in town seconded that thought as they cavorted naked in the big Olympic-sized pool. I met a few politicians from Haven Park and Fleetwood. They all seemed like slimy assholes.

Sinatra sang "The Fable of the Rose."

Rick Ross was there. He didn't speak to me, but I saw him with three strippers in the cabana cutting up a line of coke. *Great. Just what I wanted to see. Let's hear it for Ricky's rehab.*

I spent ten minutes talking about police work with Harry Eastwood, who looked ridiculous in white pants and an iridescent blue shirt. His swayback and potbelly did nothing for the outfit.

I saw the mayor's assistant, Carlos Reál, whom Alonzo had pointed out to me at A Fuego. I'd asked around and found out he was really just a political bagman. I watched him talking to some seedy Hispanics in suits by the Jacuzzi. All of them needed haircuts. Carlos never stopped moving, shifting his weight, waving his hands around. A kinetic man. Mercury on glass.

I was congratulated by half a dozen Haven Park cops for not puking or browning my pants like shit-stain Larry Miller. They all said I had balls.

I walked around greeting guys. Two topless dancers wanted to take me into the changing room and give me a party, but I managed to escape that indignity.

Then someone introduced me to Oscar Juarez. He was a well-built, clean-cut guy, about twenty-three, with a baby face and chocolate-brown eyes.

"Somebody just told me this party is in your honor," Oscar said, smiling. "So what's the deal with that?"

As I was trying to figure out that remark, I wondered if he'd also passed the orange grove test. But if he had, shouldn't he know the reason I was being honored? He looked very young and innocent. It was hard for me to picture him mixed up in this.

"I guess you know what I just went through," I said, watching his dark eyes carefully, looking for any sign.

"I'm sorry?" he said, perplexed.

"The orange grove?"

"I'm afraid I don't know what you're talking about."

I should have been relieved, but his answer presented me with a new dilemma. Was he really the only street cop in Haven Park who wasn't on the grind, or was he playing me, trying to get me to confide in him so I'd give myself up? Was I still under suspicion? Was my entire orange grove loyalty test just an elaborate head feint? When you're working undercover, you tend to overthink everything.

Rick Ross, who was currently twenty yards away inside the cabana doing a line of blow, had been the one who suggested Oscar might be okay. Did I really want to take his word for anything? I decided I'd better not trust Officer Juarez either. I moved on.

Cecil Bratano had a six-car garage and an hour later I was down there with five or so guests I didn't know, admiring the mayor's impressive car collection. All the garage doors were open and each space contained a beautifully maintained, sixties sports car. He had a Porsche 356B, two Austin Healys, and a classic MGB-GT in mint condition. But the star of his collection was a perfectly restored turquoise-and-white 1960 Cadillac El Dorado convertible. It sat on a pristine concrete floor, its chrome and big fins glittering impressively.

An elderly Hispanic man with silver hair who looked dapper in a dark suit informed me that he took care of the collection and that the Shelby was worth over two hundred thousand. He told me proudly that Cecil had paid cash for all of them. Not bad for an elementary school dropout.

At about eleven-thirty, Talbot Jones found me in the garage. "Follow me," he said. "The man wants to see you now."

# CHAPTER 31

Captain Jones led the way through the crowd of milling party guests into the mayor's magnificent mansion.

Like lots of guys who made their money late in life, Cecil Bratano needed to show it off. He had crammed way too much expensive stuff into his house. The downstairs looked like a decorator's showroom—priceless Louis XV antiques and turn-of-the-century carved wooden tables crowded each other for space on the main floor. There were oversized original paintings in gilded frames and swag lamps with fringed shades. The house reminded me of a Louisiana whorehouse with its dark velvet draperies and nude bronzed statues that seemed to stand everywhere in unabashed poses.

I followed Talbot Jones up the red-carpeted circular staircase and once we got to the top landing, he led me straight across the hall, opened a door and pulled me into a large linen closet stacked with folded sheets.

"This is different," I said, trying to keep it friendly. Even though I was grinning, I had my feet spread for balance, ready for anything.

"I gotta go through you, Shane. Sorry. Nobody talks to the mayor unless we check for a wire first."

"I thought I just made the team. Member of the posse."

"Don't argue. Turn around and hold out your arms."

It worried me that I kept getting all these body searches. Fortunately, the wire Agent Love had given me was still on my dresser at the hotel.

"Don't be a problem, Scully. This isn't about you; it's about protocol. We're very careful when it comes to Cecil, so just do it."

I patiently endured another frisk, but was beginning to suspect I would never get a murder solicitation on tape if this continued.

After he was finished Jones said, "Follow me."

We found Cecil Bratano holding court with about ten people, half of them beautiful women, in a large, wood-paneled game room that was also crammed with expensive stuff. Music equipment was jammed into every available open space. There was a full-sized Wurlitzer organ, an electronic keyboard, a drum set and at least twenty celebrity guitars on chrome stands, all signed in Magic Marker by music legends like Elvis, Johnny Cash and, of course, Frankie Valli.

An entire wall was devoted to a flat screen for video gaming. An ornately carved antique pool table dominated the center of the room. It all shone impressively, but there was so much, it only managed to seem like clutter.

Mayor Cecil Bratano was on the far side of the room. He was a man of Hispanic descent in his mid- to late fifties. I'd read numerous briefing reports on him that made him out to be a corrupt thug. In person, he was nothing like I'd expected. The mayor was a short, merry man with twinkling eyes, a trimmed mustache, and an infectious smile that was disarming even from twenty feet away. He wore a white Mexican guayabera shirt with tan linen pants and designer shoes that had to have set him back at least a grand. He also wore too many heavy diamond and gold accessories. His watch band could have balanced the national debt of Honduras. Thinning gray hair was slicked back and laid flat against a perfectly formed skull.

Talbot Jones led me up to him and introduced us. After we shook hands, the mayor smiled and said, "So you're my new patrolman." He had absolutely no trace of an accent. Behind his dark eyes, fierce intelligence burned.

"That's me," I said, my own smile widening to match his.

"Congratulations, Shane. It's damn hard to get on this department."

A week earlier I would have thought he was joking, but after kneeling in that orange grove with my own socks in my mouth, I knew he wasn't.

"This is some house," I said. Meaningless chitchat but I wanted him to make the first move.

"Yes. Yes, it is. Come here, let me show you something."

He stood, took my arm, and led me away from his admiring crowd. We stepped out onto a large balcony that overlooked his property and the twinkling city lights of Ladera Heights and Haven Park beyond. He stood almost a head shorter than I, gazing at the city below, momentarily overcome by the view. It was almost as if he were seeing it for the first time.

"When I was a boy growing up in that city down there, I only had a view of an alley wall," he said pensively. "Now I have this."

I nodded.

"It's funny how a man gets to his correct station in life," he continued. "I'm certainly not a philosopher and even though I know what I had to go through to acquire my wealth, there are still times when I stop and wonder."

"I understand that," I said, searching for some common ground. "I was also born poor. Living as a child in poverty can make you wary of good fortune." Exposing a limited grasp of philosophy with that sentence.

"Then you know what it feels like to climb from a low place. Some part of you is always looking down, afraid of the fall."

"I used to think of that all the time," I told him. "And then, two weeks ago, it actually happened. I lost everything."

He didn't comment. He seemed far back in his head somewhere. Some dark recollection had dimmed his smile, the remnants now hidden under his meticulously trimmed mustache.

"Did you know that I dropped out of school when I was only twelve?" he finally said, suddenly coming out of his reverie. "I had to get a job to feed my family. I hated having to quit my education, because I loved school, loved learning. All I wanted to do was go back there. And eventually, that's what I did."

"I read a story on you that said you quit school in the sixth grade," I said. "It didn't mention that you went back later."

"I didn't return as a student. I was hired as the school's crossing guard.

"I used to look at the children in that school, many who didn't want to be there, and wonder how they could take their education for granted. None of them seemed to understand how lucky they were, what a great opportunity they were wasting."

"School didn't seem important to me at that age either," I said. "It's a mistake you only discover later."

He nodded, thought for a minute, then said, "From my low position wearing my silly uniform, I decided to do something about it. Two years later, I ran for the Haven Park School Board. Won in a landslide. Six years after that, head of Haven Park's Public Works Department, then I ran Public Housing. Now I run the whole shebang." He focused his powerful personality at me. "So you see it's important to stay in school, even if you have to be the crossing guard."

"That's a good story." We both looked down at his amazing property and the twinkling lights of the city he controlled.

"Now that you've been here for a little while, what do you think of all this?" he asked, gesturing out at the distant towns below.

"Of Haven Park?" I asked, and he nodded. "I like it here. I'm also extremely grateful to you and to the police department for giving me a second chance. After my problems in L.A., you were the only one who reached out your hand, sir. I'll never forget you for it."

"I've observed that men often say they are grateful, but when an opportunity presents itself to return an important favor they develop short memories."

"Won't be a problem with me."

He appraised me carefully. "I know something of you. I've been told you have some unique skills."

That remark certainly made it sound as if somebody had already listened to my Sammy from Miami tape. I was hoping he'd pursue this, but his mood suddenly changed again. The relentless smile temporarily disappeared as he laid a large hand that glittered with diamonds and gold on my shoulder.

"People say I'm a throwback. That I live forty years behind the times. They laugh at my preference for old music, at my love of sixties sports cars and the way I dress. What they don't understand is a man must paint a life much as he would a picture, choosing the colors carefully. I have chosen colors from a simpler time."

He retrieved his diamond-studded hand and continued. "Back then it was much easier to see the path. Today, there are conditions. We call it political correctness, but if you want my opinion, it's really just social guilt over having so much.

"In your own field of law enforcement, there is the confusing Police Discretionary Rule, which favors the criminal and causes many valid arrests to be thrown out in court. Or there's the lunatic Miranda ruling. You must tell a criminal not to talk before you question him. In real estate it's rent control and equal housing. Education has minority quotas. There's a ton of civil litigation crowding the courts that should be covered by common sense. It goes on and on. Forty years ago, none of this existed. This attempt to be all things to all people is destroying our great country. In Haven Park I'm setting the clock back to a simpler time."

I was thinking this guy was somewhere to the right of the Mississippi Klan, but what I said was, "It's gotten so a police officer has a better chance of going to jail than the criminals he's chasing."

He nodded and suddenly the smile flashed back on. We stood listening as another old song began to play. Cecil finally turned away from the view. "I might have a way for you to pay me back for this sense of gratitude you say you feel. If you agree to help me I would be willing to compensate you nicely. If you can accomplish what I want, you will become a respected part of my inner circle. If you fail, you will fall much further than you did two weeks ago in L.A. This favor includes some inherent but I think manageable risks. . . . Interested?"

"You bet," I said eagerly. "Lay it on me, sir."

"Not now." He smiled. "I never talk business at a party. We will speak tomorrow or the next day.

Tonight you should enjoy yourself. Familiarize yourself further with my little experiment in social engineering. We'll talk shortly."

Then he patted my shoulder again, and, without another word, left me on the balcony looking down at the nude girls in the pool and the milling crowd of crooked cops and corrupt politicians.

I realized that I'd stopped breathing toward the end of our conversation. I let out a long slow lungful of air. The idea that I might be about to penetrate this corrupt politician's inner circle both frightened and invigorated me.

As I stood there the Sinatra song changed. Now Frank was singing "From the Bottom to the Top."

# CHAPTER 32

"I'm not wearing this thing." I threw the wire and recorder down on the wooden bench beside Ophelia Love. It was a little past one A.M., and we were back inside Little Swiss, in a shopping mall parking lot on the outskirts of Compton. Alexa had been replaced, but Ophelia had broken a strict FBI rule demanding interagency celibacy, and allowed my wife to attend this midnight meeting. I also thought she liked our department's cool little eight-wheel undercover truck.

"You've got to wear it. We need to get somebody to come up dirty on that wire so we can convince them to flip. Otherwise we'll never make the case. That's the reason I gave you the extra time."

"I'm still willing to do this, but I'm not gonna let a bunch of stiffs from Homeland run my play. It has to be people I know and trust. Alexa or Tony—nobody else. You can be part of it, but this gets run out of our shop or I'm done."

We sat for a moment, stewing in decades of interagency distrust. Then Agent Love said, "I'm not sure that's your decision to make."

"Get real, lady. If I pull the pin it's over."

"Something happened tonight," Alexa said softly, looking closely at me. "You need to tell us." She knew me too well. She could see that I was close to the edge.

So I told them about my trip to the orange grove and the party that followed at the mayor's house where I witnessed Rick Ross chopping up a line in the gazebo with two strip club whores. I told them I'd finally gotten next to Bratano and what he'd said to me, but that despite passing the loyalty test, Talbot Jones was still going to shake me down for a wire every time before letting me meet with hizzoner.

"I'm finally on the inside. But it's weird. They've got all these security protocols, especially where Cecil is concerned. If I'd been wearing that thing tonight, I'd be dead!"

"Maybe I could get you a DCST," Agent Love said.

"What on earth is a DCST?" Alexa asked.

"Digital covert satellite transmitter. It's very new stuff. I haven't seen one, but I've read a briefing sheet. It's out of DIA covert ops in D.C."

"Never heard of it," Alexa said.

"They're satcom transmitters designed to look like ordinary pocket equipment. Pens or car keys, stuff like that. The unit has a miniature satellite transmitter inside that beams a signal up to one of our low-flying Iridium satellites, just six hundred miles up in space. The DCST is tiny because there's no tape or digital component. It's a direct transmission to a space platform that bounces back to a covert land base."

"Is this what you people do with our tax money?"

I was starting to feel trapped. I wanted out of Haven Park, but I also knew somebody was about to get the contract on Chacon's life. If I wanted to protect Rocky, then, strange as it sounded, I had to be the one picked to kill him.

"How long to get one of those things to me?" I finally asked.

"I don't know. I've got to get you on a Pentagon distribution list first." She hesitated. "Tomorrow. Day after at the latest."

"Shane, are you sure you're okay?" Alexa reached out and took my hand.

"I'm scared out of my skull," I told her.

"Then let's end this," she said.

"I can't. We'll never get this close to the center again. Cecil Bratano said I'd be hearing from him in the next day or two. At least keep me in until then."

"I'll get the covert device to you. It'll be in your room in the top dresser drawer by noon tomorrow."

I got up to leave. "Does Alexa run this? That's the only condition I'm asking for."

Agent Love sighed. "Look, Scully, it's not perfect, I admit. But as long as you two will agree to let me ride shotgun, I'll tell my supervisors that Alexa has to run the show out of Parker Center. My guess is they'll go for it. What choice do they have?"

"Just get me that device," I said.

Then she did an unusual thing. She shook my hand. It was a strangely touching gesture.

"Thanks," she said. "I know how hard this is. I really appreciate what you're doing." She left Little Swiss and closed the door.

Alexa and I waited until we could see her car pulling away on the monitor inside the truck. After it was gone, we both stood and embraced.

"Are you sure you're okay?" she asked.

I held my wife, smelling her hair and perfume. "Ever since I took this damn job, I haven't been able to get my mind off of you and Chooch and how much I have with you guys," I told her. "It's making me play it safe. That's not the way to work one of these stings. I've been making some half-assed moves. I'm afraid I'm on the verge of screwing this up."

"I'm so sorry we took it on," she said, laying her head on my shoulder. "To hell with Ophelia and the feds. I'll call Tony. I'll get you out of there tonight."

After a moment I said, "Rocky Chacon can't be more than five-foot-seven, a hundred and sixty pounds with his shoes on. Along with his mother and a few campaign workers, he's taking on Cecil Bratano and that whole corrupt Haven Park machine.

"I'm the only one standing between him and a body bag. If I pull out now, if I cut and run, he's history. If that happens I won't be able to face myself. Then what am I really worth to you or Chooch?" Alexa didn't say anything. She knew I was right. "I wish I hadn't decided to take this damn assignment, but now that I'm here, there's no way I can leave. Not if I want to be the same guy I was before."

"I love you so much," she said softly. "You really are the best there is."

I stood there for several more minutes not feeling like the best. I was sore and scared. Alexa rubbed my back. She held me close and comforted me.

# CHAPTER 33

The next morning, I showered in the small hotel bathroom, then examined my swollen nose and black eyes in the mirror. The shiners were turning saffron, making me look like a street troll overdosing on the eye shadow. I put on my civvies and wore my belt with the tracking device. Then I drove my bugged MDX to the elementary school parking lot, putting out more microwaves than General Electric.

I felt a little better this morning despite the fitful sleep. Maybe it was extra adrenaline that came with this forty-eight-hour timeline and my new lock-and-load mentality.

As soon as I entered the locker room, it was obvious that my performance in the orange grove had elevated my status. Several of my new "friends" who had been standing in that field last night willing to watch me eat a bullet were now grinning, slapping me on the back and telling me what a stud I was.

Alonzo wasn't around. I was afraid with him out I'd be doing another eight-hour tour in the file room.

I trudged to roll call, carrying my war bag, and sat with the rest of the day watch on the basketball court's bleachers while Dirty Harry Eastwood stood splay-footed and swaybacked before us, going through his listless prewatch briefing.

"Green. You're way behind on your towing tickets," he began, looking over at Roulon. "Only ten so far this month. You all of a sudden independently wealthy or something?"

"Alonzo's had me on rollin' stolens," the black cop defended. "I been trolling for hot car tags in parking lots all up and down Pacific."

"Okay, but you're not on that now, so it's time to kick this towing thing into gear."

Then Eastwood pointed at linebacker-sized Horace Velario, the huge shaved head who, I'd been alarmed to learn, had failed the LAPD psych exam and had then gone down the street and joined Glendale PD. The story I got on that was after two months on the job in Glendale, he'd shot two unarmed liquor store bandits while on patrol. Both guys died and IA had deemed the shootings out of policy. With that ruling, Horace had barely escaped a felony prosecution by the Glendale city attorney. They threw him out, but like everyone else down here, he'd found a soft landing in Haven Park.

Eastwood said, "Congratulations to Horace on bagging our Riverbank Arsonist, who had the bad sense to pull a knife and left the scene in an oxygen tent." The cops on the bleachers gave him two Marine Corps–style hoorahs.

"Congratulations to Patrolman Scully for

passing his probationer's final exam," Eastwood continued. "You're off the turkey list and assigned to an L-unit. You'll be Car Thirteen. Way to go."

The room applauded while I nodded and pumped a fist.

Finally Lieutenant Eastwood looked down and checked his cheat sheet. "Okay, the feds want you all to make sworn statements on the gang fight at the high school. I know it's bullshit, but we gotta humor these dinks so I'm gonna cut one guy loose an hour early every night to go talk to the federal attorney in the Homeland building on Wilshire Boulevard. We'll just rotate through the roster till everybody's been over there. We'll start with the FNG." The fucking new guy was me. "Scully, you're off at four to go do that." I nodded. "That's it. Anybody got anything else?"

Nothing.

"Okay. Get out there and cook the fish."

We saddled up and lugged our gear single-file through two residential blocks to the police station and our squad cars. I'd been assigned to Unit Thirteen, one of the old units that was parked in the back on reserve. It was a '96 Chrysler that had rust spots on the trunk, a hanging muffler and needed a wash. The car smelled like most old squad cars. Vomit and Lysol.

I was getting it set up when Alonzo drove into the lot, parked his shop and walked over. "Gave you Thirteen?" He grinned. "Hope you don't have to push it."

"Thirteen's my lucky number."

"Listen, Shane. I need you for an hour or so this morning. It's already been squared away with Lieutenant Eastwood. Leave your shit locked in the trunk and come with me."

"Where we going?"

"You'll see. It's all good."

I nodded and slammed the trunk. I didn't have my covert device yet, so whatever was about to happen this morning wasn't going to be recorded. With undercover stings, you needed either a tape of the conspiracy or a corroborating witness. Most DAs wouldn't file on just a cop's word because defense lawyers could easily turn it into a he-said-he-said in court.

I got into Alonzo's shop and we went code seven as we cleared the station.

Two blocks farther on, we pulled into the parking lot at A Fuego. It was a little past eight A.M. so the lot was completely empty.

"Whatta we doing here?"

Alonzo smiled. "You're about to get kissed into something big. Just stay cool."

The door was unlocked. As soon as we entered, I saw a cop in uniform standing just inside the entry. It was Alonzo's pal Horace Velario. The guy was huge. The size of a jukebox. Making it worse, I had started picking up a nasty vibe off him.

The work lights were on inside the club and in their bright glare I could now see how tacky and threadbare A Fuego really was. The dim atmosphere lighting hid a multitude of sins. Harsh ceiling lights exposed chipped paint and hundreds of scratches on the dance floor.

"Come on," Alonzo said.

I followed him into the bar area while Horace Velario lumbered along in my wake.

We went through a door marked OFFICE located behind the bar. Then we single-filed down a long white fuorescent-lit corridor. I spotted Manny Avila on the phone in his office, up early, getting a jump-start on his long list of profitable extortions.

We continued down the corridor into a small but well-equipped kitchen. Alonzo suddenly reached out and stopped me, then turned me gently around.

"Don't tell me I'm gonna get another cheap feel," I said.

"If I was going for this ride Horace over there would be going through me. It's the way it's gotta be."

He ran a hand over my chest, under my armpits and down to my crotch. Then he went to my back, searching my shoulders down to the waist and down each leg to my shoes. Very professional and thorough.

"Was it as good for you as it was for me?" I said as soon as he finished.

We walked down the corridor and a few seconds later we were standing on the back dock.

Alonzo triggered his shoulder rover. "We're ten-twenty-three on the loading platform," he said.

"He's on his way," a voice crackled back.

Five minutes later the restored turquoise and white El Dorado convertible rounded the corner with its top up and all four windows down. As it approached I could hear Sinatra singing "I Believe I'm Gonna Love You."

Alonzo led me down the loading dock steps and we waited as the car pulled up.

*"Buenos días, amigos,"* the mayor of Haven Park caroled over the music coming from his retro eight-track. He was wearing a turquoise guayabera shirt to match the Eldo's paint job and a large snap-brim Panama hat. It would have been very sporty if we had been in Argentina or Cuba.

"Shane, let's you and me go for a ride," Hizzoner suggested.

I slid onto the matching leather seats and Alonzo slammed the door. A black-and-white squad car with Horace at the wheel pulled up behind us. Alonzo got in the patrol car beside his best friend and for the next several seconds both cars sat parked behind A Fuego with their engines idling.

"I wanted to have a little talk and show you my city," Cecil said. "Sound like a plan?"

"Sounds good."

He smiled and put the column stick shift into

drive. The straight pipes rumbled as we rolled out of the nightclub parking lot with a Haven Park patrol car right behind us, riding the El Dorado's bumper, staying up close in a chase position.

# CHAPTER 34

Cecil Bratano turned the heavy turquoise Cad onto the street. He was smiling, tapping his left hand on his thigh, keeping time to Sinatra's music as he drove.

"Man, this guy had some pipes, didn't he?" Bratano said, pointing at his eight-track. "Nobody sings like this anymore."

He turned the volume down a little and Frank settled into a lower decibel level. Then Cecil glanced at me, widened his smile. I knew by now that the smile didn't indicate much of anything, least of all humor. His too-white teeth flashed an alabaster warning.

"I'm often referred to in the press as Haven Park's Mexican mayor, but that's not what I am at all," he said. "My genealogy defines me as Hispanic, but I'm American. However, the Mexican in my blood understands how the people who live in Haven Park and Fleetwood think. I know what they need."

He put on his blinker and we turned onto a street that ran along the slimy banks of the L.A. River. The black-and-white tailed close behind.

"Our population in Haven Park is around thirty thousand," the mayor continued. "Well over seventy percent of those are illegals.

"These are simple people with simple tastes. They like parades, so I give them parades. They like *fiestas tradicionales*, so this town officially celebrates all the major Mexican holidays. We have big, publicly sponsored parties with music and games in the park. On Cinco de Mayo the city puts on a fireworks display and I pass out candy to the children. On Día de los Muertos I wear the skull mask and light candles at the altar. Because I respect the traditions they love, I'm loved and respected in return."

I was thinking, *This is priceless. You're the asshole who's booting and towing their cars, ticketing and closing their businesses.* But I didn't say anything. I waited for him to get to his point.

"But despite all this, these two towns are not easy places to govern," he continued.

I threw some bread on the water. "Anything I can do to help?"

"It's why we're riding together," he said, his smile again widening. Then he reached over and patted my hand. It was a strangely paternal gesture.

"Some interesting facts, which might help you help me. New immigrants pour across the borders and settle here every day. Because there are so many, they stick to themselves and have shown a surprising resistance to assimilation. They don't learn English, they don't intermarry with Anglos, and as a result their ties to Mexico remain very strong."

He was in the zone, spinning his tale. But it felt like he had said this too many times before and was doing it mostly by rote.

We were now entering Fleetwood and the mayor pointed at the little Spanish-style duplexes that were sliding by on his left. "Did you know that Fleetwood was founded by the meatpacking baron Michael Fleetwood way back in 1908?" Completely switching tacks on me. I was suddenly in for a history lesson.

"These properties on my left were originally called Fleetwood lots because they're a hundred feet wide and an amazing eight hundred feet deep. Mr. Fleetwood's idea was that the residents here would be able to have gardens and keep horses like in the old agrarian societies of Mexico. He designed this place to Old World standards. Now, a hundred years later, it's been left for me to look over his dream."

The song ended and "The House I Live In" began to play.

"Our politicians at the state and federal levels don't understand that the millions of Hispanics who are living here and not assimilating will inevitably want to revert to a political system closer to the one they had in Mexico. Even though

I know that system is often uneven, it's also, in its own way, very fair, because once you understand the rules, everyone can play."

It was tortured logic to forgive the massive theft and political corruption south of the border, but I hung in there, nodded and tried to look enthralled.

"What we currently have in California is a concerted, if unintentional, effort by our federal and state governments for Third World communities like Haven Park and Fleetwood to flourish with no loyalty to the United States. In order to continue to govern, I must provide a system that resembles the one these people are accustomed to."

He glanced over at me to see if I was buying any of it. I tried to look like he was parting the Red Sea, driving his turquoise Cadillac through the divide, leading his flock out of a desert of racial misunderstanding.

"But there are those who see this as corruption," he went on. "People like Rocky Chacon who want a system that can't possibly hold up under the pressures created by this huge tide of unchecked immigration."

With the mention of Rocky's name, I knew we were finally getting to the point of my ride-along.

"I don't think it's likely that Rocky Chacon is going to win the election," I said.

"You're wrong," Cecil replied. "Unless something important happens, he's bound to win. Perhaps even in a landslide. Not because he's right, but because he's popular. These last months, Rocky Chacon has become a very big problem for me. I can't let him win. It will destroy everything I've been building here." Then he turned his head and glanced at me. "Any suggestions?"

"Eliminate the problem."

"But as I've just explained, the problem is complex and deals with many diverse social and economic factors."

"You're wrong," I said. "The problem is just one guy. One dirt-town Mexican with limited resources. I'm sure somebody could jack him up and talk some sense to him, or, if that fails, employ a more direct solution. Either way, once he's no longer in the political picture, your problem disappears."

"Interesting theory," he said solemnly, as if he were pondering this for the first time.

"Nothing theoretical about it," I replied. "It's your call, but somehow I think you already know what you want to do."

His face was now a mask that I couldn't read.

We finally arrived back at the police department lot, where my rusting squad car was parked alone in the back row. As Cecil Bratano turned in his seat to face me, Sinatra began to sing "My Way."

"If I had something for you to do, something important that would preserve what we have created here but needs to be done in the next several days, would you be willing to take on such a project?"

"I would very much like to help you preserve what you've built here, sir. I've already told you that." I held his solemn gaze.

"In that case, how would you feel about taking care of this problem for me?" he asked.

"Are you asking what I think you are?" I replied.

"I would rather leave this solution in your hands. You are a man of considerable talents."

Then Bratano reached across me and opened the passenger door. "*Vaya con Dios, compañero,*" he said.

I got out of the car realizing I had just been given the contract on Rocky Chacon's life.

He waved and smiled before turning up the volume on the eight-track. The lyrics hung in the air as the turquoise Cad disappeared around the corner. Frank Sinatra sang:

*I did it my way.*

# CHAPTER 35

I was released from duty an hour early to go down to Wilshire Boulevard and give a statement to Homeland, but I decided to blow that off and get Ophelia to cover for me.

I dragged my ass back to the hotel, went up to

my room, and checked inside the top dresser drawer. One of Ophelia's case agents must have visited my room, because hidden underneath my socks there was a small, innocent-looking ballpoint pen with a mike hole in the top.

I put the ballpoint in my pocket and checked my messages. There was a package for me at the desk. Nobody at the LAPD or the FBI would contact me here, so I was naturally curious who might be leaving me packages.

I went downstairs to the front desk. The clerk reached into a file and handed me a thin #10 envelope—no identifying marks, but my name was printed on the front in block letters. I found a secluded place in the back of the casino bar and opened it.

One sheet. Three lines.

**Come alone. Five PM**
**Under the Pacific Blvd. bridge**
**$R^2$**

I was already pissed at Rick Ross for what I'd seen him doing at the party. Now I was even more pissed at him for leaving me a message that anyone could open at the concierge desk and read. But I knew Ross's police history and he'd never been on an undercover assignment, so I tried to cut him some slack because, quite obviously, he didn't know what the hell he was doing. Either that or he was actively trying to get me killed.

I didn't want to have a clandestine meeting with this asshole. But there was one overriding factor influencing my decision to go. He might know something that I needed to hear in order to stay alive.

I went back to my room, stripped off the belt with the tracking device, activated Ophelia's pen satellite transmitter, and headed back downstairs. If Ross was luring me out there to ambush me, at least the LAPD and the feds would have a good recording of my murder.

I took the scenic route through Vista, into the City of Commerce. It was 4:20 and I had forty minutes before my meeting. I felt the reassuring weight of my backup AirLight .38 riding comfortably on my hip.

As I drove, I looked across the river and saw the city of Haven Park just beginning to darken in L.A.'s smog-filled late afternoon sunlight. I made a right and took the bridge back to the Haven Park side of the river, then parked on a residential street two blocks from the meeting spot and locked the Acura.

There was a strip of dead grass about ten yards wide that ran along the riverbank. The rusting chain-link fence that protected the wash had been cut long ago by 18th Street tagger crews. I slipped through the rusted edge of the clipped opening and slid on my heels down the forty-five-degree poured concrete bank to the river floor. When I reached the bottom I found myself standing in mud, looking at old juice cartons, moss and water-logged garbage, thinking, some picturesque river we have here in L.A.

I picked my way through old tires and soggy junk, reading 18th Street Loco graffiti as I walked. It had been sprayed on every flat surface and concrete piling. I was heading back toward Pacific Boulevard, trying to keep the muck out of my shoes. The idea here was if I approached the meeting spot from the river, anybody waiting to ambush me would be looking the wrong way, with their back to my approach. At least that was the theory.

Finally I saw the Pacific Street bridge span up ahead and when I was near, I scrambled up out of the wash, climbing the steep concrete bank quietly on rubber-soled shoes until I reached the lip above. Then I started moving slowly along, staying close to a line of trees, trying not to make any noise as I approached. When I was less than fifty yards away from the bridge, I knelt in the shadows to check out the meeting site.

There was enough light for me to see up under the abutment. No one appeared to be there, but that was the reason I'd arrived thirty minutes early.

I crept closer and found a good hiding place in some browned-out shrubbery that was clinging in death to the concrete base of the bridge. I cleared a space behind the dead brush, then squatted down, concealing myself. I wasn't sure what was coming, so I pulled my gun and waited.

At seventeen minutes after five I heard a single set of footsteps crunching through dead leaves, carelessly kicking stones and gravel, making more noise than a stumbling drunk.

Finally Rick Ross came into view. He was alone and wearing his same stupid disguise—windbreaker, tennies and a baseball cap pulled low. I watched as he worked his way down under the bridge and stood with his hands on his hips, looking around. Then he glanced at his watch.

"Hey, Scully," he whispered. "You down here yet?"

I didn't answer. I wanted to see what he would do.

After a minute he pulled an abandoned shipping crate over, brushed it off with his hand and sat. He looked at his watch again and scuffed his feet. He let a few minutes pass, then he took out his phone and speed-dialed a number. I leaned forward.

"He's not here. He's late," I heard him say. "Look . . . I'll get there as soon as I can. Stop bitching at me about it."

He rang off, then got to his feet and started looking around again. "Hey, Scully. You down here? Shit."

It didn't look like an ambush, so I palmed the AirLight in my right hand, held it down by my leg, parted the dry brush, and stood. Ricky spun around, a panicked look on his face.

# CHAPTER 36

"What are you doing back there?" he challenged angrily.

"I'm careful. Before we talk, you need to answer three questions."

"Look . . . You . . ."

"First question. Who did you just call?"

"My new girlfriend."

"What's her name?"

"Chrissie."

I holstered my AirLight, then reached over, took the cell phone from him, and hit redial. After two rings it was answered.

"That was quick," a woman's voice purred.

"Who's this?" I demanded.

"Chrissie. Who's this?"

I closed the phone and handed it back to him.

"Next question. Did you know those guys were gonna pick me up last night and threaten me out in that orange grove? And if so, why the hell didn't you warn me?"

"I didn't know. I got hired onto this department by Charles Le Grande before Cecil was elected four years ago, so I wasn't part of Mayor

Bratano's crew. I was isolated. I think it's why he wanted me as chief. Up until about a month ago I was so wasted all the time I didn't know what the hell was going on and they never confided in me. I got my envelopes, my money, but nobody ever told me much of anything. After what happened with Le Grande, that's the way they wanted it. I only found out last night at the party about them taking you out to that orange grove."

"You told me you were drug-free. Then last night I saw you snorting up lines in Bratano's cabana."

He was quiet for a long moment, uncertainty, or maybe it was shame, playing across his face. Then he said, "I relapsed, okay? I'm trying to stay straight, but I'm under a lot of pressure here myself. I had a weak moment."

I looked at him, not sure how I wanted to frame this. I finally decided to just say it. "When I first came here, I wasn't sure you weren't trying to make good on your old threat to kill me. But I've been thinking about it a lot and if that had been your plan, you would have done it long before now. After what happened in that orange grove I have to figure you're telling the truth. They didn't know I was a UC, so I figure you're probably being straight with me. But you need to stay in the program, Rick. I can't have the guy holding my back buzzed on drugs."

"I'm in just as much jeopardy as you are," he

said. "I'm doing the best I can, but I'm vulnerable and scared. If you'd caved in out there and told them I put you undercover, I was going to end up just as dead as you. I was going nuts at that party, not knowing if you were about to give me up. I needed to settle my nerves. That's why I did the lines. From now on I'm clean."

We stood looking at each other. Selfish bastard that I am, I hadn't really stopped to consider that Ross was in just as much jeopardy from me as I was from him. I now saw that he was very close to the edge. His hands were shaking and, like me, he looked like he hadn't slept much lately.

"Okay," I said. "Let's put all that behind us for now. Why did you leave me the note? What's up?"

"I just found out this afternoon that Talbot Jones hired an independent polygraph operator to come down and put the entire police department on the box. All the blues plus command staff."

"Why?"

"Because they think there's a mole on the force somewhere. They're totally freaked about it. They know somebody gave them up to the feds on the Haven Park High gang fight. They just don't know who. Until last night everybody thought it was you, but now they're not sure, so everybody gets tested top to bottom."

I couldn't catch a break. "Who did they hire? What company?" I snapped.

"I don't know, but the poly's been fast-tracked.

The guy will be here soon," Ross continued. "As soon as he shows they're gonna start pulling people in and putting them on the box one at a time. I don't know what to do. I'll never pass. I'm a nervous wreck. If either one of us fails that poly, it's over for us both. Whatta we gonna do?"

"Either change the game or the timetable."

Rick's cell phone rang. He answered. "For Christ's sake, not now, Chrissie." Then turned off the power and shoved it deep into his pocket.

"You haven't told Chrissie what's going on here, have you?"

"I may be fucked up, but I'm not an idiot," he said. "Give me a *little* damn credit, okay?"

I was trying.

"How are we gonna stop it?" he said.

"I haven't the faintest idea. But since neither of us wants to die, we better come up with something fast."

# CHAPTER 37

So that was my five o'clock powwow with Ricky Ross. After we split up I walked again through the L.A. river muck to the Acura and arrived back at the Bicycle Club a little before six. I went straight to the lobby, picked a pay phone and dialed Alexa. I told her about the pending polygraph. I could feel worry and frustration coming from her end of the line.

"Here's what I was thinking," I said. "In L.A., there can't be all that many qualified independent polygraph experts or companies. Eight or ten, max. We need to find which one of these people Talbot Jones hired and get that person off the Haven Park job, put our own guy in there instead."

"There's a polygraph licensing board," Alexa said. "I think it's called CAPE—California Association of Polygraph Examiners. Ophelia and I can start calling each name and offer them an immediate job for Homeland Security. If anybody says they're busy in Haven Park, we'll order them to cancel that because national security is involved."

"I probably can't beat a poly and Rick Ross is shaking apart," I said. "You gotta do it tonight. If he shows up here, I'm gonna have to get out fast."

I was about to hang up when I felt someone standing right behind me. I turned around. Alonzo Bell was two feet away. *How much of this had he overheard?*

"Who you talking to?" he asked.

"Dentist. I was clamping my jaw down so hard in that orange grove, I think I cracked a molar. It's killing me. I'm gonna have to get it out fast," I said, repeating most of the last sentence I'd just said to Alexa, praying my B.S. would fly.

He took the phone from my hand. I could hear

Alexa's voice talking as he raised the handset to his ear.

". . . could fit you in next Friday at two, Mr. Scully," I heard her say. "Dr. Swanson has an opening then and you're due for a cleaning anyway."

Alonzo hung up on her and turned to look at me. "We're outta here. You've been called on."

"Let me get my jacket."

We took the elevator to my room. Alonzo stood in the doorway as I grabbed my coat. I also snatched up the belt with the transmitter, stringing it through the belt loops and cinching it tight, hoping Ophelia had a track on it, by now. Then I followed Alonzo back to the elevator and out of the casino. Parked out front in the red zone was his white Escalade.

"Where are we going?" I asked. "I should follow you in my car."

"Don't worry, I'll bring you back."

The windows of the SUV were tinted, so I couldn't see inside, but when I opened the door to get into the passenger side Horace Velario was seated in the back. He bulled his buffalo neck and glared with hard eyes.

"Where are we going?" I repeated.

Alonzo didn't answer, but put the Escalade in gear and pulled out. We drove across the bridge and out of Vista. I wanted to get the ballpoint transmitter out of my jacket and move it up into my shirt pocket where it would be better located to transmit, but it felt like too obvious a move so I left it where it was.

We turned onto a two-lane street, which ran along the edge of the river into the city of Haven Park. Alonzo made a final turn and pulled up in front of A Fuego. As usual, he parked in the red zone by the front door.

With Alonzo in front and Horace behind, I headed into the club. I found a moment when my back was to them and reached into my jacket, clicked the ballpoint pen, and transferred it into my front shirt pocket.

Inside the club, mariachi music blared. People laughed loudly, shouting over the racket. Whatever ended up being transmitted by my little DCST was going to be killed by this racket.

Alonzo motioned for me to follow him into the men's room. "Keep everybody out," he instructed Horace.

The men's room was empty. Once we were inside, Alonzo said, "Assume the position, darling."

"Okay," I said. "But if this keeps up, I'm gonna need to get a ring."

He was very thorough just like last time, but he was looking for a wire and completely missed the pen.

When he finished, we exited the bathroom and, with Horace trailing us, walked across the club to his booth in the bar. Horace jammed his huge hulk in next to me on the upholstered bench, crowding me uncomfortably. Velario obviously didn't like me and was making no attempt to hide it. Alonzo slid in across from us.

"Beers all around?" he asked. Horace and I nodded, so he beckoned to a waitress and gave the order.

Then Alonzo spotted someone across the room and waved him over. A minute later Carlos Real Deal Reál, the mayor's whippet-thin, hyperactive assistant, walked over to our booth and slid in next to Alonzo.

"Carlos Reál, meet Shane Scully," Alonzo said. We shook hands across the table.

Without preamble, Carlos said, "I understand you're good at cleaning up messes."

# CHAPTER 38

Reál had more ticks than a sleeping hound. He jiggled his leg, he picked nervously at his shirt cuffs. When he talked, his hands flew around over the table like a guy conducting an orchestra. His eyebrows kept flicking up and down maniacally. If I didn't know his rep, I wouldn't have believed this speed freak could be the mayor's number one political assistant.

"I talked to C.B. He tells me you already know what needs to be done," Carlos said.

"Yeah. I'm down."

"We've recently discovered we have some serious timetable restrictions." He lowered his voice. His fingers now drummed relentlessly on the tabletop. "We have several phone taps on the target. Because of what we've recently learned, we gotta pull everything way up."

"Okay," I said, "as long as it doesn't get stupid, I'm flexible."

"The individual in question needs to go tonight."

"Tonight? What's the big rush?" I asked.

"We just learned that there are several people who have decided to involve themselves in his safety—people who have proven skills."

"I thought you guys controlled the gangs," I said.

"Not gangs. Marines from Camp Pendleton. Mexican guys. The target has an uncle who's on extended leave from Iraq. His *tío* recruited some Force Recon guys from the base. They're arriving tomorrow and plan to be with your man day and night until after the election."

I couldn't help but wonder if the Marines might be Agent Love's doing.

"If we go tonight, are you still up for this?" Carlos asked. He had suddenly developed a tic at the corner of his right eye.

"We haven't discussed price. The mayor said it was a paying job." I wanted to lock in a premeditated murder-for-hire solicitation.

"I asked around up in L.A. I believe ten thousand is a good number," he said, quoting the exact price from my Sammy from Miami meeting.

"That works."

Carlos put a brown paper bag on the table. It didn't look like money, so I laid my hand on top of it. I could instantly feel the contours of a small automatic under my palm.

"It's a six-shot Para Covert Carry with a three-inch barrel," he said, as his eyebrows did a little jig. "It's nontraceable, so drop it at the scene. Alonzo and Horace will cover you."

"I want the cash up front."

"Half now. Half when the job is done." Reál pulled a fat envelope out of his pocket and slid it across the table. "That's five," he said. "The rest comes after proof of death. We good?" Twitching and jerking like a hooked flounder.

"We're good."

He slid out of the booth without another word and disappeared into the throng, leaving behind a cold street gun, five thousand dollars and the smell of cheap cologne.

"I hope this money isn't part of our cafeteria policing deal," I said. "I'd hate to pass half of it back up to the same guy who just gave it to me."

"All yours," Alonzo said.

He looked at his watch. "Okay, we got a tight timetable if we're gonna get this done tonight. Let's go."

Once Horace, Alonzo and I were outside, I stopped them.

"I need to hear how you guys think this is gonna work," I said.

"Rocky's gonna give a campaign speech tonight at a rally over in Municipal Park in Vista," Alonzo answered. "We wouldn't give him a rally permit for Haven Park or Fleetwood, so he's doing it over there. It's at ten o'clock. According to one of the phone taps we got on him, after the speech he's gonna visit his new girlfriend, that lawyer bitch we met at the jail three days ago. Rocky's got a secret fuck pad somewhere over in Fleetwood. We don't know where it is yet so we need to go to the rally, and once it breaks up we follow him to the tuna. That's where you do the job."

"I just shoot him? That doesn't sound too sharp. The guy's very popular. We need a good reason for the murder or this will never be off the six o'clock news. We need an old enemy or something."

"Rocky's got a lot of jealous girlfriends," Alonzo said. "We stage it to look like he got shot by this *abogada*, this Carmen Ramirez person. The story is she shot him, then shot herself, because he wouldn't stop seeing that reporter, Anita Juarez. A classic taco triangle. You leave the gun in the dead bitch's hand. It goes into the books as a murder-suicide."

"That's still a tad loose, guys. What about forensics? Blood splatter? My hair and fiber?"

"None a that shit matters," Alonzo said. "After you shoot him, you call a guy I got waiting by a phone. He'll make the 911 call in Spanish. Since you're gonna be the first blue on the scene, your hair and fiber aren't a problem. After the department puts out the shots-fired call, you grab it, then ask for backup. Me and Horace roger that. We all work the case together. Talbot Jones will handle the one-eighty-seven investigation. It's gonna go down the way we want and get booked exactly the way we say 'cause we're the ones working the crime scene."

"It's starting to sound a little better," I said.

"Good. Now get in the Escalade."

I climbed in and Horace piled in behind me. Alonzo pulled out of the parking lot and headed back into Haven Park.

"I thought you said the rally was in Vista," I said. "We're going the wrong way."

"Gotta stop at the station first."

"How come?"

"Before you do this, you've gotta take a polygraph."

# CHAPTER 39

As soon as we pulled into the parking lot of the Haven Park PD, Alonzo and Horace got out of the Escalade. I just sat there. I was almost certain that Alexa and Ophelia hadn't had enough time to locate and block the polygrapher. While I was trying to figure out what to do, Alonzo jerked open the passenger door. "You coming?"

"Yeah," I said as I climbed out, "but is this really necessary?"

"The mayor wants it," Alonzo said. "He's a cautious guy. So let's just get it done. That way we all know there's no rats, okay?"

"Okay."

The three of us walked into the station. From the look of the lobby, the swing shift was having a busy night. There were half a dozen tense brown faces—mostly women. Mothers and girlfriends sitting in worn leather chairs, their knees tight together, clutching worn fabric purses, waiting for ugly news about loved ones courtesy of the corrupt Haven Park PD.

I followed Alonzo into Talbot Jones's empty office.

"We're gonna do it in here," he said.

He picked up the phone and dialed an extension. "There should be a guy out there from ESA. That's Electronic Systems Analysts. He's a polygraph operator. Hunt him up and send him back to Tal's office." After he hung up he said, "Who wants to go first?"

I certainly didn't. I had a wide, dishonest smile that felt like I'd borrowed it from a drugstore Halloween rack. Horace Velario was still staring at me suspiciously.

Alonzo picked up the phone again. "Let's go. Where is the guy? We need to be over in Fleetwood by ten-fifteen." He listened, then said, "You can't be serious!" He slammed down the phone and left the office without saying anything.

Velario continued to stare at me.

I endured his gaze for almost half a minute. Then I said, "My fly open?"

"You need to know how it is with me and Alonzo," he finally said. "We played high school football together at Long Beach Poly. The press called us Omelet and Toast. I was Omelet. Weak-side linebacker. They called me that 'cause when I hit somebody I scrambled their eggs. Bell was on the strong side and made the toast. We were fucking dangerous. You didn't want what we were dishing out. Between the two of us we logged almost two hundred tackles our senior year."

"That's real nice," I said, tuning him out. My mind was elsewhere, trying to come up with a way to avoid taking the damn polygraph.

"The reason I'm boring you with this shit is you need to know that since then, I never stopped watching Al's back. He looks big and tough, but underneath all that he's got this dumb trusting side, which dickheads always try and take advantage of. When that happens, I scramble up an omelet. My job over the years has been to pick off the bullshitters. I've been looking at you for two days now, and I've come to the decision that you're a lying sack a shit."

That got my attention.

"You're the fucking mole," he said.

"You need to stop taking yourself so seriously," I responded. "This isn't the Long Beach Poly defensive backfield."

"I told Alonzo you're the rat, but since he vouched for you with the Avilas, it's in his best interests for you to be okay, so he don't believe me. But I'm still over here covering the weak side, just like always."

"You were there in the orange grove," I said. "He fired a shot at me. If I was the mole, I would have talked."

"I'm not saying you don't have balls, Scully. I'm saying you're a spy."

"You're probably gonna have to prove that."

"I don't gotta prove shit. This fucking poly is gonna do all the proving for me. You fail, you're gonna go outta here feet first."

Just then Alonzo came back through the door. He was pissed, on the verge of losing it, his brown complexion red with anger.

"Fucking guy isn't here!" he shouted at us.

Alonzo pointed at Horace. "Call Tal. Use the WC's office. Tell Captain Jones the polygraph examiner is a no-show. He booked this guy. Have him get on the phone to ESA. He needs to get the man here now. We need to be out the door in twenty minutes."

Horace shot me a hard look, then exited the office.

Alonzo paced around the room fuming. "Fucking civilian agencies. We used to have our own poly guy, but now because of budgets we're subcontracting all this shit out."

Two minutes later Horace was back. "Talbot can't reach ESA. Their phones go straight to voice mail. He says he don't have no personal contact number on the guy they assigned to us."

Alonzo stood in the center of the office for a long moment, then he looked at his watch. "Okay, then we gotta go without it. From here out, we do this as a team. Once it's done, the conspiracy to commit guarantees everybody's silence."

"I'm good with that," I said.

Horace said nothing, but kept his gaze on me.

"Let's go," Alonzo said. "We got no time left."

We headed back to the Escalade and squealed out of the police lot. We hit Lincoln Boulevard chirping rubber.

# CHAPTER 40

By the time we arrived, close to a thousand people were gathered in the park. A balmy Southern California night undoubtedly helped Rocky's turnout. The twenty sheriffs from the Vista substation could easily have been overmatched by the crowd, but everybody was in a festive mood.

High school bands from Haven Park and Fleetwood were playing Mexican and American music under the park's sulfurous halogen lights. A large platform had been constructed and was festooned with ROCKY FOR MAYOR signs. Campaign posters depicting the candidate stripped to the waist, fists high, ready to vanquish Haven Park's corrupt politicians were stapled to every available wooden post and palm tree. Volunteers circulated through the crowd selling ROCKY FOR MAYOR T-shirts and baseball caps.

When we pulled in, Alonzo couldn't find a place to park.

"Lookit all this illegal parking," he growled. "We oughta get the Avilas over here to tag and drag a few of these rust buckets." Except we weren't in Haven Park or Fleetwood and Vista was policed by the sheriff's department, which had banned Blue Light from operating inside the city limits.

Finally, in frustration, Alonzo pulled up over a curb and left the Escalade on the grass. He draped his handcuffs over the steering wheel, the universal warning that this was an off-duty cop car, then chirped his locks. Horace and I followed him across the grass toward the bandstand.

A Mexican radio station had supplied a few popular disc jockeys who, along with an assortment of local politicians and minor celebrities, were onstage speaking in both English and Spanish, whipping up the crowd over the loudspeakers.

At that point, a beautiful woman stepped to the microphone and was identified as Anita Juarez from the *Haven Park Courier.* Oscar's second cousin and one of Rocky's girlfriends.

As she began to address the crowd, Alonzo, Horace and I finally reached a spot near the east side of the bandstand. "Can you believe this?" Alonzo said, surveying the large turnout. "This fucking guy wasn't even that good a fighter. They act like the little shit walks on water."

Alonzo told us to wait where we were and went off to do something, leaving Horace and me angrily bumping shoulders in the confined space.

"It's not my fault the polygrapher didn't show," I said into Velario's flat glare. "Get over it."

"You're gonna kill Chacon tonight or I'm gonna drop you like a sack of hammers," he threatened.

"You wanta take a step away? You're on my foot." I shoved him back. He was a big guy, so he didn't move far, but the push definitely pissed him off.

At ten-twenty the mayor of Vista introduced Rocky Chacon. He walked across the podium dressed in slacks and a polo shirt. Even before he spoke, the place went nuts. He struck his classic fight pose and they screamed even louder.

As this was happening, Alonzo returned. "I found his ride," he shouted over the racket. "A five-year-old black Mercedes 220 behind the barrier in the park maintenance area. After he's finished speaking, follow him over there and keep him in sight. I'll pick you up." He handed us each a ROCKY FOR MAYOR ball cap that he'd bought from a vendor. "Disguise," he said with a grin.

*"Hola, compañeros,"* Rocky shouted into the mike.

*"Hola, Rocky!"* the crowd shouted back.

*"Como están ustedes esta noche?"*

*"Muy bien, hermano,"* the crowd roared.

"Tonight I will first speak to you in English. Then, for my brothers who just got here, I will talk again in Spanish." The crowd cheered.

"I came here tonight to tell you why I have decided to run for mayor. It is very simple. Haven Park and Fleetwood are run by criminals. Their only desire is to prey on you, taking advantage of your families. We must put an end to this corruption and vote these criminals out of office. Six days from today, this can happen. Six days from today we can send a message that will begin a new life for all of us. This is America. In America, unlike Mexico, the government exists by and for the people. The kind of government I intend to run will be by and for each and every one of you."

"He better have a damn good plan, 'cause he's gonna be running his government from inside a fucking coffin," Alonzo whispered into my ear.

Rocky told the audience how he would end corruption. He promised that no extortion would happen in his Haven Park administration. He promised to fire the entire existing police department and give the job back to the L.A. County sheriffs who had policed both towns until Mayor Bratano had been elected and had canceled the contract, forming his own department made up of police rejects. He said the corrupt Haven Park PD was little more than the mayor's goon squad and vowed that after he was in office the residents of Haven Park would be treated with respect, that his door would be open to any grievance. The crowd went wild. When he finished, he gave the speech again in Spanish.

By eleven o'clock, the rally began breaking up. The bands played "The Star-Spangled Banner" and the "Himno Nacional Mexicano." People waved Mexican and American flags and cheered.

Rocky jumped down off the platform and waded

into the screaming crowd, shaking hands. He hugged people and they shouted their encouragement. He was surrounded by well-wishers on all sides. As he passed us, I could see inspiration and hope shining in his dark brown eyes.

# CHAPTER 41

I followed Rocky through the crowd, with Horace right on my shoulder, never more than a footstep away. The little fighter was being stopped constantly by admirers.

"God bless you," one elderly Hispanic woman said as she took his hand in both of hers. "You have come to save us."

"*Mamá*, you vote for me and we will save each other," Rocky answered.

It took him almost a full thirty minutes to make his way to the staging area where his Mercedes was parked.

We hung back and tried to remain inconspicuous, which was nearly impossible for two Anglos in a park full of Hispanics. We both had our new ROCKY FOR MAYOR ball caps pulled low over our eyes.

We tailed along a few yards behind Chacon until we reached a wooden barrier that had been constructed to partition vehicles with special passes. Two large sound trucks were parked among the VIP cars. After Rocky got into his old Mercedes, we made our way over to the white Escalade parked nearby and climbed inside.

"This nimrod actually thinks he can just waltz in here and take this," Horace growled. Then he pointed at Rocky's departing sedan. "He's pulling out."

Through the back window of the old Mercedes, we could see that Rocky was alone. We slid out into traffic and followed him, staying a block back, as he drove down Scout Avenue, then turned onto the bridge that spanned the L.A. River, heading into the neighboring town of Fleetwood.

"Okay, Shane, here's the 4-1-1," Alonzo said as he drove. "Dirty Harry reassigned you, Horace and Roulon Green to the swing shift. As of tonight you're all on the deployment sheet for Fleetwood. Roulon is waiting over here somewhere right now with your black-and-white. As soon as we locate Rocky's fuck pad, I'll radio him and he'll drive your unit to a spot near the apartment. That's where we'll meet up. Then you walk back, sneak into Rocky's place and double-tap those two. Your squad car will be parked out front of his apartment waiting for you when you come out."

"We're rushing this," I said. "If I'm on patrol, I can't show up in civvies."

"It's covered. I got both your uniforms out of your lockers. They're stashed in the black-and-white. You two change into your Class C's when we meet up with Roulon. After you do the job, you call dispatch and ask for backup. Horace and I will roger the call and the three of us will lock down the crime scene and hold it for Captain Jones, who will handle the one-eighty-seven investigation."

"I'm going with Scully," Horace interjected.

"No, you're not," I replied.

"I'm going with you," Horace reiterated. "Get used to the idea. I'm gonna be there to make sure you do what you're supposed to."

"I'm not taking a fucking observer," I said hotly. Our voices were now rising in anger.

"Calm down, both of you," Alonzo ordered. Then he glanced over at me. "He's right. We agreed, since there's no poly, we're stuck in this together. If Horace wants to back you up, what's the big problem?"

"The problem is I don't want him. I don't like him."

"I told you Scully was dirty," Horace challenged. "He doesn't want me there 'cause he's not gonna do it. I keep telling you he's our rat."

"Velario's going with you," Alonzo snapped. As far as he was concerned, the subject was closed. I let it drop.

Alonzo continued to follow the black 220 across the bridge into Fleetwood. After going about a mile, Rocky made a left, passed three intersections, and then pulled up to a building on the corner. It was a big boxy apartment with the architectural significance of a parking garage in Watts.

A sign on the roof identified it as the Garden Apartments. I could see no gardens, just a strip of dead grass out front.

Rocky turned his 220 into the underground garage using a security card, which opened the sliding gate. Then the little Mercedes sedan disappeared down the ramp, flaring red from its taillights.

Alonzo continued past the apartment complex and hung a U-turn in the middle of the street that went north. He triggered a hand rover as he drove. "R.G., we'll meet you on the seven hundred block of Walnut Street."

I heard two static squelches as Roulon triggered his walkie twice to indicate an affirmative.

Alonzo pulled to the curb and a minute later my old rust-spotted '96 Chrysler squad car pulled up behind us and parked. As Roulon got out, I could see that he was already in uniform.

He opened the trunk and was pulling our war bags out as we joined him. He handed Horace and me our duffels. "You two can take turns changing in the back of the patrol car."

I opened the back door of Car Thirteen. As I was doing this, Horace leaned in close and whispered, "You and I are about to have some fun, asshole."

As I was finishing putting on my uniform, I had a decision to make over which belt to wear. If Agent Love could track me using the Haven Park PD device, it might give me a slight advantage because the little pen was only a satellite transmitter and probably not too accurate as a GPS. Alonzo knew where I was anyway so I strung my civilian belt through my uniform, then grabbed an extra pair of black socks from my duffel, shoved them into my pocket and got out.

After Horace and I were in harness, Alonzo reached into his pocket and handed me the murder gun. He had put it in a police evidence bag to keep our prints off it. I looked through the cellophane at the blue steel Covert Carry automatic with six in the clip. There was a smooth spot above the trigger where the serial numbers had been filed. Your basic throwdown gun.

"What about the cartridges? You wipe the brass?" I asked.

"We're not idiots, Scully," Alonzo said. "After you shoot both of 'em, wipe the gun clean, then put it in the bitch's hand. Fire it once so she tests positive when CSI does the gunshot residue test, then call this number." Alonzo handed me a slip of paper. "The guy on that phone will report gunshots to 911 in Spanish. I'll tell dispatch I'm passing the apartment on my way home and will cover the front. Don't screw it up."

"Don't worry," I told him.

I took off walking, with Velario on my heels, never more than a foot behind. He was so close that I could feel his hot breath on my ear.

In less than two minutes, one of us would be going on alone.

# CHAPTER 42

My uniform shirt was beginning to stick to my back as we neared the four-story Garden Apartments. The building loomed ahead on the opposite corner like a big stucco shoe box. It was after midnight, and most of the lights were off inside. I paused in a recessed doorway on the corner to look the place over before crossing the street.

"What're you waiting for?" Horace prodded.

"You wanta just stroll up the front walk and start knocking on doors? That's your plan? We're here to clip this guy. It might be better if we're not seen."

"It's late. They're all fucking illegals. They won't mess with us. Nobody wants to risk getting deported. We need to check the mailboxes, see which apartment he's in. How the fuck else will we find his room?"

I didn't answer and stepped off the curb. I crossed Wilcox and started up the street heading along the west side of the apartment building. I found an alley that ran perpendicular and turned left.

It took two more minutes to get to the rear of the apartment complex, where I saw an eight-foot-high wooden fence with an unlocked back gate. I swung it open and we walked into a small backyard area. Four wooden planter boxes containing water-starved citrus trees supplied the meager courtyard landscaping. We crossed that weed-choked space, staying next to the apartment wall so we wouldn't be seen by any residents who might be sitting on their narrow balconies. Then we went through a large door into the main building.

Once we got to the lobby elevator, I saw a sign Scotch-taped to the metal doors that said FUERA DE SERVICIO—UTILIZA LA ESCALERA. Out of Service.

I bypassed the main staircase, preferring to use the fire stairs. Then I descended into the subterranean parking garage.

"The fuck you going?" Horace growled as he lumbered along behind me. "Whatta we doin' in the damn garage?"

I went down one more flight until we reached a large open parking level that contained at least fifty cars. Most of them were old and in pretty bad shape.

"Ain't gonna find him down here," Horace complained. " 'Less he's bangin' his bitch in the backseat."

I found Rocky's empty Mercedes parked in a stall marked 456.

"Apartment four-fifty-six," I told him. "Happy now?"

He wasn't happy. He didn't like being outthought.

We headed back into the stairwell and started up. If I was going to unload Velario, now was the time.

For the last five minutes, I'd been coming up with and discarding different ways to go about it. He had a reputation as a barroom brawler and was supposed to be cat-quick. Since he didn't trust me, he was being careful to always walk a few feet to the left and behind, staying in my blind spot.

As we reentered the staircase, I heard the creak of leather as he unholstered his sidearm. Then I heard his aluminum street baton coming out of its metal belt ring. I had an ugly image of that murderous Neanderthal trailing behind me with a .38 in one hand and an eighteen-inch aluminum bat in the other.

I stopped on the third-floor landing and reached for the murder weapon, pulling the street-clcan nine-millimeter Para automatic out of the cellophane bag.

"What're you doing?" Horace said, backing away, raising the nose of his .38 to the vicinity of my groin. His baton was belt-high at the ready.

"I'm checking the gun," I said. "Don't want a misfire." I motioned toward his .38. "And stop pointing that at me."

Horace ignored the request and instead took another step back, giving himself a better range of motion in case I tried anything.

I went through an elaborate weapons check on

the Para. I dropped the clip, checked the loads, and jammed it back up into the handle. I carefully slipped the safety forward to the on position. When I finished I looked over at Horace, who was standing there like a video game assassin—shaved head, weapons in both hands, ready to spill some sauce.

"Safety's broken," I said, and pointed the gun at the concrete wall, pulling the trigger helplessly. The hammer wouldn't move.

"Bullshit," Horace said.

"You try it, then." I handed Velario the Para. This caused him a logistics problem because he had the metal baton in one hand and his police .38 in the other. He had to holster something. He finally slid the metal baton back into his belt ring and he took the automatic from me. Once he was holding it, he seemed to drop his guard slightly, because he now had all the unholstered weapons and, except for my police-issue sidearm in its flapped holster, which would be hard to draw quickly, he thought I was momentarily defenseless.

He lowered his own weapon and glared down at the little palm-sized automatic, quickly discovering the problem. "There's nothing wrong with the safety, dummy. You just gotta push it down."

As he said this, my right hand snaked into my back pocket. Horace was still looking down at the Para as I yanked the leather sap out and made a mighty, swing-for-the-fences pivot toward him with the sap at full arm extension. Two pounds of encased lead whistled through the air and hit him square in the teeth. Little pieces of chipped enamel flew like broken pottery. His giant head snapped back and hit the concrete wall. He dropped the street gun and barely managed to hang on to his .38. It dangled precariously from his fingers, momentarily forgotten.

I took one step forward, gave him a backward shot to the temple using my elbow. As soon as that landed, I stomped on his right foot to hold him in place and threw a hard left cross followed by a vicious uppercut with the sap. It was a great three-punch combination, but despite all this, the big ex-linebacker didn't go down. He was stunned, but still standing, his gun hanging loosely from his fingertips. I swatted it away. It clattered to the ground, bouncing down two steps.

He looked up at me with dull eyes, then grabbed feebly for the sap. I let go of it and he came away with the two-pound lead weight in his hand. Then he tried to get his arm back to swing it, but by now he was moving at half speed. I finished him off with a double left jab over a chopping right. I landed all three perfectly and he slammed back against the wall and started to slide down with a puzzled look on his face. His expression seemed to say, *But I never lose one of these.*

"We having fun yet?" I asked, then I kicked him

in the head. But one eye stayed open, staring. He was slumped over. *What's this guy using for a skull?* I thought. *Forty-gauge iron plate?*

I snatched the handcuffs off his belt and cuffed both his wrists through the metal handrail in the stairwell. Then I grabbed the extra pair of socks I'd taken from my duffel earlier and stuffed them into his mouth. He was bleeding from four places on his head and four of his teeth were gone. The rest were shattered. I picked up both guns and turned off his shoulder rover. I was just getting ready to go when I glanced down and saw him staring up at me through one open bloodshot eye. I'd given him the best I had and he was still not out.

"I gotta hand it to you, Horace. I'm impressed."

I turned and left him there.

# CHAPTER 43

I exited the stairwell on the fourth floor and glanced out a window that overlooked the street. No white Escalade. No federal backup.

Apartment 456 was in the middle of the top-floor corridor on the courtyard side of the building. I carefully tried the doorknob. Locked.

It had a solid wood core so I didn't think I could kick it in.

I stood in the hallway looking for a likely hide-a-key spot. I checked over the doorjamb. Dust bunnies and spiders. No potted plants or wall art. I checked the fire-extinguisher box down the hall. Nada.

I certainly didn't want to climb up to the roof and try to rappel down onto the balcony like some character in a Bruce Lee movie. It felt too much like comedy.

I also knew that if Alonzo didn't get the 911 call soon, he and Roulon Green would come looking. With the elevators broken, they'd probably also use the less-traveled fire stairs and would find Horace. I had used up too much valuable time already and knew I couldn't stand around scratching my head.

The damned roof gag boiled down to my only decent choice. I returned to the stairwell and looked down one flight at Velario, who was still cuffed to the railing with my socks in his mouth. His left eye was now swollen completely shut, but the other one was glaring up at me with murderous hatred.

"Comfy?" I whispered down at him.

Then I turned and climbed up the one additional flight and came out onto a flat, silver-painted roof. There was a half-moon lighting the night and I could see a minefield of hardware-store clutter up here. It looked as if the apartments' residents used this roof for a sundeck. Beach chairs and hibachis shared space with several flourishing marijuana plants with protective signs that read HECTOR'S

BUD or PROPERTY OF JUAN GARCIA—NO TOCA.

I picked my way across this campground of flowering happiness and crossed to the interior edge of the building, then walked along counting apartment windows below me until I got to the spot I hoped was directly above Rocky's balcony. I looked down at the dead citrus trees in the courtyard below. To do this, I was going to have to hang down from the rain gutter, dangling four stories up. I hated it, but there was no other way.

I lay on my stomach and slowly lowered myself over the edge, gripping the rain gutter with both hands and extending to my full five feet eleven inches. Then I searched for the balcony railing with my toes. After half a minute of this, the gutter started to pull loose, coming away from the eaves of the roof with a loud metallic shriek.

It suddenly gave way and I crashed painfully onto the balcony below, landing on some wooden patio furniture, shattering a small glass-top table. Electric pain buzzed up my arm from my funny bone. I felt a sharp stab in my side like a rib had just broken.

I groaned and tried to collect myself.

Just then the door to the balcony flew open and Rocky was standing there butt-naked, fists up, ready to kick my ass again. Despite the pain, I scrambled to my feet.

"You!" he said, quickly recognizing me from the jail.

He started to advance. I didn't want to waste any more of my blood on this guy, so I pulled the Para and aimed it at him with the safety still on.

"Stop," I ordered. "This isn't what you think."

Despite the automatic in my hand, Rocky was still advancing, about to deck me.

"Juanito, what is it?" a woman's voice called from inside the apartment.

"I need four minutes," I said. "Put on a robe and listen to me."

"You're the cop with that *culo* Bell."

"Rocky, I'm not with Bell. I'm an LAPD officer working undercover inside the Haven Park PD. Your life is in danger. Not from me, from them. You need to hear what I have to say."

He still had his fists up.

"I was sent here to kill you, but I came to warn you instead. There are others outside the building to make sure I do the job. We don't have any time. I know you have no reason to trust me, but you've got to take a chance."

"You're the one holding the gun, and *I'm* supposed to take a chance?"

I needed to do something dramatic to turn him, so I handed the Para automatic over and said, "You hold it, then."

He stood there with the small automatic in his hand, trying to decide what to do. Then he turned his head and yelled, "Carmen. Put something on. We have company."

# CHAPTER 44

We went into the small one-bedroom apartment, where Rocky grabbed a silk fight robe with EL ALBOROTADOR embroidered on the back. The furnishings in the unit were sparse. No pictures or personal effects. A queen-sized bed dominated a small bedroom barely large enough to accommodate it.

I caught a glimpse of a naked woman as she slipped into the bathroom and closed the door.

"Okay. Who's trying to kill me?" Chacon said suspiciously.

"C'mon, you can't be that dense. You really think you can take all this away from Bratano and still get to city hall?"

"I've got people coming to protect me."

"Yeah. The Marines from Pendleton." He looked surprised. "Your phones are tapped. They know those guys aren't coming till tomorrow. That's why this is going down tonight. Right now there are two cops outside to make sure I do it right."

"You're Bell's partner. How can I believe anything you say?"

"Come here," I said, moving to the front door. "I want to show you something."

I stepped into the hallway. He hesitated, not moving.

"Whatta you afraid of? You got a gun."

He followed me reluctantly into the hall and then into the staircase. We walked down one flight, where Horace was still cuffed to the railing, glaring malevolently out of one swollen eye.

"Remember this guy?" I reached down and yanked my socks out of Horace's mouth.

"You're gonna fucking die, Scully," he growled through broken teeth. "You're a corpse."

"That's enough," I said, holding out the socks. "Open wide."

He clenched his broken jaw, so I kicked him in the shin. He opened his mouth to scream out and I jammed my socks back in.

"You really fucked him up," Rocky said.

"I'm supposed to kill you and Carmen, put the gun in her hand so it looks like a street divorce."

He thought about it. "Okay, let's say I believe you," he said. "Whatta we do about it?"

"Not here."

We left Horace where he was and climbed back to the fourth floor and entered the hallway. As I passed the window, I looked at the street out front. Alonzo's white Escalade still wasn't there.

We went back into the apartment and locked the door. Carmen had changed into a conservative black pantsuit. Rocky immediately stripped off his robe and started to get dressed while I filled both of them in on the rest of the plot and how Alonzo had instructed me to do it.

After I was finished, Carmen said, “Is Bratano insane? How does he think he can get away with that?”

“He controls the cops, so he controls everything from the crime scene to the booking desk. Believe me, if I hadn’t managed to slip in between these guys, it would have worked.”

Just then, my shoulder rover clicked twice. Alonzo’s impatient signal for me to check in and tell him what was taking so long.

“Have you got a car we can use to get out of here? We can’t use Rocky’s Mercedes. We’ll never get it out of the garage.”

“I have a little red Mustang,” Carmen said. “It’s parked on the street half a block down.”

“Okay. We’ll use that,” I said. “We have to get out of this jurisdiction. There’s supposed to be some FBI or Homeland agents around here somewhere to back me up, but so far I haven’t seen them.”

“It’s gonna be next to impossible to get out of Fleetwood going east,” Rocky said. “All they have to do is block the three bridges that cross the L.A. River. We’re better off trying to head toward Monterey Park or Cypress.”

I nodded, then explained exactly what we needed to do.

# CHAPTER 45

I had Rocky go down the hall carrying the gun and take a position by the front window overlooking the street. My shoulder rover had squelched twice more in the last minute. Alonzo was impatient, demanding a reply. I pulled my sidearm and looked over at Carmen.

"I've got to fire this thing because I'm supposed to be committing a double murder," I explained. "They could be close enough to hear the gunshots. Ready?"

She nodded.

I aimed my police revolver at the wall that overlooked the courtyard and pulled the trigger. The first bullet punched through the plaster and started bouncing around inside. The second and third rounds hit a wall stud, thunking loudly. I jammed the gun back into my harness leather, then used the apartment phone to dial the number Alonzo had given me.

After two rings a man answered, "Yeah."

"Make the call. Apartment four-fifty-six," I said and hung up.

The shots had awakened our neighbors. We could hear people out in the corridor, slamming doors and talking loudly in Spanish.

"Let's go." I led Carmen out of the room. There were about ten people milling around in the hall.

*"Que es?"* a young *vato* wearing a wife-beater tee said. He was only about seventeen, but was holding a blue steel .45. His skin was crawling with 18th Street gang tats.

*"No es nada,"* Carmen said as we hurried past.

Rocky was next to the window, watching the street for Alonzo. The people in the corridor started to pick up on the fact that a celebrity was in their midst.

"El Alborotador," an old man said.

"Hey, it's Rocky Chacon," somebody else exclaimed.

Then my shoulder rover squawked. "One-L-Nine and all available units in the vicinity of Vista Street and Park. You have a four-fifteen with shots fired in the Garden Apartments, seven hundred block of Vista Street, apartment four-five-six. L-Nine, your call is code three."

I triggered my shoulder rover. "This is One-L-Thirteen. I'm in front of the location right now and will handle. Notify L-Nine that I'm in the building."

"Roger that. L-Nine, your call is now code two. L-Thirteen is inside the location."

A cacophony of radio calls followed. I grabbed Rocky and Carmen by the arm and led them to the fire door.

As we entered the stairwell, I glanced down to make sure Horace Velario was still cuffed to the railing. We hurried up to the roof.

My rover lit up again. Alonzo Bell calling the dispatcher.

"This is Sergeant Bell. I'm just pulling up to the Wilcox location now. All responding units and L-Thirteen, I've got my gun out and am in plainclothes wearing a green short-sleeved shirt and tan pants."

"Roger that. All units. All frequencies. The shift sergeant is on the location in plainclothes, green over tan."

Then I heard Roulon Green roger the call and announce his arrival. In another minute we were going to have enough cops out front to put on a police fundraiser.

I threw open the roof door and ran across the top of the building, with Rocky and Carmen a few steps behind. I didn't want to be a moonlit silhouette, so I stayed toward the center of the roof and kept low. Only once did I veer to the edge, crouching down to survey the activity in the street below. I could see four squad cars at the curb and one more boiling in a block away about thirty seconds out. The front of the apartment building was now lit by a strobing cherry orchard of red and blue Mars lights.

I spotted the white Escalade with the driver's-side door open. No sign of Alonzo. That meant he was in the lobby and would probably find Horace any minute. I wanted to stay up here just long enough to get the majority of the cops into the building. I had to time it just right.

I checked my watch and let fifty seconds tick off the dial. Then I nodded at Rocky and Carmen. We ran to the far end of the building, where the rooftop fire-escape ladder was located. Rocky went down first. I helped Carmen over the edge and then followed. As I clambered down, I heard Alonzo's voice come over my rover.

"All units, all frequencies, be advised—we have an attempted murder of a police officer by our own patrolman, Officer Shane Scully. He and two armed Hispanics, male and female, are in the building. Set up a perimeter. I'm authorizing deadly force." Then Alonzo was talking directly to me. "Scully, you won't make this. The only way you can save your ass is for you and the two beaners to give yourselves up."

I didn't respond, just kept descending the fire ladder, finally dropping to the ground on the north side of the building.

When I hit the pavement, I could hear at least five or six police radios blaring calls from two overlapping frequencies. The lights from the patrol units wigwagged furiously, strobing the neighborhood. Three fresh units arrived.

We took off running, trying to keep close to the buildings so we wouldn't be spotted. It didn't work.

"Over there!" someone yelled.

Carmen's red Mustang convertible was parked

at the curb half a block from the front entrance. I glanced back and saw a wall of blue uniforms running toward us, all with guns drawn.

"Freeze! Police," somebody shouted.

"I'm driving," I said to Carmen, grabbing the keys from her hand. I triggered the door remote and slid in behind the wheel. Rocky and Carmen jumped in the back.

I jammed the key into the ignition and started the engine just as the first shots rang out. A bullet slammed into the trunk. The next one careened off the pavement under the car, hitting the asphalt, bouncing like a skipped stone before whining away into the night.

I floored the Mustang and left half a pound of rubber at the curb.

*"Mamá mia!"* Rocky exclaimed.

We roared down Vista and made a hard right.

I heard a flurry of pursuit calls over my shoulder rover. "All units, One-L-Seven reports the fugitive vehicle is now westbound," one said. "The suspect vehicle is red 2007 Mustang convertible."

"Requesting air support. We need a chopper!" another voice chimed in.

Then Alonzo's unmistakable growl: "All units. The shoot-on-sight authorization is still in place. Don't let these scumbags out of Fleetwood!"

"Keep going straight!" Rocky yelled. "This street takes us into Monterey Park!"

I was doing almost eighty by the time we passed

Pacific Boulevard. I got lucky and caught the green. At Lincoln, I had to break a red light. I almost hit a produce truck and swung the wheel frantically, fishtailing wildly, barely missing the rear end before flooring it again and continuing on.

"Only six more blocks to go!" Rocky yelled. "We're almost there!"

We didn't even come close to making it.

# CHAPTER 46

"Scully! Give yourselves up," Alonzo screamed over the shoulder rover. "Don't die for these shit-stains!"

I didn't answer, and lowered the volume instead.

"You've committed an attempted murder on a police officer," Bell continued. "I've got a full police response, Air One on the way and a shoot-on-sight order. I'll cancel it now if you pull over, throw down your guns and give up!"

"Maybe we should stop," Carmen yelled over the screaming engine. "What are they going to do, shoot us all?"

"That's exactly what they'll do," I answered. "He'll say we initiated a gunfight and then just execute all three of us. They'll have ten cops to swear witness."

"He's right," Rocky shouted. "In this town, they do what they want."

I had my foot to the floor and within a block the little red Mustang was again going almost ninety. The engine was wound tight, screaming. We flashed past Pacific going south heading out of Fleetwood a block from Monterey Park.

Just then I saw two Haven Park black-and-whites make smoking turns into the intersection ahead, braking to a tire-shredding stop, blocking both lanes.

"You can't get through!" Rocky yelled.

I slammed on the foot brake, pulled the hand brake to lock the tires, and threw the Mustang into a heart-stopping 180-degree bootlegger's skid. All four tortured tires screamed as I completed the maneuver, burning rubber, bouncing onto the curb but finally getting the vehicle turned around, speeding through my own tire smoke, heading north back into Fleetwood.

"Go right! Try to make it into Vernon," Rocky yelled.

I hung a quick right. Sirens blared all around us, closing in from every direction.

Then I heard a cop screaming at the dispatcher through my shoulder mike. "This is One-L-Nine! I have the suspect's vehicle in sight. He's south-bound on Otis Avenue heading into Vernon."

"Scully, you'll never make it," Alonzo's voice came over my shoulder rover. "The air unit will be over you in a minute. Be smart, man. Don't die over this. We can still work something out."

I triggered my shoulder mike with my right hand as I drove.

"This is One-L-Nine," I screamed, trying to mimic the frantic sound of the pursuing cop. "The fugitive vehicle just turned onto Huntington Park Drive passing Bristol heading west."

As I put out the phony call I heard Alonzo's voice immediately step on it. "Cancel that! He's still westbound on Otis."

"One-L-Six has the suspect vehicle in sight," Roulon Green said.

I glanced in the rearview and saw a second set of pursuing headlights about two blocks back.

We didn't make it into Vernon either. Just as we were about four blocks from the city boundary, two Haven Park squad cars turned onto the street ahead, blocking our way.

I pulled another smoking one-eighty and reversed course, passing between the two trailing black-and-whites, splitting them, knocking off side mirrors, going almost eighty. I caught a glimpse of Roulon Green's startled expression as we flashed past. Both patrol cars made screeching turns and came after us.

Rocky yelled, "You're heading toward the river. They'll have all those bridges blocked. Go left here. Try for Monterey Park again."

I took a thirty-mile-an-hour left on the next street and almost flipped the Mustang as the right-side tires slammed hard against the far curb. But we stayed upright as I hit the gas and headed west again.

We had gone almost six miles, but had gotten nowhere. Alonzo and the Haven Park cops had managed to herd us in a big useless circle.

Over the noise of the sirens, I heard the chopper moving in. Carmen cursed in Spanish under her breath.

"Almost there!" Rocky shouted. "Two more blocks!"

We drove through the underpass that bordered Fleetwood and Monterey Park. For a minute I thought we'd made it. We were out of Fleetwood and that meant we were out of Haven Park PD's jurisdiction. I didn't think Alonzo would shoot us down in county sheriff territory because the sheriffs would be in charge of the investigation, putting another controlling authority into the mix. Then Alonzo's voice came over the rover.

"All units. All frequencies. We have just been given hot pursuit authorization by Monterey Park Sheriffs. Do not break off. I repeat, do not break off at the city line. Continue into Monterey Park. Take this guy down."

Just then, two Haven Park PD squad cars rounded the corner ahead and skidded to a stop, blocking the road. I had no choice but to make another smoking, tire-shredding U and retreat again into Fleetwood. As I came out of the underpass, the xenon sun in the belly of the police chopper suddenly lit us in a halo of white light.

"I've gotta lose this chopper," I shouted. "We'll never get away with him on top of us!"

"How about Live Oak Street?" Carmen suggested.

"What's on Live Oak?" I shouted.

"Oak trees," she said.

# CHAPTER 47

As soon as I turned onto the street I knew Carmen's suggestion was a good one. It was lined with massive hundred-year-old oaks. Huge branches completely overhung the street. I shut off the headlights as we streaked under the sheltering canopy. I was looking for an open garage or deep driveway where I could ditch the Mustang. The night sun from the chopper was shooting hot streaks of white light through pinholes in the leafy overhead. They shifted and moved, dancing on the asphalt as the chopper changed position above, trying to spot.

"I have an aunt who lives on this street," Carmen shouted over the din of the lowering helicopter.

A few blocks back, two Haven Park patrol cars, going almost fifty, were smoking turns onto the street.

"Which one is your aunt's?" I shouted.

Carmen pointed to a brightly painted stucco house with barred windows in the middle of the block.

"I'm turning at the next corner," I shouted. "Once I've stopped—everybody out. Get behind the bushes in front of the corner house, then we'll make our way back up the street to your aunt's."

"They're too close!" Rocky shouted.

"I've got a plan for that," I told him.

I floored the car, picking up speed. The two squad cars also sped up and were now only a block and a half back. I made a quick right at the corner, then immediately slewed the Mustang sideways to a stop, blocking the narrow street. I set the emergency brake and the three of us jumped out, abandoning the car. We sprinted for the shrubs and dove behind them, flattening out in the dirt. A few seconds later two cop cars rounded the corner with lights and sirens blaring. The lead unit T-boned Carmen's car, slamming into the passenger door. The second shop immediately pounded into the back of him.

While the cops were busy getting out of their busted units with guns drawn and advancing cautiously on the Mustang to clear it, we rose up and sprinted across the lawn in the dark, keeping low, working our way toward Carmen's aunt's painted stucco.

"I know where she keeps the hide-a-key," Carmen shouted and dug it out of a nearby pot. We ran for the back porch and Carmen slipped the key into the lock, then swung the door wide.

"Auntie Anna, it's Carmenita," she called out as we entered the house. I closed and locked the door behind us.

"Keep the lights off," I instructed.

"I'll check her bedroom," Carmen said and headed down a dark hallway.

Overhead, Air One was coming lower, working back and forth above the street. I could hear its rotor pitch whine and buzz as the pilot worked the chopper's collective and cyclic controls to circle overhead.

A few minutes later Carmen exited the back hallway with a short, middle-aged Hispanic woman who was belting her robe and pushing a sleep-ruined hairdo back up into place.

She was looking up at her ceiling, where, above the roof, the helicopter was making a racket.

"Auntie, it's the police. They're trying to kill Rocky."

"Aye, aye, aye," Carmen's Aunt Anna said, but asked no further questions. She knew how justice was delivered in Haven Park.

"Carmen, get out of those clothes," Rocky said. "Put on one of your aunt's nightgowns and wrap your head in a scarf or something. Maybe if they come in here they won't recognize you."

Then he turned to me. "If we stay, we could get them both killed!"

"I agree." I turned to Carmen. "Rocky and I are gonna take off. There's an FBI agent named Ophelia Love. Get in touch with her through the Homeland Security office on Wilshire. Tell her what's going down."

"What are you going to do?" she asked Rocky.

"I'm not that far along with my plan yet," Rocky said.

"We've got a better shot if we split up. I've got a tracker in my belt. If they're using it, maybe I can lead them off you," I told him. "One of us has to be alive to testify against these guys."

*"Querido,"* Carmen said, putting her hands up to Rocky's face. "I love you. I couldn't stand to lose you."

He leaned forward, kissing her, putting his arms around her waist. "I couldn't stand to lose me either. *Te amo. Soy tuyo.*"

"This is a really nice moment," I whispered. "But can we please get the hell out of here?"

Just then there was a heavy knock at the front door.

"Police! Open up!" somebody shouted.

# CHAPTER 48

Rocky and I waited until we heard Carmen's aunt open the front door, then I slipped out the back. The helicopter's belly light was blasting through the dense tree cover, dappling the backyard from overhead. We ran across the grass and both dove for cover under a huge leafy oak.

"I'm going east," Rocky said. "You should go north. There's a bunch of old decommissioned water runoff drains all over this part of town. They're big underground pipes from the fifties, almost five feet in diameter. They've been sealed up with big metal plates, but it's possible to pull them off. If you can find one, get inside and follow the drain down into the L.A. River."

"Okay, thanks. Good luck, Rocky."

"You too, *amigo. Adiós.*"

As soon as he took off, I turned and leaped over the low fence bordering Aunt Anna's property and promptly landed in her neighbor's trash area, setting up a loud clatter as I knocked over metal cans, spewing garbage. Lights were going on in houses all over the neighborhood as police radios blared from the street out front. Late-arriving squad cars growled their sirens as they pulled in. The helicopter continued its loud, low hover.

I stayed close to the house next door, creeping along under the eaves, working my way carefully forward toward the street so I could get a better look at what was going on out front. Once I got to the corner of the house, I saw about ten cops and squad cars parked randomly on Live Oak. Almost the entire mid-watch.

Residents of the neighborhood were beginning to come out of their houses and stand on front lawns to watch. A few Haven Park patrol officers were going up and down the block with bullhorns, ordering them to get back inside. The rest of the blues were fanning out, searching the block, knocking on doors and pushing their way into houses. Most of the residents were frightened illegals, so the officers sure weren't bothering with warrants.

I'd been involved in enough helicopter-assisted searches in my career to know that it was next to impossible to get away once they put that night sun on you.

I was trying to figure out how to get some distance between me and this mess. My immediate plan was to lead them away from Rocky. Then I would ditch the belt by throwing it in the back of a moving car so it would lead them farther away from both of us while I made it to freedom. My police uniform was both a blessing and a curse. They were looking for a cop, so my blues made me instantly vulnerable. But the uniform also gave me immediate authority over these immigrant residents. Most would do whatever a policeman ordered. I had to make a choice.

I decided that because of my dark hair, if I lost the uniform blouse and wore only my white undershirt and pants, I had a decent chance of looking like one of the Mexican neighbors. I dumped my uniform shirt in a neighbor's trash bin, but held on to my rover unit and the rest of my police equipment, including the DCST transmitter I'd gotten from Agent Love. I also kept my .38 and jammed all of this equipment in my belt.

I found a white dishrag on a clothesline and wrapped my head. My best shot was to try to blend in and then mingle my way out of range, into the next block. I went out into the yard and stood with everybody else, in plain sight, squinting at the night sky, shading my eyes from the helicopter light.

Then a police speaker blared.

"Back inside your houses! Get inside or you will be arrested." A moment later the same voice announced, *"Regresa a su casas inmediatamente o quedan detenido!"*

I moved along with the flow of people back toward the sidewalk, then ducked into a space between two houses and ran into somebody else's backyard. I found the rear gate and went out into a narrow alley.

The helicopter had moved a block to the east, so I started running down the alley. I didn't know where I was going. I saw the lights of a strip mall with a big Vons market up ahead and ran in that direction. Just then the helicopter turned and started back.

I came out from under the leafy oak foliage at the intersection, put my hands in my pockets and strolled casually across the four-lane street heading toward the market in the center of the mall. I might be able to find a phone and call for help.

I was halfway across the parking lot heading for the sliding double doors when two squad cars roared by. One of them threw on the brakes and squealed to a stop, then made a power turn and blasted into the mall parking lot where I was.

I started to run and immediately heard a broadcast for backup over the rover in my pocket.

Two more cars boiled into the strip mall. I was cut off. Nowhere to go. I turned, threw down my gun and put my hands on top of my head.

Alonzo Bell and Horace Velario got out of the second car. Horace was moving like everything hurt but managed to follow Alonzo across the lot. I was about to get a serving of omelets and toast.

"Turn around and lace your fingers behind your neck," Alonzo ordered.

I did as I was told. They spun me around, cuffed me, then shook me down.

Agent Love and her FBI SWAT team needed to get here fast and break this up. But that wasn't in my future either. I was abruptly spun again and found myself looking into the toothless and swollen face of Horace Velario.

"Now comes the fun," he said through split, bleeding lips.

Then he pulled out his sap and slammed me in the side of the head. The blow was aimed at my temple. I saw it coming and tried to pivot away, but was a beat slow and my brain exploded, engulfing me in a starburst of white light. I stumbled and fell.

"Okay, Horace, enough payback," I vaguely heard Alonzo say as my world narrowed and darkened.

"No problemo." Horace sounded like somebody whispering in a dense fog. "Just gonna give him a little tune-up." Then I felt something smash into my ribs. A foot or his metal baton. Just before I lost consciousness I heard Horace say, "This is more like it, asshole."

# CHAPTER 49

When I came to, I was in a huge food warehouse located God knows where, maybe in one of the big storage complexes in the nearby City of Industry. It looked too big to be the storage room at the Vons market, so I'd been moved. I was looking at a pallet stacked high with large boxes labeled SAFEWAY KITCHEN-STYLE GREEN BEANS.

My mind was, somehow, miraculously functioning. In fact, a strange sense of calm now dominated me.

I was tied to a metal chair with my hands cuffed behind me and I had a blinding headache. I tried to turn my head, but as soon as I did, my temple flashed a current of unbearable pain that threatened to take me out, so I took several long breaths, tried to refocus, waited, then slowly turned my head again. I found myself looking into the frying-pan-shaped face of Sergeant Bell. He was about two feet away, seated backward, his chin resting on huge, overdeveloped forearms that were crossed over the back of his metal chair. He examined me without expression.

"Hi," he finally said.

Some time passed. We looked at each other. "Lucy, you got some 'splainin' to do," he said, softly.

I didn't answer.

He stood up and moved the chair out of the way, placing it carefully to the side. "How much did you tell Agent Love?"

I was having trouble keeping up. I needed to slow this down. I had sustained a concussion and it occurred to me that this false sense of clarity I was experiencing might just be a trauma-induced illusion.

"You need to know that right now, sitting where you are, you're a dead man," Bell said. "You're not going to walk away. I got my orders straight from Carlos Reál, which means they came from the man himself. Short and sweet. 'Kill the bastard!' That's what he told me. But before that happens we need to know what we need to know."

"Agent Love hates me," I whispered weakly. "I didn't tell her shit."

"Yeah. Then how come I stopped her on the

Pacific Street bridge an hour ago? She was busting into Haven Park all full a spit and mustard, looking for you."

I felt a wave of nausea and thought for a moment that I was going to throw up. I barely managed to hold it down.

"You're working for her, Shane. I think you somehow managed to get a distress call out and she was hustling over here to back your play. She said she had orders to arrest you, but dumb bitch that she is she forgot to pick up a charge sheet or an arrest warrant. Captain Jones told her you were wanted in Fleetwood for attempted homicide. She only had two guys, Tal had six. She didn't get across the bridge. So all this tells me is you're the federal plant after all."

"You're wrong, but I probably can't change your mind."

"That's right, you can't." He smiled. "You need to pony up some info. Start by telling me what the feds know."

"There isn't anything to tell. You got this all wrong."

"Really?"

He motioned with his left hand. Horace Velario stepped out of the shadows behind him. He must have undergone some emergency first aid while I was knocked out. His split lip was stitched up and his head was bandaged, but his teeth were still a mess and they must have been killing him because when he talked, he kept his mouth closed to keep cold air off exposed nerves. I didn't think there was much I could say that would change the outcome of this, so I tried to prepare myself for what was coming.

But Alonzo wasn't through. "That write-up on POLITE was bullshit," he told me. "You and the little wifey set that up, which means you're not bangin' the famous actress like everybody thought. Means you're still married, still got shit to worry about at home."

"Alexa threw me out."

"I gotta operate on more credible instincts." Alonzo smiled. "I need to know how deep and wide this mess is. If you convince me you're not holding back, I might take pity and leave wifey alone. But if you keep up this hard-guy routine, I'm gonna make a move. I'll fuck her up big, put her on the bitch bus and send her to a hole out in Visalia. It's up to you what happens."

"You kill her, the sixth floor will never stop hunting you. But do what you want, 'cause I could give less of a shit about her."

I was hoping he didn't hear the fear in my voice, couldn't read the distress in my eyes. The only way to save Alexa was to convince him I didn't care.

He motioned to Horace. "Your turn. But don't kill him yet. He's still got a job to do." Then Bell started to walk away.

"Al." He stopped and turned back to face me.

"Change of heart?"

"Whether I'm dead or alive, the cafeteria line is closed. You're all going to prison."

"All good things gotta end sometime," he said philosophically. "But I'm pretty sure nobody's going to prison. You're gonna be indicted and tried in absentia for crimes committed against the people and police department in Haven Park. We'll put out a warrant, but you're never gonna be found. You're gonna be moldering in your own hole somewhere."

Then he turned and left me with Horace Velario, who immediately pulled the sap out of his back pocket. He moved over to stand in front of me.

"We got us a couple a hours. You'll be conscious for all of it."

"I got stacks of money from the street hits I pulled up in L.A. It's all yours, Horace. How does a hundred thousand sound?"

He didn't answer. He hit me with the sap instead. I was out before the starburst in my head even happened.

# CHAPTER 50

"Scully . . . hey, Scully . . ." Somebody was whispering. "Wake up, homes. Hey, wake up."

Little pieces of my senses started to return, first smell, then the pain.

"Scully! You gotta wake up! I need help."

God had blessed me with a very hard head, but I was often too careless and my brains always seemed to be getting hammered.

"Wake up, man. Hey, Scully, wake up!"

I was looking at a carton of creamed corn. Last time it was green beans. All I needed to enjoy a hearty vegetable feast was a settled stomach.

I was lying on my side on a floor that appeared to be moving. Never a good sign after a head injury.

"Scully? Shit, man, are you awake?"

"Trying," I said with great deliberation. Something was wrong with my mouth. I felt around with my tongue. Several of my front teeth were gone, others broken. *Shit.*

"Scully, over here."

I turned my head and was now looking at crates of asparagus and lima beans. I was in the magic vegetable kingdom . . . The Jolly Green Giant was probably going to kick my ass.

"Scully, wake up, man."

I finally figured out why the floor was moving. I was in a truck, and the truck was moving . . . Deduction. As I came to a little more, I could hear the hum of big truck tires on pavement. I turned my head farther to the right and saw Rocky Chacon a few feet away. Like me, he was tied up. He'd also been beaten and was propped against the inside of the big semi truck full of produce and canned goods. The trailer we were in was at least fifty feet long.

"Thank God you're alive," he said.

"I'm not talking to you," I finally replied.

"What'd I do?"

"You were supposed to escape. Sound the alarm. Get help."

"So were you."

"Yeah, but you're El Aboratador."

Every time I spoke there was a terrible pain in my mouth. The exposed nerve endings from my own broken teeth were killing me.

It really pissed me off that Horace had knocked out my choppers while I was unconscious. That guy needed a new rule book.

"Where are we?" I was talking now like a ventriloquist, keeping my mouth closed. I had to get past my broken teeth, will myself to ignore the pain. I had bigger problems.

"Why are we in a truck?" I asked.

"I heard 'em say we're heading to Calexico. We're in a big eighteen-wheeler."

Calexico was on the California side of the Mexican border, off Highway 8. That was pretty much everything I knew about the place.

"Why Calexico?" I asked, taking a painful physical inventory of my injuries.

It was more than just my head and my mouth. I'd been really worked over with that sap, head to toe. I had damage everywhere.

"I think they're going to move us across the border to Mexicali on the Mexican side."

"In a produce truck?"

The truck suddenly bounced over some bad highway and there were sharp pains in my rib cage, hip and, of course, my head. Even my nuts ached.

"I think Calexico is a big Customs stop," I finally said once the testicular pain had subsided. "Customs will go through a big truck like this with dogs. They'll never be able to smuggle us across the border in this."

"I think they're taking us there to kill us," Rocky said, making it worse with every sentence. "But why take us there? They could just as easily kill us here."

"Different laws," I said. "I'm a cop and you're a famous prize fighter. Here it could cause problems. They can't get extradited for capital murder in Mexico."

"We need to come up with a plan," Rocky said. "In every fight I've ever had, no matter how bad it's going, there's always a moment where victory can be snatched from defeat. The same will be true here. We've got to find and exploit that moment."

"Yeah, good thinking." I wanted to curl up and die. My head was beginning to get fuzzy. My thoughts blurred.

"How should we handle it?" he pressed.

"I don't know. I think maybe I'll go back to sleep for a while. I feel like shit."

"Sometimes a man must ignore pain. Focus on the goal. In a fight you've gotta keep punching."

"I like it," I said. "While you do that, I'm just gonna close my eyes for a minute."

# CHAPTER 51

The highway changed to a bad stretch of pitted road. We were bumping along, and the pain from the rough ride shot through my body and jolted my senses, bringing me fully awake. I was still on my back trying to deal with it when Rocky spoke.

"I think we're almost there."

"Seems so," I groaned.

I rolled over on my side. If I puked, I didn't want to choke on vomit. Those were the kind of choices I was down to.

"We still need a plan," Rocky said. "I don't think we've crossed into Mexico yet, because the truck hasn't made a border stop."

After a minute, I realized I might have a better chance of keeping my stomach down if I was upright. With my hands still cuffed behind me, I tried to scoot across the floor to the far wall of the trailer and push myself up into a sitting position. After four or five pain-filled minutes, I finally made it. Once I was settled, I was able to look across the trailer at Rocky and see him better.

"These guys aren't going to chance a Customs stop," I said. "It would give us too good a chance to call for help."

I took several long breaths and again tried to block out the pain.

"They're also not going to be able to drive this thing into Mexico," I said. "That means we aren't going to be crossing the border in this truck."

"How, then?"

"I don't know. We've got to wait until we can see the layout of the place where they take us. We have to guess at their plan and then do this on the fly. We need to find a way to get these cuffs off. A con I know showed me once how to pick police cuffs with a nail or a straight pin. Start looking around for something I can use."

Of course, we couldn't move far, so inside the trailer we found nothing.

After another half hour, the truck came to a stop and began backing up. The driver was jackknifing a reverse turn. Finally, I felt the back bumper tap a loading dock. A minute later the rear door was unbolted.

"We'll make this happen, amigo," Rocky said bravely. I wasn't as optimistic.

The trailer's rear doors opened and I was surprised to see Manny Avila standing there wearing an expensive leather coat and wraparound shades. The sun was coming up over his shoulder. While we'd been rolling south, night had turned into morning.

"Get 'em out. Take 'em into the warehouse," Manny ordered.

Two Mexican thugs I'd never seen before moved into the truck and pulled us out. They were young bangers with 18-L tattooed in gang-style lettering across their chests like meatpacking stamps. Rocky and I were hustled onto a large loading dock where big sliding doors led into a newly constructed concrete tilt-up warehouse.

"Put 'em in the back," Avila ordered. As I was pulled forward, I saw the white Escalade pull into the parking lot.

There were at least twenty more 18th Street Locos inside the warehouse. Some were pushing dollies, others were driving forklifts loaded with boxes of canned vegetables. They were all wearing wife-beater tees and baggy pants. There was lots of gang ink on display.

It was going to be hard to make a move with this many *esse* hitters standing around.

We were shoved inside an empty windowless storage room and the metal door was slammed closed and locked. There was nothing to do but wait.

"I think we're pretty close to the border," Rocky said. "I crossed near Mexicali when I was four. You can smell the sulfur and human waste that floats in the Rio Nuevo River. I remember it as a boy—a smell you don't forget."

"We won't get more than one shot at this," I said

through broken teeth. "My guess is they aren't going to keep us here long. You gotta help me find something I can use to pick these cuffs."

"If I can, I will," Rocky said, looking around the empty room. "What is this place? What's with all the canned goods?"

"The produce is just cover. If I had to guess, I'd say we're in the Avilas' main transshipping point for all the Russian machine guns, Mexican dope and immigrant labor they're smuggling into L.A."

# CHAPTER 52

"*Mamá* brought me across the border about five miles east of here. The coyote was an old man with tangled white hair, who smelled of pigs. He had an empty five-hundred-gallon water truck, and six of us, all members of my family, were jammed inside. He drove us across the desert. It was over a hundred degrees—so hot I didn't think I could live for even a minute longer. *Mamá* held my hand and whispered in my ear. She told me Jesus would protect me, and up till now He has."

Rocky and I were still sitting on the concrete floor of the windowless room waiting to see what our fate would be. It had been over an hour and nobody had opened the door.

"After the old pig farmer let us out, he led us across into the California desert," Rocky went on. "Two of my little cousins and Uncle Pepe died from heat exposure. I was only four years old, but I can still remember every moment of that trip. Sometimes, in the ring, I'd be getting hammered senseless, but in the back of my mind that little four-year-old kid would be saying, *Hey, Juanito, you've been through worse.*"

Sitting here facing death on the border, I realized for the first time what the Mexican immigrant experience must be like. Admittedly, I was going the wrong direction, being sneaked into, not out of, Mexico. But still, it gave me some perspective.

In L.A., emotions over undocumented immigrants are high and conflicted. Our schools and hospitals have become swamped with non-English-speaking illegals. Liberals want their votes, conservatives want their sweat, but nobody wants *them*. The situation had already triggered one riot.

Bratano was corrupt but he was born in L.A. Rocky was born in Mexico, but was the gold standard. It didn't change any of the state's social or economic problems, but if I survived this, it gave me something new to consider.

"*Mamá* told me that from dark, dank places, beautiful flowers often grow," Rocky continued. "In America, she said we would be flowers. We would add to, not subtract from, the value of life there. She cleaned floors in other people's houses. I had a paper route, sold magazines door to door and worked after school in a market, but we survived. In

’81, we both got amnesty. Two years later, I became a citizen. It was the proudest moment of my life.”

An hour later, they came and got us. Manny Avila checked both of our cuffs, then spun each of us around and faced us.

He turned and spoke to Rocky. “You have given up everything and gained nothing.”

“Despite all you’ve stolen, it is you who have nothing,” Rocky told him.

We were marched to the rear of the warehouse, where a young, tattooed *vato* on a forklift was moving a stack of heavy pallets piled high with cartons of canned goods. For some reason he was lifting one pallet at a time off the pile, then repositioning it only a few feet away.

A group of 18th Street Locos stood around watching. After the last one was moved, I finally saw the reason. The pallets had covered a framed, four-foot-square hole in the poured concrete floor. Inside the opening I could see a staircase that led down into a tunnel below the building. It was lit by fluorescent tubes that ran along the east side of the ceiling.

Manny Avila pulled a cell phone out of his pocket and spoke softly. *“Orale ahora, esse.”*

A few minutes later a heavy wooden box was handed up out of the tunnel and passed to the waiting 18th Street Locos. It was placed on a fresh wooden pallet. Seven more boxes followed. They were each about four feet long by three feet high and were made of reinforced pine nailed together with heavy two-by-four side braces. Russian writing covered the sides of each box. More of the AK-100 machine guns that Agent Love had been tracking.

Eight boxes came out of the tunnel and were loaded onto the pallet. I estimated from their size that they contained six submachine guns each. Then four men I hadn't seen before came up the stairs. I wondered how they had carried the heavy crates.

"Inside," Manny Avila said, and pulled Rocky up from the box he'd been leaning against.

I was pushed forward, with Rocky directly behind me. We were led down a short wooden staircase, which descended about twenty feet. Once we reached the bottom, we were standing on the floor of a long, well-lit tunnel. Sitting before us was a small trolley, which ran on half-gauge tracks. Question answered.

"Walk," Manny ordered.

With two gangsters in front of us and two in back, we started down the tunnel, leaving Manny Avila near the staircase, watching us.

The tunnel narrowed and descended on a ten- to fifteen-degree slant. After descending for about a quarter mile, I estimated we were another twenty feet down, leaving Calexico behind, heading toward Mexicali, where we were undoubtedly going to be murdered.

# CHAPTER 53

The tunnel became damp, collecting ground moisture the farther down we went. At its deepest spot we were forced to slog through almost an inch of blackish brown water before making the slow climb back up on the Mexican side.

Somewhere well past the halfway point Rocky stumbled and fell into me, knocking me into the *vato* guard in front. The man spun and in the next few seconds it got very busy. He started raining blows onto me. I ducked and dodged, with my hands cuffed helplessly behind my back. He ended the short, vicious routine with a right hook, which caught me high in the forehead, the part of the skull where the bone is the thickest. I heard one of his knuckles break as the punch landed. He screamed in pain. Rocky was being wrestled to the ground a few feet to my right. For the next couple of seconds we were back to back, sprawled across the narrow-gauge tracks on the tunnel floor.

Then I felt something sharp poking me in the kidney. I moved my cuffed hands up to the middle of my back to try to stop it and got jabbed again, this time in my left palm. Why the hell was Rocky stabbing me?

I finally figured it out. He had somehow gotten his hands on a sharp piece of metal. He jabbed it out again and this time I caught it in my right hand

and wrapped my fingers around it. It was a four-inch nail, which he'd probably pulled out of that gun crate he'd been leaning against in the Calexico warehouse.

Just then I was snatched back up to my feet. The punk with the busted knuckle was standing in front of me, cradling his hand and glowering angrily. He finally pulled out his gun with his good hand, then slammed me in the head with the flat side of the automatic.

*"Carechimba hijueputa,"* he shouted, then hit me with it again. I went down on one knee, and struggled to retain consciousness. As I teetered there, half out of it, I fought to get my head to stop spinning.

*"Flaquito,"* he screamed and spit on me.

Rocky and I were then pulled up to our feet and pushed roughly through the dimly lit tunnel. I managed to slowly collect myself during the next few minutes.

The air was damp and fetid, despite the ventilation tubes punched into the tunnel's ceiling every fifteen feet or so. Whoever designed this thing knew what they were doing.

I'd been through a few captured drug tunnels in the past and they usually looked like fun house exhibits where the floors and walls serpentined all over the place. Somewhere around the middle of the passage there would be a hard left or right to accommodate the fact that the diggers tunneling in one direction had to make a sharp course correction to meet up with the ones coming the other way. This tunnel was straight and true. It had been carefully engineered, attesting to the organization behind this smuggling operation.

We finally reached the far end, where another staircase waited. Rocky and I were stopped. The *celador* in front of me snatched up a phone mounted to the wall at the base of the staircase.

*"Es Ramon. Tengo los prisoneros."*

Ramon listened for a moment, hung up, then climbed the stairs and opened a reinforced wooden door.

We were led up into a carpeted basement hallway. Halfway down the corridor Ramon opened another door and flipped a light switch. Then we were pushed inside what looked like a very large laundry area containing several commercial-sized washers and dryers. There were two long folding tables in the center of the room attached to the floor with metal brackets. Along one wall were several porcelain sinks.

While his partner pointed an automatic pistol at me, Ramon removed my handcuffs and recuffed my wrists in front of me through a wrought-iron wall brace that supported a huge metal drying rack that contained half a dozen small, three-foot-square Mexican blankets. Rocky was cuffed to a similar rack on the opposite side of the room.

The four guards started patting us down,

stealing everything we had in our pockets. One of them saw my belt, which had a silver buckle. He undid it and pulled it off, taking the satellite transmitter with him. Then they left, closing and locking the door behind them. I was pretty sure they were just outside waiting, so I kept my voice low.

"I thought you were trying to kill me in that tunnel," I whispered.

"You said you wanted a nail. Now get going and pick these cuffs, homes."

I shifted the nail carefully between my index finger and thumb, making sure I didn't drop it. Then I went to work on the new Hookfast stainless steel handcuffs that were securing my wrists to the thick metal bracket.

# CHAPTER 54

It only took me two minutes to pop my handcuffs open. Once I was loose I moved across the laundry room and freed Rocky. We both started looking around for anything we could use as a weapon. Almost everything in the room was bolted down.

I finally pulled one of the large commercial dryers away from the wall and found a heavy extension cable coated in an eighth of an inch of black rubber. It had a heavy rubber-encased plug on one end. I disconnected it and started to knot the end of the cord around the plug until I had a three-foot cord with a tennis-ball-sized monkey knot at the end.

While I was doing this, Rocky hunted around in back of the washing machines and finally came out with a two-foot-long brass pipe. Not much of an arsenal but it was better than being chained to a wall and getting beat to death.

"You got a way you want to do this?" he asked.

"Let's make some noise. We'll pretend we're still chained to these racks. Once they're inside, whammo—take them from behind."

"I like it, homes."

I positioned myself where I was before. I had the knotted extension cord stuffed under my belt where I could yank it out quickly. I nodded at Rocky and he started banging on the front of one of the washers that was pulled away from the wall. As Rocky returned to his place by the drying rack across the room, we heard the door being unlocked.

A second later two of the G's rushed in, guns out. After a quick glance at us, they turned their backs and studied the room.

As they were trying to figure out how the hell one of the washing machines got moved, Rocky and I stepped quietly away from the metal racks.

"Hey, Ramon," I said softly to the *vato* with the broken hand who'd pistol-whipped me. He spun quickly and I let him have it with my makeshift mace. The monkey knot hit Ramon flush in the throat. His Adam's apple cracked loudly, sounding like a Ping-Pong ball being crushed. The gun fell from his fingers, clattering to the cement floor.

I didn't see Rocky's guy get it because Ramon immediately dropped to his knees with both hands clutching his throat. He started gasping for breath, then gagging. I had one eye on the door waiting for the other two thugs to come busting in.

A second after Ramon hit the floor, he pitched forward, his face turned purple, and he began writhing at my feet. I stepped forward and scooped up his gun—a state-of-the-art nine-millimeter Kimber automatic with a four-inch barrel and a laser sight.

I turned to check on Rocky. He'd knocked out his guy and was frisking him for a gun. He pulled out a nine-millimeter Glock, then used the cuffs to lock the guard's hands through the leg of the bolted-down metal table. He shoved a towel, which he'd found inside one of the dryers, into the *vato*'s mouth.

Ramon was still writhing on the floor, making an odd keening sound. In the Marines, we'd learned that the larynx was one of nine vital kill points. I didn't have time to try an emergency tracheotomy. Seconds later he was gone, his mouth stretched wide in a silent scream.

Rocky checked the square-muzzled nine-millimeter Glock he'd just taken off his man.

While he was doing that, I looked out the doorway into the hall. It was empty. Apparently they'd only left two men to guard us.

"Okay, let's see how quickly we can get out of here," I said.

"Hey, Scully. The blankets hanging on those racks—you know what I think they are?" I shrugged. "Horse blankets."

I was mystified. "So what?"

"There's gotta be horses around here," Rocky explained. "There are places that horses can go that cars or Jeeps can't. I remember this area from before. There's a chain of mountains between Mexicali and Ejido Tabasco. It can't be too far. If we could get there—"

"On horses? You out of your mind?"

"What's your problem? Didn't you ride as a kid?"

"Hell, no. I was raised in a damn orphanage. I rode stolen bicycles."

"If we can get to the rocks near here on horseback, they can't follow in vehicles. I'm pretty sure the Hills of Tabasco are close."

He was probably right. If we tried to get away on foot, we wouldn't get far. If we stole a truck, they would hunt us down in Jeeps. "Let's deal with it once we check this place out," I said.

We exited the laundry and climbed a flight of stairs up to the ground floor of the building. We came out in a large tack room that was loaded with bridles and fancy, silver-studded saddles and martingales hanging from pegs on the walls. When we opened the back door of the tack room, we stepped into an impressive new barn with at least ten stalls, each holding a beautifully brushed Arabian Thoroughbred. Aside from the animals, the barn appeared to be empty. I could hear a radio playing nearby, tuned to a Mexican music station.

"Hang on," Rocky whispered, and moved toward the stalls.

"Where you going?"

"Gonna go select the two best horses," he whispered.

I groaned and held his back, aiming my newly acquired Kimber out the open door of the barn. It took several minutes for Rocky to pick our mounts. He chose a huge bay and a dappled gray, putting on their bridles and leading them out of the stalls into the center section of the barn. As I held the reins, he began to saddle up, getting equipment out of the tack room and first placing a blanket, then a huge silver-adorned Mexican saddle on each animal. When he had cinched up both, he pointed to the big dappled gray.

"The gelding is yours," he said. "His name is Humo Blanco. It was painted on the gate of his stall."

"White Smoke?" I said. "Must be a dope dealer's horse."

Rocky nodded and mounted the bay.

"Wait a minute," I told him. "Don't want to leave the other horses here so those assholes can follow us."

Rocky held my reins as I moved back toward the stalls and opened all the doors, shooing the rest of the horses out. I slapped the last horse on the withers and shouted loudly. The entire herd took off, heading out the front of the barn. I mounted White Smoke and followed Rocky as we cantered out of the building. It was all I could do to stay in the saddle.

I had actually been on a few swayback park-ride-type horses in the past, but I was still pretty busted up and my scrotum felt like it had been attacked by wolves. White Smoke and I got off to a bad start. I was dude-ranch material at best. Rocky, on the other hand, rode like it was in his DNA.

Once we got out into the open, I could see that the barn was part of a huge complex that sat right next to the border. Farther away on the horizon, I could see the twin towns of Mexicali and Calexico.

The expensive ranch we were escaping from was located on a grassy patch of land right at the edge of the Baja desert. There were beautiful corrals and low, tile-roofed buildings surrounding a large Spanish-style hacienda and courtyard. The main house was three stories with a red-tile roof and arched doorways.

I didn't use up much time admiring the spread because almost immediately half a dozen men in windbreakers carrying long guns began running out of the houses into the yard. I knew from the way they cradled their weapons at port arms that they were trained bodyguards. Some of them jumped into Jeeps. Others tried to stop the eight fleeing horses with no luck. As the last of the unsaddled Arabians cleared the courtyard, Rocky and I followed. We streaked under a large arch emblazoned with the words CIELO RANCHERO—Heavenly Ranch.

We rode out into the desert, close behind the eight escaping horses. In less than a minute, four Jeeps full of armed men were racing under the arch, pursuing us, less than two hundred yards behind.

# CHAPTER 55

As we rode away from Cielo Ranchero, I was pumping so much adrenaline I didn't even feel the beating Horace had given me. I struggled to stay behind Rocky's bay, eating a lot of dust in the process.

The other fleeing stallions were fanning out, each heading in a separate direction. As Rocky had predicted, there was a low chain of mountains about half a mile to the southeast. If we could get our horses up into the rocks, we would be able to leave the pursuing Jeeps behind.

As I was calculating those odds, the first shots rang out. They made a flat popping noise, like a distant backfire. I pulled my Kimber and shot back. The instant I fired, White Smoke shied to the left, almost throwing me off. It looked way easier when John Wayne did it. My balls were engaged in round two, taking a brutal pounding on the silver pommel. I tried to ease this by getting into the horse's rhythm, but no matter what I tried, I was in agony. Every time I glanced back the Jeeps were closer.

"We aren't gonna make it," I shouted. "We need to find a place and make a stand."

"Over there," Rocky shouted and pointed to the right, where, about two hundred yards away, there was a tin-roofed line shack surrounded by a low adobe wall. It looked like some kind of storage shed for field equipment. Rocky wheeled and rode in that direction. I followed, bouncing like a rag doll in the saddle.

We made it to a spot behind the building. We didn't want our horses to get hit when the shooting started, so we turned them loose, slapping their flanks. They bolted, running away into the desert.

When I looked up, the Jeeps were now about five hundred yards away, slowing down and spreading out, attempting to surround us on three sides. Without warning, Rocky aimed his automatic at the closest Jeep and started firing.

"They're too far away. Save your ammo. We only have one clip each. Let 'em get in closer, then make every round count."

We hunkered down behind the low adobe wall and waited. In the distance, I saw the Jeeps coming to a stop. They were still about three hundred yards away, not out of range for a nine-millimeter handgun, but unless we got damn lucky, an impossible shot.

Several of the bodyguards were already out of the Jeeps and taking cover behind the fenders of their vehicles, aiming their long guns across the hoods at us. Then a voice blasted from an electronic bullhorn.

"Throw down your guns. Put your hands in the air! You won't be killed if you give up."

"Is that Manny Avila?" I asked.

Rocky said, "Whoever he is, he's got a great sense of humor."

"This must be his place. That rancho is probably the Avilas' Mexican gun- and drug-running base. They smuggle their contraband through that tunnel, then truck it up in produce vans and distribute it in L.A." Rocky didn't respond. His eyes were locked on our assailants. "Look, if Manny Avila is in that Jeep and we can get our hands on him, we could really change the dynamic here."

"How the hell we gonna do that?" Rocky said, cocking a worried eyebrow at me. "They're just gonna lay back and pick us off with those carbines."

"Hold them back, but don't waste too many rounds. I'm gonna try and get inside this shed."

"Why the hell are—"

I didn't wait around to explain. I headed for the front door of the line shack. Gunshots rang out almost immediately and little pieces of adobe dust flew off the edge of the building as I rounded the corner. I got to the front door, shot the lock off and, as bullets peppered the wall and wood above my head, I dove inside.

The shed held mostly field equipment—a big pipe wheel sprinkler that watered grass, lots of rusting metal farm stuff. *Where's that spare submachine gun when you need it?*

As I rummaged around in the junk, I heard the Jeeps moving again. The engines revved and growled as they moved in closer. Then I heard two more shots from Rocky's handgun.

I started pawing desperately through the mounds of junk stacked in the shack. There wasn't much, but I had come in here with an idea and finally found something I thought might work. It was a small pewter hose nozzle with a trigger, which was shaped roughly like a gun.

I snatched it up and ran back out of the building.

As soon as I was visible, more carbine slugs flew, but the shots were hurried and the bullets went wide, whining off into the distance. After another desperate run, I dove back behind the wall next to Rocky.

"What'd you get?" he asked.

I showed him the hose nozzle.

"Perfect. We can challenge these pricks to a water fight."

"How good a shot are you?"

"I'm a prizefighter. I never needed a gun to win an argument."

"Okay, here's how we do this. I'll yell out that we want to give up. We'll put our hands up, walk out. You throw your gun down, I'll toss this nozzle. Once they think we're unarmed, my bet is they'll get careless and come in closer. As soon as they're ten or fifteen yards away, I'll put down some cover fire with the Kimber. While they're ducking and dodging, you make a move, get to Manny's Jeep and drag him out. I'll be right behind you. Once I screw this nine in his ear, we got a whole new game."

"Are you kidding? That's all you got? What's to keep them from just shooting us once we stand up?"

"They've had plenty of chances to kill us in the last nine hours and haven't. My guess is they want to set it up so it looks right. Stage it, so they can say we got in a beef and killed each other. Manny's got a lot going on in Haven Park. He doesn't want to be stuck down here as a U.S. fugitive in a double homicide."

Rocky looked at me like I'd just grown antlers.

"I don't like this plan, homes."

I shrugged. "Let's hear yours."

The Jeeps were in gear and again moving up closer. Two more shots rang out, ricocheting off the low wall we were behind.

"Shit. This really sucks. Let's try it," he said.

# CHAPTER 56

The Jeeps were still spaced out but were now only about one hundred yards away. Still a tough pistol shot.

"We're coming out, don't shoot!" I shouted painfully through my broken teeth.

"Stand up and throw your guns out in front of you," the bullhorn commanded. It definitely sounded like Manny Avila's voice.

I glanced at Rocky. "Ready?"

"How the hell do I get ready for a dumb-ass move like this?"

But Rocky stood up anyway and stepped around the wall with me. Then he held his gun up high so they could see it. I held up my hose nozzle. I saw the sun glint off a pair of field glasses, so I knew they had a magnified view.

"Throw your guns down," the bullhorn repeated.

Rocky tossed his gun away. It landed a few feet in front of him, kicking up a little puff of sand.

I was ten feet to his right as I threw the pewter hose nozzle away.

"Now move forward," the electrified voice ordered.

As we walked toward the Jeep, I could feel the comforting weight of the Kimber jammed in my jeans out of sight at the small of my back.

"Move toward me," the bullhorn screeched.

We started slowly toward Manny Avila's Jeep.

We were about thirty yards away when I saw something in the sky. It started out as a strange, distant movement camouflaged in the heat waves coming off the desert. A distortion of the horizon. A few seconds later, I heard the distant thump of a helicopter blade beating the air. Before I could react, I saw a muzzle flash over by the Jeeps and heard the simultaneous whine of a bullet streaking past my ear.

Rocky and I dove headfirst into the sand.

I snatched out the Kimber and started shooting from a prone position. Thirty yards is still a long ways out for a pistol with a four-inch barrel. The Kimber wasn't much good at that distance. But they didn't know what I was shooting and my gunshots were definitely changing their plans. The Jeeps suddenly went into reverse, backing away from us, throwing up clouds of sand and dust.

As I laid down a withering fire, Rocky used the moment to dart out and snatch his Glock from the desert floor.

I continued to fire the slide lock.

A large green and gold Schweizer 333 helicopter appeared out of the heat distortion and headed rig toward us. It was hugging the deck, the sound of the thumping blade growing louder as it choppered toward us at over a hundred miles an hour.

Then all hell broke loose.

Jeeps were scattering in every direction. One of them broke from the pack and headed back toward us. As it got closer I recognized Manny Avila in the passenger seat, still wearing his cool leather jacket and wraparound shades. He was clutching the electronic bullhorn, his mouth stretched wide in panic.

Rocky suddenly jumped up and charged in the direction of Avila's Jeep. I scrambled to my feet and followed. As we ran, the helicopter banked just overhead. I looked up and saw a big PJDF logo painted on the side—POLICIA JUDICIAL DEL DISTRITO FEDERAL. As the Schweizer flashed past, I caught a glimpse of Ophelia Love hanging in the open doorway, gun out, intensity etching her face.

The Jeeps were all in four-wheel drive, going about twenty miles per hour in the deep sand. Manny's was closing fast. Rocky was still four strides out ahead of me when Manny's driver swerved and headed right at us. The front bumper clipped Rocky, knocking him onto his back in the sand. He dropped his Glock, but I was able to scoop it up as I ran past. I dove into the Jeep and landed in the backseat.

In the next instant I was trading shots at point-blank range with the carbine-wielding bodyguard next to me. However, at three feet, Rocky's Glock was a far superior weapon. The bodyguard discharged an awkward, errant shot as he struggled to swing the three-foot-long barrel around in cramped quarters. I placed my muzzle on his shoulder and blew him right out of the speeding Jeep.

As my gun discharged, Manny Avila screamed in fright and started clawing for his sidearm.

But when the Glock fired, the driver flinched and jerked the wheel, flipping the Jeep. Everyone flew out of the vehicle and landed face-first in the sand. I rolled, and came up on my feet with the Glock still out in front of me. Manny Avila was ten feet away, trying to stand. I ran to him and jammed the automatic into his chest and shoved him back to his knees.

"Stay put," I ordered, then snatched his chrome-plated pistol out of the belt holster and threw it a safe distance away. The driver of the Jeep was out cold.

The mop-up was right out of a Bruckheimer movie. The helicopter was herding Jeeps from the air, turning them and forcing them to stop. Finally, the green and gold Schweizer settled low and landed. Flak-jacketed, machine-gun-wielding

PJDF cops poured out of the chopper door and surrounded the startled ranch bodyguards, who quickly threw down their rifles, jutting their hands in the air.

Ophelia ran over to me. "You okay?" she asked.

"Yeah, but we better check Rocky."

We moved over and helped Rocky to his feet. He was shaken but unhurt.

*"¡Maravilloso!"* the little fighter said with a grin.

"How the hell did you find us?" I asked.

Ophelia reached into my shirt pocket and removed her DCST unit. In all the excitement, I'd completely forgotten it was still there.

"You left it on and we backtracked the signal from space." She grinned at me. "How's that for your tax dollars saving your ass?" Then she triggered her hand rover. "Alexa, it's me. I got him. He's safe."

"Thank God," I heard Alexa say. "Get him over here."

"I'll have him to you in ten." Then Ophelia turned off her radio.

"Ten minutes?" I said, and Ophelia nodded. "Where is she?"

"We split up. I was following this signal, but she insisted on following the belt tracker because she was sure that was where you'd be." She pointed at Cielo Ranchero. "She's over there."

# CHAPTER 57

With Rocky driving and Ophelia in the back, we raced one of the Jeeps across the desert sand toward the ranch house.

I could see another green and gold PJDF Schweizer parked in the large plaza out in front of the main house with the rotor just winding down. We streaked under the archway and swerved to a stop as a uniformed Mexican colonel and several helmeted judicial *policia* were herding ranch hands into a large rec building. Alexa saw me and ran out of the farmhouse toward us. I jumped out of the Jeep and took her into my arms.

"Thank God you're alive," she said, holding me close. She leaned back and held me at arm's length. "When I found this I didn't know what to think."

She was holding my belt with the tracking device sewn into it. "I took it off one of those Eighteenth Street gangsters."

She leaned in to kiss me, but I pulled away. The pain from the exposed nerves in my broken teeth was beginning to saw a hole through the adrenaline. "Got a little problem with my teeth," I said.

"Open your mouth," she commanded.

"You don't wanta see it."

She reached up and pulled my lip back. "My God! What the hell happened?"

"Got those rearranged courtesy of the Haven Park PD. But the LAPD is gonna get 'em fixed up better than before. This time next week, I'll have a better smile than Brad Pitt."

Alexa and Ophelia introduced me to Colonel Felix Mendez, the head of the PJDF for Baja del Sur. He was a tall, no-nonsense cop with a crisp uniform, a polished Sam Browne and a neatly trimmed mustache. He had worked several joint ops with Ophelia and was trying to help Homeland and the FBI stem the flow of Russian-made guns and Mexican brown that was coming into the U.S. He had taken over command of her operation in Mexico and supplied the helicopters, then led the mission into Mexican airspace.

"It will be necessary to move fast," he said in near perfect English. "To protect this operation, I have temporarily decommissioned the phones for this sector, including cell towers, so they shouldn't have been able to call out and alert anyone. But there is still a risk somebody got through to Mayor Bratano before we closed communications."

"There's a tunnel that leads from the barn under the border to a warehouse in Calexico," I told them. "You need to go through it and bolt down the U.S. side." I turned to Ophelia. "I think you'll find a big stash of AK-100 series submachine guns over there."

"We have to get back up to L.A. in a hurry and

organize our takedown in Haven Park," Alexa said. "We're going to need a bunch of FISA warrants."

Rocky and I showed Colonel Mendez where the tunnel was. Six Mexican PJDF agents headed into it while Ophelia radioed FBI SWAT and instructed them to move in and close down the Calexico warehouse. Twenty minutes later, the warehouse had been secured and ten more 18th Street gang members had been arrested. Two hundred AK-100s and at least a ton of Mexican heroin were also booked into evidence.

Less than an hour later, we were back on the other side of the border, climbing into a U.S. Coast Guard Sikorsky for the helicopter ride back to L.A. Once we were airborne, Rocky sat on the seat beside me, looking out across the expanse of Baja desert.

"The town where I was born is called Progreso. It's over there somewhere." He pointed south. We all looked in that direction, but couldn't see anything. Just endless miles of brown sand and a cloudless blue sky.

As we flew, I gave Ophelia the names of everybody I had seen committing crimes in Haven Park. It came to about fifteen people. Ophelia was on the helicopter's tactical frequency, talking to a FISA judge. To be safe and to save time, she asked for twenty additional John Doe warrants.

At one-thirty, we landed on the roof of the

LAPD Air Support Division on Ramirez Street. I got out of the Sikorsky with Alexa and Ophelia and we hurried over to four police vans that were waiting there, engines idling, side doors open. Before I got in, I turned and said goodbye to Rocky.

*"Tuvinmos bueno suerte, amigo,"* he said.

"Didn't need luck. All we needed was each other."

Then he grabbed me and gave me a Mexican *abrazo*.

I got inside the police van and we sped off, heading toward the secure situation room in the basement of Parker Center. Alexa and Ophelia were in the lead van ahead of the one I was riding in, drawing up operation plans.

As I watched the city of L.A. fly past my window, it was hard to believe that Haven Park was only six short miles from downtown L.A. and Parker Center. Up until a few hours ago, it had felt to me like that corrupt city existed in a parallel universe, far from the justice I believed in. It had seemed secure from assault, moated by its own laws and the slimy Los Angeles River, policed by men capable of almost anything.

I thought about how quickly some realities change. What had once seemed like a massive criminal conspiracy, controlled by brutal power elitists, now just looked like a collection of sorry losers scattering for their lives like tenement cockroaches when the lights came on.

# CHAPTER 58

The situation room at the Glass House is located two stories belowground in a subbasement. It's designed to be used as a command center during major earthquakes, terrorist attacks or incidents of massive civil unrest. It was also frequently used for secure operations like this one. There was a large computer bullpen, a TV media room and television center, along with a tricked-out communications center that utilized half a dozen satellite uplinks.

When we got there, Chief Filosiani was already in discussions with Homeland Security's special agent in charge, Teddy Fielding. The Homeland SAC was pure vanilla, with a bland face and a comb-over hairstyle. He also had Ivy League manners, no personality and a beige suit. He and Tony Filosiani were huddled over a map of Haven Park, working on the takedown.

Captain Calloway greeted me and told me he was proud of what I'd done. He seemed strangely subdued. He'd just been told that my obstruction-of-justice crime had been orchestrated by the chief's office. I could see, as I looked into his dark eyes, that he was torturing himself that he hadn't put up much of a fight defending me. However, after what he'd been told, and given my confession, there wasn't really much to fight for.

Nonetheless, he prided himself on his dedication and loyalty to his troops and, despite my protest, he wasn't about to cut himself much slack.

He hovered over me, making sure I got medical attention. An EMT looked at my mouth, checked me for broken ribs and gave me some pain pills, suggesting I get right to a dentist.

But I wasn't about to sit in a dental chair listening to piped music while the Haven Park takedown was in progress.

"Okay," Filosiani was saying as I returned to the briefing room. "We're gonna hit them at a little before four o'clock. Two federal teams will scoop up the day watch guys as they come off shift at four. Two more will get the mid-watch at Haven Park Elementary School before they hit the street. They'll swarm the gym and make the arrest at roll call. Keep it contained. Then we go door to door on everybody else."

Chief Filosiani looked up. "Agent Love and Agent Fielding will run the takedown. Both Ted and I think it's better for federal agents to be on point and do the arrests. I don't want to get into a jurisdictional shouting match. LAPD SWAT will operate as backup only."

The plan was agreed to and signed off on by everyone.

It took longer to get the FISA warrants than anticipated. I found myself sitting alone with Alexa in the empty media room, waiting. She was holding my hand—a strange thing for her to do in a police setting, but everyone who saw us in there seemed to understand.

"We need to call Chooch," she finally said.

We went to the com center and made the call together.

"Thank God," was all he said, and then he told me how much he loved me, how he had been praying constantly. I felt tears well in my eyes as I talked to him.

I wanted to get Ricky Ross out of Haven Park before this went down, both for his own protection and to preserve the integrity of the case. He had surprised me once again. He surprised me in L.A. fifteen years ago when he turned out to be much worse than I ever thought. But since I went undercover in Haven Park, he'd surprised me again, turning out to be exactly what he promised. I still didn't catch his vibe, but this time he'd stood up when it mattered. I owed him.

An hour later, a plainclothes unit had picked him up and deposited him in the chief's office at Parker Center.

The FISA warrants were delivered at three in the afternoon. A federal attorney brought them over from the courthouse. We left the situation room and headed up to the garage roof, where a dozen LAPD and FBI SWAT and Tactical Weapons vans were staged. Two LAPD SWAT teams piled into their black armored rescue vehicles, five to each truck. The commanders got into Tactical Support vehicles and they all started rolling, heading down from the roof of the Glass House parking structure. The twenty FBI SWAT officers were leading the way in their ARVs.

Alexa, Filosiani and I rode in one of the LAPD plainclothes cars with his department driver at the wheel, following the six SWAT teams.

"You did good, Shane," the chief said, looking over the seat at me. He'd been so busy it was the first time we'd spoken.

"Thank you, sir."

"I'm putting you in for the Medal of Valor."

"I don't want a medal. The right guy is going to get elected in Haven Park. That's enough for me."

"Good take," he said. "But you're getting the fucking medal anyway. Think of it as police department PR." Then he turned back and watched the SWAT van in front of us as we tracked silently down Third Street, the last vehicle in the motorcade.

# CHAPTER 59

Given all that had gone before, the takedown was ridiculously easy.

FBI SWAT in riot gear with faceplates and street sweepers scooped up the day watch as they pulled into the Haven Park police parking lot. Nobody tried anything. One by one, they were lined up in cuffs, Mirandized and loaded into federal jail vans.

I was watching as Alonzo Bell drove in and got hooked up. They dragged that monster cop out of his car, disarmed him and slapped the bracelets on.

I walked over and waited until the Miranda was finished. Bell glared at me with insolent hatred.

"I tried to help you. I tried to be your friend," he said.

"Was that before or after you tried to kill me and let that asshole Velario beat the shit out of me while I was tied to a chair?"

"You know this ain't over. All kinda stuff can still get done," he said softly, so nobody else would hear. "I don't have to be on the street to make toast."

"Another threat, Al?"

"Just information, pal."

"Thanks for the heads-up. Now go do your time and try not to get short-stroked in the prison shower."

They took him away.

Horace Velario was off duty, taking some sick days. I heard later that after he was arrested, he cried in the car when they were taking him over to the federal building on Wilshire.

Talbot Jones got busted at home. Same with Carlos Reál.

Mayor Bratano was hooked up in his plaque-filled office at Haven Park City Hall a little before five the same night. The turquoise Cadillac was in his special parking space under a custom car cover. The sign at his parking place said HIS HONOR THE MAYOR.

I was standing in the hall with Alexa as he was brought out of his office in handcuffs. He was in the middle of an indignant rant as he was led past.

"Conspiracy to commit murder?" he said. "And just who's going to testify to that?"

"Me," I said. He stopped and turned back, seeing me now for the first time.

A lot of things played across his face. Anger, betrayal, and finally, despair.

The first big defection was at 6:16 that same evening. Talbot Jones's lawyer asked for a meeting with the DA. Jones copped a plea and turned state's evidence. That started the ball rolling. A deal-making free-for-all followed, with the main players in the Haven Park corruption scandal getting hung out to dry.

I wasn't around to witness it. My mouth was killing me. Chief Filosiani had cashed in a favor with a top Beverly Hills oral surgeon and in an hour I was in the dentist's chair getting a set of beautiful new teeth.

Seven pain-filled hours later I walked out of the office with a numb jaw and a new set of plastic temporaries. Great from a distance, but I had strict instructions not to eat corn on the cob, peanuts, or any hard candy until my new porcelain caps were manufactured and installed.

I got home at eleven and Alexa and I were again back in our lawn chairs watching the still waters of the Venice canals. Franco wound incessantly back and forth around our legs. Cat love. He was glad that things were finally back to normal.

The numbness was beginning to wear off, and my mouth felt different with each passing hour. The teeth seemed somehow too big, like they belonged to someone else. They looked great, but when I spoke I could hear a slight lisp that I had to work hard to control.

"We really lucked out on this, babe," Alexa said, holding my hand.

"Luck has nossing to do wif it. I'm a trained proseshinal," I lisped.

She laughed and squeezed my hand.

It ended up pretty much the way it had begun, with Alexa and me in our queen-sized bed making love.

Most people never find happiness. You're lucky if you get close—get a glimpse. As I held Alexa, with Franco fussing at the foot of our bed looking for a place to lie down, I knew this was more than just a homecoming. This was redemption.

Tomorrow I would go back to work. Tomorrow I would listen to my friends and colleagues telling stories about how bad they'd felt when I'd been fired. I'd tell some stories of my own. The orange grove, the truck ride to Calexico and the trip through that tunnel. The shoot-out in the desert. Cops love war stories, and I had a slew of great new ones.

Tomorrow I'd be back on the job where I belonged.

But tonight, right now, in my wife's arms, I had peace. And with it, finally, came true happiness.

# ACKNOWLEDGMENTS

They say that being a novelist is a lonely profession, however I have so many people helping me get these books to you that loneliness is hardly a problem.

To begin with, there is my office staff. Kathy Ezso is my right hand and serves in so many other ways, not the least of which is as a valued assistant and great first and last pass editor. Jane Whitney is my other hand. A gifted writer on her own, her helpful suggestions always enrich.

Jo Swerling, longtime friend (and, for thirty years, my number-one senior producer in television), is always my first reader. Thanks, Jo, for providing encouragement and honest responses. Daisy Marco is a secret weapon, helping supervise everything from budgets to marketing. Theresa Peoples is a film development executive at my company who also pitches in and does pages when I have a big weekend and bomb the office with new material.

I have great help and support from St. Martin's Press. Sally Richardson, my publisher, is always there for me. She's a great leader and friend. My editor, Charlie Spicer, is the best. This is our eighth Scully book together, and I treasure the friendship, gentle support and creative encouragement. Matthew Shear has worked tirelessly to help me achieve success. Matt Baldacci is another secret weapon—a marketing genius who comes up with the best ideas of anyone. My thanks to Steve Troha and Tara Cibelli, Yaniv Soha and David Rotstein.

I want to thank Michael Lloyd for his amazing help. Michael, you are the best. Also, thanks to Dylan Chaufty for help on jacket design.

My family is my emotional center. My wife, Marcia, has kept me honest and changes the air in my head when it occasionally turns to helium. She's performed this valuable task for more than fifty years, ever since I asked her to go steady in the eighth grade. My children, Tawnia, Chelsea and Cody, give me the greatest joy in my life. If personal joy has anything to do with good writing, then they are a big part of this.

**Center Point Publishing**
600 Brooks Road • PO Box 1
Thorndike ME 04986-0001 USA

**(207) 568-3717**

**US & Canada:**
**1 800 929-9108**
www.centerpointlargeprint.com